SWORD HEIRESS

Violet Moon Series

Book 3

Alisa Hope Wagner

Sword Heiress
Violet Moon Series Book 3
Marked Writers Publishing
Copyright 2024 by Alisa Hope Wagner
www.alisahopewagner.com
Written by Alisa Hope Wagner
Illustrated by Albert Morales
Cover Colored by Bryan Arfel Magnaye
Author Photo by Lori Stead
All rights reserved
ISBN: 978-1-963190-01-4

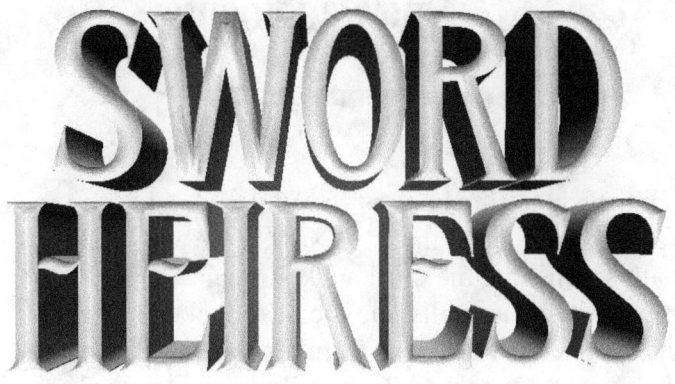

SWORD HEIRESS

Violet Moon Series

Book 3

Alisa Hope Wagner

Acknowledgments

I published the first book of the Violet Moon Series in 2018 and the second book in 2019. Now at the end of 2023, I am finally publishing the third book. Though I will be aggressive about publishing the next book in the series much sooner, it was a wonderful experience getting to rediscover the planet of Rodesh, and I am honored to expand this beautiful world with its intriguing people groups and exciting happenings.

I want to give my heartfelt gratitude to my husband, Daniel Wagner, who supports my work financially and with his words of inspiration. Thank you for always believing in me. To my children, thank you for cheering me on and keeping me motivated.

I want to acknowledge my amazing editing team. Writing a book is only half the battle. The other half takes a team. Thank you to my copy editors Patricia Coughlin, Faith Newton, Jennifer Smith, Daniel Wagner and Bernadine Zimmerman and to my content/copy editor Emerald Barnes. I needed every single comment, suggestion, correction and encouragement you all gave me.

And as always, I'm grateful to the talent and friendship of my illustrator, Albert Morales. Your creative and excellent illustrations always bring the characters of Rodesh to life.

Finally, without the Holy Spirit guiding my writing, I would not be the author I am today. He is my Writing Partner, and I listen to His insight and wisdom. I want my work to have eternal value, and I only gain that through obedience to His voice.

Dedication

To my high school sweetheart and husband, Daniel, my stories live because you cherish me.

To my three loves, Isaac, Levi and Karis Ruth, I write with excellence to make you proud.

To anyone who has suffered trauma and had to go through the process of healing, may the blood of Jesus heal you, the guidance of the Holy Spirit lead you and the love of your Heavenly Father comfort you.

Thank You, Father, for giving me purpose.
Thank You, Son, for redeeming my world.
Thank You, Spirit, for guiding my journey.

"He heals the brokenhearted And binds up their wounds." – Psalm 147.3 (NKJV)

Two Worlds Combined

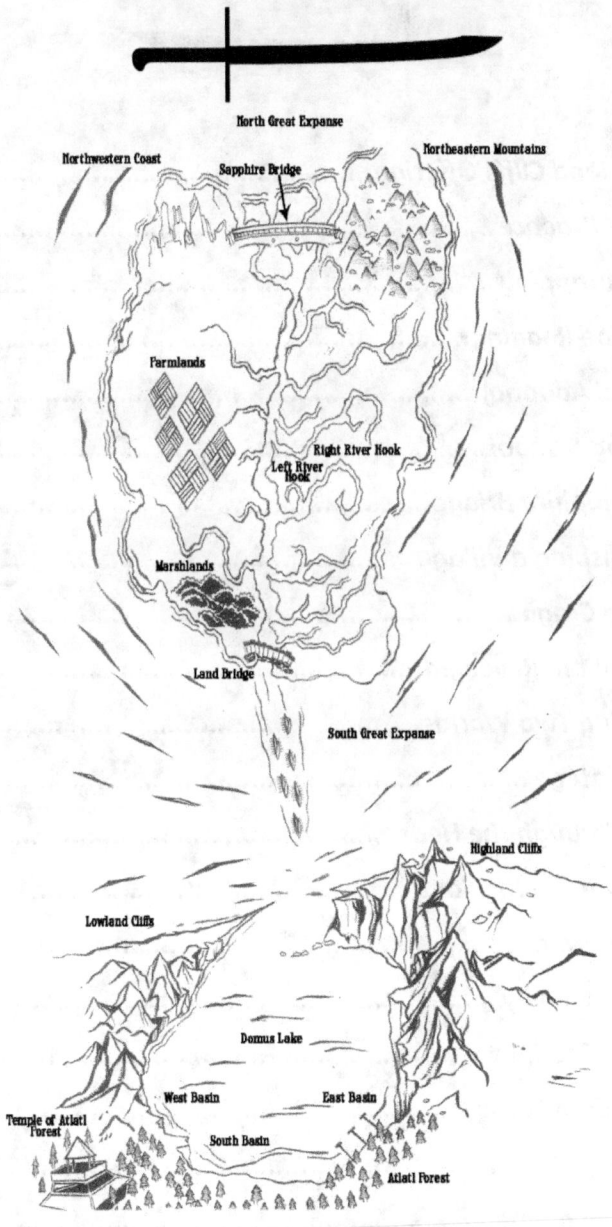

North Great Expanse

Northwestern Coast

Northeastern Mountains

Sapphire Bridge

Farmlands

Right River Hook

Left River Hook

Marshlands

Land Bridge

South Great Expanse

Highland Cliffs

Lowland Cliffs

Domus Lake

West Basin

East Basin

Temple of Atlatl Forest

South Basin

Atlatl Forest

Table of Contents

A Lowland Cliffs Offering

Corven's lame foot made it difficult to step out of the boat. He hated getting help from his mute servant, Reece, but his pride was wounded long ago when his father disowned him at the age of twelve. He turned his body and tried to put his good foot onto the rocky shore, but his lame right foot buckled under the pressure, causing him to fall back against the wooden seat of the boat.

"Ouch!" A piercing pain shot through Corven's back. Finally, he held out his arms to Reece who patiently waited for his command. Reece, with his healthy, strong physique easily reached down and scooped up Corven and placed him onto the shore. Corven found his balance and straightened his back. "That's going to hurt for at least a week." He reached and felt the bump on the center of his spine. "Small price to pay for finally arriving. I'm glad I thought to bring extra food. Took you long enough to row us here. Didn't realize how vast the waters would be. Though, it was better than walking through sand. I'd have to be carried the entire way."

Reece shrugged. The muscles on his tanned shoulders and arms contradicted the innocent compliance of his green eyes. His blonde, shaggy hair made his appearance even more youthful. Though Corven's servant couldn't talk, at least he could hear. It made it easier for Corven because he enjoyed speaking his thoughts out loud and having a listening ear helped construct his ideas, especially since Reece couldn't speak back. Corven knew he himself was the smartest of all Sand-shapers—though, he had kept that information a secret—and he didn't need servants offering inferior ideas. His father may have disowned him, but at least he had given him a quiet servant and a ledger of money that had gotten him this far.

He decided to take his destiny into his own hands once his father forced him to be the steward of Lord Rencon's archives of cylinders. Lord Rencon and his father had more cylinders than all the Sand-shapers of the Northwestern Coastal Cities combined. Little did they know that the reason he was good at categorizing them was because he had read every symbol on every parchment before his childhood memories closed at age fourteen. He knew the history of Rodesh all the way back to *The Great Engulfing*. He had even found old cylinders with memories written of the time before *The Great Engulfing*, which was why he was here now. He pieced together a new life for himself that included power, prestige and abundance. He would no longer be a mere steward.

"Bring the boat on shore and leave our bags here but grab the basket of auraium and my bag of cylinders. We needed to have a gift for the current bar Hathway Chieftain." While Reece did what he was told, Corven took a moment to inspect his surroundings. "So this is Lake-keeper territory. Funny. I don't see a lake. The earth shakes must have also changed their topography like it has ours. All I see is that the ocean has finally ended against this land. There are no longer underground tunnels and rivers hidden by a massive desert."

Corven looked south. A sandy shore spread a great distance to the east and west in a half-moon shape, but the sand on the east and the west transformed into rocky shores. Directly south, piers and decks lined a wooden boardwalk with fishing boats tied to their wood planks. Behind the shores he could see small wooden homes, and beyond that the making of a great forest. However, the trees in this forest were no match for the Achion trees that the River-dwellers still used as homes.

To the left of him were towering cliffs and a magnificent stone castle with winding, stone stairs on the perimeter. The grand castle cast a shadow over the waters. It was still early, and the sun would be above them in a few hours. Then he looked right. The cliffs were lower but broader. And instead of the castle towering with hundreds of steps winding to the pinnacle, this castle laid low, wide and long with all entrances level to the ground. This meant the steps were few, and he smiled. He was glad his lineage led to the Lowland Cliffs Clan rather than the Highland Cliffs Clan.

Reece walked up to him with the basket and bag in each hand. He gave his normal compliant smile. Corven knew that both the auraium and the cylinders were heavy loads, but Reece held them like they were filled with feathers and leaves.

"Be careful with the bag of cylinders. They are old. I wrapped each one with cloth, but they are still extremely fragile and could break and tear apart the parchments along with my evidence."

Reece nodded. As Corven turned back toward the low castle, a dozen swordsmen exited various doors of the castle and began to march his way. He knew they were swordsmen because they wore similar leather uniforms and carried great swords by their sides.

"So that is steel," Corven whispered under his breath. When the men arrived at his position, he gave the customary greeting he learned from one of the parchments which he had practiced. It was difficult with his lame foot, but he believed he had mastered the subtle bow and leaning back of his leg.

The swordsmen started to laugh.

One of the men walked up to him. His skin was several shades darker than his own light ebony coloring, but the swordsman had the same emerald eyes as his. His hair was light brown, though. Even lighter than his own. It was also much longer and held back together in a long braid. "My name is Durstin le Guyel. I am the Swordmaster of the Lowland Cliffs. And you just gave the bow of a woman." Durstin snickered and stared at Corven's lame foot. "Maybe it is fitting for you."

"My apologies," Corven said as his cheeks flushed. "I have come a great distance and with boundless peril to my life to talk with Chieftain bar Hathway."

"You look like us, but I don't recognize you. And where, by the Befores, are your horns? And where are his?" Durstin asked, pointing to Reece.

"I am from the land beyond the waters," he said, motioning to the sea they had crossed. "My name is Corven, and this is my servant Reece. I am a Sand-shaper. We work with sand and make glass for our homes, cities, decoration and even to wear. We started extracting our horns after *The Great Engulfing*, finding them cumbersome. We write the symbols you have no doubt been finding on your shores in the floating glass cylinders. I purchased this boat, and my servant rowed us here. It took almost two weeks, but I have information that your chieftain will want."

Durstin said nothing for several moments. He stared at Corven's hornless head and then toward the boat. "You know about the Chieftain Lothar bar Haven's inherited daughter, Amorfia?" he finally asked.

"Yes, her real name is F'lorna, and she is his biological niece."

"Impossible!" Durstin yelled. "Lothar has no heir."

"No, it's true. His mother died in the tunnels where the land bridge is now. A healer of the River-dwellers found her and got the baby out before the mother died. His name is Jaquarn, and he is F'lorna's father. They were both raised as River-dwellers, and they do not extract their horns."

Durstin looked skeptical. "As they shouldn't. You look like a baby with no horns."

Corven overlooked the insult. He was used to it, and he didn't want to offend anyone who could deter his plan. "F'lorna is only a tiny taste of what I know. I have information which will change the lives of every man and woman living in the Lowland Cliffs. I've come to make the bar Hathway Clan the most powerful clan of all the Lake-keepers and then all of Rodesh."

"The word *clan* is of the old dialect. We don't use it anymore. Now what do you have in the basket and bag?" Durstin asked, nodding at Reece who quietly continued to hold the heavy loads.

"The bag is full of auraium—or what I think you call gold—a gift to your chieftain. It is a rare metal that is used to make jewelry and other works of priceless art but not strong like your swords."

"We know what gold is," Durstin scoffed.

"Yes, of course. My apologies. And the bag is filled with cylinders that have the history of the bar Hathway family written in symbols."

"You know how to decipher the symbols?" Durstin asked.

"Not only that, but I also have thousands of them memorized in my childhood memories. I even have information that comes from before *The Great Engulfing,* which I believe you call the Great Shaking or the Great Shake. I may be lame in foot, but what I can offer your chieftain will give him an edge over every other chieftain. Plus…" Corven hesitated.

Durstin crossed his arms. "What? Say it now or I will not bring you to see Chieftain Rugar bar Hathway."

"I have a cylinder from my family's vault that tells of my grandmother from long ago born before *The Great Engulfing* who found herself cut off from her family and in new territory."

"So," the Swordsman said.

"She was a Lake-keeper and her last name was Hathway."

"That is a bold claim to say you have lineage with the bar Hathways."

"I know," Corven said. "But I can prove it."

"Let us hope so because if you prove to be false, you will be banished or killed."

Corven swallowed. "I understand the risks, but I've done extensive research and double checked all my findings."

"Well then," Durstin said, "you will present your gift and your proof and let the Befores decide your fate. Follow me and keep up."

Corven nodded but Durstin had already starting walking back toward the Lowland Cliff castle with the other swordsmen. Corven waved for Reece to come to his side, but he was already there still holding the heavy basket and bag. He grabbed hold of Reece's stable body in case he tripped. Corven trekked behind the swordsmen staring at the ground just before each step he made. He had fallen many times before jeering faces, and he wouldn't allow that to happen today. This day was his point of no return. A way to start the honored life that was stolen from him the day the head of the massive solid glass statue of his father fell on his foot, snapping his ankle in half and shattering every bone. The healers could not fix it, and it became twisted and weak.

Corven thought of Lord Rencon's traveling case and his servants who carried him south away from the Northwester Coastal cities. He had sent it to him knowing it would take months for him to travel to the farmlands on foot. He probably knew that Corven did not show up in the traveling case with the cylinders by now. Lord Rencon needed a way to make a material stronger than obsidian, and he hoped that information could be found in his large collection of cylinders. Corven had discovered the steel material of the Lake-keepers years ago, but he would not share such information. Lord Rencon already had too much wealth and power. The steel material would just elevate him further while he was stuck in the dingy cylinder vaults. He discovered that the Lake-keepers used the steel to forge weapons, and Lord Rencon desperately wanted it to create a tool that would cut the coveted auraium out from the face of the land bridge.

The travel south was extremely enlightening. The news about F'lorna, the River-dweller girl who had returned from the distant lands of the Lake-keepers, traveled fast. As he rode in the traveling case to Lord Tarmian's farmlands, whispers of startling events surrounded him at every stop. Corven's keen mind made quick connections, using all that he read in the cylinders as his reference point. When Corven received information about Lord Dexarian's illegitimate daughter and granddaughter, and that the grand-daughter, F'lorna, was related to Chieftain Lothar bar Haven on her father's side, he formulated his own plan. If she could be accepted into the bar Havens, there was a chance for him—though his relationship with the bar Hathways was more distant. Still, he had something more enticing to offer if he were accepted as a bar Hathway.

Suddenly, an odious odor filled Corven's nostrils. "What is that awful smell?"

"We are passing the Swarve stables. What? Do you not have Swarves in the lands beyond the waters?" Durstin asked.

"No, only the one F'lorna brought back. It supposedly ran and flapped its wings up the massive rocky incline to get F'lorna and her father to safety before the waters swallowed up the sands."

Durstin stopped. "Swarves do not fly. Their wings are as useless as that foot of yours."

"I was told this one had long golden feathers that gave him enough flight to make it up the land bridge, and I've seen that mass of rock. It is extremely high, even with the waters now gathered below."

"How is that possible?"

Corven smiled. "Again, I have information about that, as well. It will change everything you know about Swarves."

Durstin stood silently for several seconds. He looked toward two of his men. "Carry the basket and bag for Corven's servant, so he can assist Corven up the stairs to the throne room. When I present Corven, I want everything to go perfectly." He looked back at Corven. "If you do get accepted as a bar Hathway, you'll have to get your horns back. I have plenty of bulbs, it may take some time, but we'll find the right pair. We will have you looking like a proper Lake-keeper from the Lowland Cliffs."

Corven nodded. He hadn't read about the bulbs in the archives of cylinders, but he heard rumors that F'lorna had grown back her missing horn and even her mother was growing them. The two swordsmen took the heavy loads from Reece, and he offered his arm to Corven. Corven grabbed hold of it and began his walk looking straight and not at the ground. He was finished looking down. It was time for him to use the knowledge he had gained from years of quiet study to become a man of renown and prestige, not a man of shame hidden in dark vaults alone. He would never look down again.

Chapter 1

Sword Practice

F'lorna drove her sword forward from the center of her chest into the air with both hands on the grip and thrust her right foot swiftly ahead of her on the grassy floor. Her foot had been broken by a boulder during the land shudders, but it was almost completely healed now. Though, she still needed to be careful not to put too much weight on it. Her father was a great healer and made sure she mended properly. Then F'lorna swiped the sword down diagonally with her right hand, touching the hilt of the sword to her hip and bowing her torso low to the ground. Finally, she turned full circle to the left—switching the sword from her right to her left hand—and slashed the sword horizontally through the air crossing her body before turning her sword vertically and sliding it gracefully into the sheath belted on her right hip. Attack, guard and counterattack were the three principles of sword fighting. The younglings—both River-dwellers and

1

Marsh-landers—followed suit. She had over twenty students who wanted to learn the bar Haven Swordcraft. Many elders of both South Village and the Marshlands watched from a safe distance.

The younglings fought with spears made heavy by pouring melted sand mixed with grounded shells around them—a trick her mother showed her. F'lorna noticed her mother standing near the crowd. She had the midday meal prepared for the younglings. She wore a horn brace since her horns had already grown past toddler age. The process of planting the bulbs back into her forehead was painful. Her father almost didn't want to do the procedure, but T'maya insisted. She wanted horns and didn't care how painful the process would be. F'lorna assisted her father in the planting of the bulbs she had saved from her own horn. Her mother never cried out. F'lorna knew that years of being shunned because of her hornless head made the pain worth it, like the pain one has while giving birth.

Once the faux swords were secure by each youngling's side, F'lorna inspected them. Some of the younglings were only eight turns of the moon, but many of them were close to having closed Eternal Memories. The bar Haven Swordcraft would be a secondary Adoration for most of them. She stopped in front of Dezzy, the granddaughter of Limmian, the Spiritual Elder of South Village, and turned to face her. Her dark skin was drenched with sweat and strands of her auburn hair that she kept in a tight bun at the nape of her neck like her mother and grandmother were sticking to her cheeks and neck. She was close to being two turns and about to have her Doublemoon Ceremony. Her Eternal Memory would shut at any moment, but F'lorna gave voiceless words that Ra'ash would give her more time. Dezzy was her best student.

"So have you decided which Adoration you would choose to present at your Doublemoon Ceremony?" F'lorna asked. "Hunting or Swordcraft?"

Dezzy gave a mischievous smile. "My grandmother, father and mother went to the Circle of Elders with my request. I want to offer two Adorations for my Doublemoon Ceremony."

2

F'lorna paused. It was difficult for many River-dwellers to change tradition, but the people of South Village had more to think about than formalities. The Sand-shapers would be coming for the auraium and could use their obsidian blades to attack the villagers. F'lorna also knew that Lothar bar Haven, her uncle and chieftain of the Highland Cliffs, wanted an interrupter for the Sand-shaper symbols. Though she doubted he would leave his territory vulnerable, he may find a way to send servants across the great waters that were once the Desert Plains. F'lorna looked at her young apprentice. Her grandmother, Elder Limmian, was an excellent Spiritual leader of South Village. She and the Circle of Elders would choose what was best for the village.

"What was their answer?" F'lorna asked.

"They said I can offer both Adorations. I will simply harvest my animal before the ceremony. Your mother has already said she will prepare it for me. Then I will present the Swordcraft on the Village Achion cluster."

F'lorna nodded. "Good. But now I must teach you all of it. We do not have much time. I would like to do one-on-one training with you each day before our evening meal."

"I was going to offer that exact request," Dezzy replied.

"Has Lemmeck finished all your hunting training?" F'lorna didn't want to intrude in his work with Dezzy. His brothers, Rashion and Dashion, went back home to Left River Hook with Sage. Le'ana joined them but went back home to Right River Hook. Zelara had written her twice since their return and many families from Right River Hook had gone to live at Left River Hook and other tributary villages further south. It seems that with the absence of Jaquarn, Zelara's father, Elder Trenton, has become more aggressive about leading the village, and he is no Spiritual Elder. He's currently trying to eradicate the Shoam-sha, saying that spiritual matters should be done at home. The Circle of Elders are split on the decision.

"Yes, he says I was a quick study. I am honored that you and Lemmeck visited our village and stayed, or I believe I would not have gone down the path Ra'ash wills for me."

3

"Ra'ash has His ways. We simply must trust Him." F'lorna turned toward the rest of the younglings waiting for her next command. "That is all for today. I expect you to practice at your Achion cluster until our next meeting. You have the moves memorized, but now you must add the power and finesse needed. Your swordcraft should appear as a formidable dance."

"Yes, Novice Elder F'lorna," they all repeated in unison. Then they hurried to where T'maya was waiting with the midday meal.

F'lorna felt the cool spring air flow across her sweat-drenched tunic. She thought she might go back to the Visitor's Achion cluster to rest and clean up, but she needed to talk with Lemmeck. If he was finished teaching Dezzy the Hunting Adoration, there was no reason for him to stay so far away from his family. She felt for the small glass pendant around her neck with the strands of the White Diamond Stag inside. She found it on the shores of the Highland Cliffs when she had forgotten her true identity. It felt like a cycle of moons ago that he had given it to her. She and her birth friends were almost about to celebrate their sixteenth turns of the moon together. However, deep within her chest, she carried the weight of two worlds and two lives, and the abundance of knowledge and memories made her feel aged.

F'lorna saw her father coming alongside her mother to help pass out the food. Her mother's growing horns were now secured with a horn brace to ensure their proper growth. She quickly walked toward her parents. "Father, did you see some of our practice today? The Younglings are learning quickly, especially Dezzy."

He put his strong arm around her shoulder. "I offer you my apology of healing, my daughter. I was busy with my team. We are still trying to find the iron rocks you need to create steel and forge swords like yours. As of now, we have been unsuccessful. All we can find is auraium, and that metal is too soft and heavy. It wouldn't last long against a steel sword."

F'lorna knew the various iron ore rocks used in the making of steel because a Highland Cliff Sage showed her the various rocks and then explained the process of extracting the iron from them with fire, but F'lorna feared the rocks were only found in the High and Lowland Cliffs because Chieftain Lothar and Chieftain Hathway were the only Lake-keepers who had armies of swordsmen. The South, East and West Basin chieftains had bowmen, using arrows of wood from Atlatl Forest.

F'lorna thought. "What if you tried underwater? There were tunnels of rock and dirt. I traveled the length of them. Maybe some of the ore rocks made their way to the bottom of the new waters that swallowed up the Desert Plains."

Jaquarn scratched his chin with his free hand and his countenance brightened. "Maybe you are right. Riverend Village on the other side of the land bridge makes boats. Maybe we can borrow some and go diving. I don't think the waters are too deep close to the land bridge. Maybe Ra'ash will be gracious and have some of those rocks collecting against the land bridge floor. I will go speak with their Spiritual Elder now."

"Father, before you go, I've had some of those headaches again. Can I go into your medicine pouch and get out the herbs for my tea?"

Jaquarn wrapped his other arm around F'lorna and brought her to his chest. "I know you have been through a lot. We all have, but you have gotten the worst of it. I believe your headaches are from having two Eternal Memories. It will take time to get used to them and learn to use them in tandem. But yes, my medicine pouch is on the top shelf of my and your mother's Achion tree. Just put it back when you're done."

"Of course, Father. I give you my gratitude of understanding."

"Here, F'lorna. I saved you a portion of the soup. I believe your size is thinning like the saplings around the Achion trees."

F'lorna eyed the soup. "Thank you, Mother. I'm sure it's from all the exertion of training the swordcraft. I must tie my tunic belt a little tighter. Can you save my soup? I will come back and get it. I need to speak with Lemmeck."

T'maya gave her daughter a stern look. "I will be here only until the Heat Source moves west two-finger widths. Then I expect you to eat."

F'lorna nodded. "Yes, Mother." Then she turned to walk to the Visitor Achion cluster where she, her parents and Lemmeck were staying. Once she got to her parents' Achion hole, she crawled in and reached for her father's medicine pouch. She knew what herbs she wanted, but it wasn't for headaches. Once she opened the pouch, she saw the herbs tucked into a separate smaller bag and her heart became tense. She looked out through the Achion hole to make sure no one was watching her. First, she unstrapped her own medicine pouch from her tunic belt. It was a lot smaller than her father's. She rolled it open. She opened the small bag with the special herbs and pinched a double helping of the dried, red leaves. If she didn't replace them soon, her father would notice. She carefully placed the herbs into a pocket in her pouch and rolled it back up. Finally, she closed the small bag and put it back into her father's pouch and closed it.

After F'lorna reached up to put it back on the top shelf, she looked down and saw another medicine pouch on the bottom shelf next to her right knee.

"It's Aunt Eline's medicinal pouch," she said breathlessly.

F'lorna quickly rolled the large pouch open. Then she saw what she was looking for. But instead of opening the small bag of herbs, she took the entire thing. She hoped her father wouldn't notice. Then she placed the pouch exactly as she found it. She quickly shoved the bag into her medicinal pouch and reattached it to her tunic belt. Then she exited the Achion hole with so much haste that she ran into Lemmeck.

"F'lorna," he said catching her. "Are you in a rush?"

F'lorna felt her cheeks flush, but hopefully, they were still red from her vigorous training. "I was looking for you, in fact."

He let his hands gently slide down her arms as he let go. "You were, weren't you?" He smiled.

As F'lorna stared into his emerald eyes, she thought of the old sage from the Lowland Cliffs. They looked very similar, and she wondered if he too had Lake-keeper blood in his family lineage. "I wanted to ask you that since you are finished with Dezzy's training, would you be making the trek home to be with your family?"

Lemmeck's smile faded. "I've been waiting for you and your family to return, and I shall join you."

"I haven't told you yet," she whispered, looking at the ground.

"What? F'lorna, what haven't you told me?" he asked.

F'lorna could hear uneasiness in his voice.

"My mother and father agreed that we would stay here for a while longer. Then my father wants to take Aunt Eline's place as a traveling Healing Elder, training villages as we go. And I will train the bar Haven Swordcraft to all who want to learn."

"But," he said, lifting her face with his finger, "we are almost sixteen turns. I wanted to ask your parents if I could begin the process of courting you."

Tears threatened to sting the corners of F'lorna's eyes. "I care about you, Lemmeck. But I also care about Boru."

Lemmeck let his hands fall to his sides. "I thought he was merely a friend. A companion to keep you company when you were with the sages."

"He was and so were you—just a friend. But now I have these two memories and these two sets of emotions, and I'm confused and almost—" She stopped.

"Almost what?" he pressed.

She stared into his eyes and grabbed his hands into hers. "Please don't tell anyone. Not yet. I'm not ready. Everyone is so happy that I am alive and home."

"I promise I won't tell anyone unless I fear you are in danger."

She looked away for a moment and took a deep breath. "I feel tormented. I have nightmares every night. I can't sleep. I can't eat. It's hard to explain, but I feel like I'm struggling between two warring worlds. My own mind is conflicted, and it is no longer a safe place for me. My thoughts have no peace. I keep myself busy, but it's not enough. I keep thinking time will make things better, but I fear I'm getting worse. I don't know how to live as two people, and I'm struggling to bring them together."

Lemmeck brought F'lorna into his arms and she began to weep. "What were you getting out of your father's Achion tree?"

F'lorna could no longer hide the truth. "It's an herb to help me sleep. It's the only thing that calms my thoughts. I don't know what else to do. I wasn't sleeping. Images and thoughts bombarded my mind all night every night. I couldn't stop the noise of my fighting thoughts."

"You know you will have to tell your father."

F'lorna pushed away from Lemmeck. "That is the worst of it. I called another man *Father*. I feel like I betrayed my own father. Why couldn't I remember? Why did I forget my life and start another one?" Fresh tears wet her cheeks.

"Look, F'lorna," Lemmeck said, bringing her back into his embrace, "this is not your fault. Ra'ash allowed this for a reason. You couldn't remember. There was nothing else for you to do but to begin again. Trust me, though. I know you will overcome this struggle and be stronger on the other side, but you can't do it alone. We are all here to help you. Do not let shame or guilt stop you from receiving love from your family and friends. Do you understand? I'm hurt about your feelings for Boru, but I am not angry. I understand you were looking for companionship, and I will understand regardless of what you choose to do because I care about you. Your father will understand too. You must speak with him and your mother. She is of two worlds, as well. She can help you understand the experience in a better light."

F'lorna stayed in Lemmeck's arms for a moment longer. She experienced some semblance of peace, which she hadn't felt since she arrived over the bridge.

"Why don't you go to Croga? Maybe he can help."

"Poor thing." F'lorna gave a soft laugh. "He's just as confused as I am. He can help me with my Mountain Terror, but now he's dealing with two people in one body. He soothes the Amorfia part of me, but he doesn't know what to do with this new

F'lorna of his. Thankfully, he cures the Mountain Terror in F'lorna also or else I couldn't be close to the land bridge."

"Maybe he needs to figure it all out too. You both can do it together. We always have hope with Ra'ash walking with us and the Indwelling guiding us."

"You're right. Thank you, Lemmeck. You have been more than a friend to me."

Lemmeck finally let go of his second embrace. "I will stay until Dezzy's Doublemoon Ceremony, and then I must travel home. I want you to talk to your parents before then. I don't want to leave being the only one who knows your struggle."

"You are right," she nodded. "Give me a few more rises of the moon. Let me go to Croga. Maybe he'll finally accept and soothe the F'lorna part of me."

"He should. The F'lorna part of you has lived many more turns of the moon than the Amorfia part of you." Lemmeck moved his hand toward F'lorna's right horn and allowed his fingers to slip through her silken, amber hair. "Your hair has gotten so long, and you don't braid it anymore."

She allowed him to stroke her hair. The feeling of his touch comforted her. "I know. Braiding hair around our horns seems like a silly custom now. My mother always wanted to braid my hair because I think she was so proud of my horns. I never really learned to do it by myself. And, honestly, I don't want to learn. There are some things about the River-dwellers that I don't agree with," she said. She quickly repressed memories of her mother being politely—and sometimes not so politely—tolerated at Right River Hook all her life.

"I know," he agreed. "There are some things that I do not like, but it is my home—though, not Right River Hook. My family serves Left River Hook now." Then he looked at the golden cuff on her left horn. "And you have allowed the crest of the Lake-keepers to remain on your horn." He moved his hand to feel the carved symbol of the Highland Cliffs Chieftain. "It's made of auraium or what the Lake-keepers call gold."

"Yes, but the teeth of the cuff are made of steel and are embedded in my horn. Plus—" she hesitated. "I lost my left horn here and regained it with the Lake-keepers. Somehow, I feel like it is meant to be there."

Lemmeck allowed his fingers to have one more stroke of her vibrant hair. He finally brought his hand back to his side and replaced the longing in his voice with a tone of protection. "And F'lorna, everyone sees it. You have lost weight. People think it's because you train the younglings with the sword or because you just came back from the Lake-keepers, but the truth will come out eventually. Please tell your father and mother. They are understanding and wise. They will help you through this difficulty."

F'lorna smiled and nodded. "I will. I just need a few more Rises of the Heat Source." Then she squeezed his shoulder with her hand in the River-dweller's customary way of saying hello and goodbye. "I will see you at evening meal."

"Yes," he said. "I will save a seat for you at your parents' table. F'lorna, promise me that once you make peace within that you will think of me. Maybe deeper feelings for me will arise."

"I promise," she whispered and turned to make her way further in the forest to find Croga. She gave silent words that the animal could finally come to know the F'lorna part of her. Lemmeck was right. Amorfia hadn't even lived a full turn of the moon. However, because of the Supreme Sage's insistence on her learning, the Amorfia part of her had an entire civilization stored in her Eternal Memory.

Chapter 2

Eavesdropping

F'lorna tried not to make a noise as she stepped through the mossy ground of the forest floor. Croga was more than likely napping, and she enjoyed creeping up on him. She saw a flash of golden wisps of fur between the many Achion tree leaves. He loved eating the leaves, and since spring had arrived, they were in abundance. Finally, when she got close enough, she jumped out from behind a big tree and yelped. Croga yawned and rolled onto his back, exposing his large underbelly.

"Croga, I can't scare you anymore," she said giggling. She knelt next to him, and his fur automatically began reaching for the exposed skin on her arms. She reached over his large belly and began to rub. He stretched his torso and made the grunting noises that signified he was content.

"You are getting so massive, Croga. And you are eating too many leaves. I've seen you crawl up the Achion trees to eat more.

11

You must flap your wings to help carry the weight. Your feathers are long and beautiful, but they could never carry all of you across the sky," she said and laid her upper body across his belly. His fur did soothe her, but she wished he could reach all of her. She remembered the Lake-keeper's stories of Swarves making two connections, not just one. She needed him to connect with the F'lorna side of her. That was the only way she would get better.

She got up from his belly and sat on the ground directly behind his head. Then she scooted up while lifting his head and placed it on her lap, allowing the wisps of fur to once again wrap around her bare arms. "Can I tell you a story, Croga?"

He closed his eyes like he was listening and allowed her to stroke his face. "About three turns ago, my best birth friend was taken from me by her grandfather. Her name is Raecli. When I lost our friendship, I was devastated. I grieved every day. Then, I shut down my feelings and stopped engaging in the daily life of our village. I did what needed to be done, but I could never put my heart in it. I think I feared being hurt again. Then I saw my friend, Raecli, for a moment on the land bridge just before I fell." As F'lorna spoke, she allowed the memories to fill her mind along with the emotions attached. "I fell and forgot who I was. I forgot that I was F'lorna, a River-dweller from Right River Hook. I became Amorfia, and when you came to me, you only connected with a small part of who I am." F'lorna's voice shook while she talked, but she kept going. "Now I am back to my homelands, but when I asked to see Raecli, Weston received a note from her that her grandfather was taking her back to cities of the Northwestern Coast." F'lorna felt more tears wetting her face. She rarely cried as F'lorna. Maybe she had become more like Amorfia.

She placed her face against Croga's cheek, and his fur began to wrap gently around her neck, cheeks and forehead, allowing space under her nose for her to breathe. She said nothing more but opened her heart and mind to the pain of the loss she felt. She wanted to stop the painful feelings from flowing in her mind, but she yearned for Croga to reach them somehow and to understand and ease the hurt. She almost stopped the painful process, but Croga's eyes suddenly opened. She looked deep within the blacks of his pupils. Finally, an ease poured down her body from head to toe like oil. For the first time, she felt at peace with her loss of Raecli, and the pain she felt after her birth friend left dissipated. Croga had touched a part of F'lorna.

As Croga cradled her face, she began to pet his neck and shoulders. That's what she would do. She would expose parts of F'lorna to Croga a little bit at a time. Eventually, he would get to know her fully and respond to both the F'lorna and Amorfia parts of her. If Croga could merge the two worlds, so could she. Lemmeck's words resonated in her mind. She would overcome this struggle. Ra'ash would have not allowed it unless He had already planned her victory.

Raecli's grandfather, Lord Rencon, kicked over a glass floor vase and the intricate design smashed to the ground exploding in piercing shards. One of the servants went to the kitchen to retrieve the sweeper. Intricately etched and stained artwork adorned the walls of the vast townhouse. One of many Raecli's grandfather owned. The building was constructed with stones from the Northeastern Mountains and hardened, thick glass flowing through the uneven rock for a uniform shape of the building's design. Out of all their townhomes in the various cities, this one was her favorite because of the friends she made in the city.

"Are you sure your team can read every symbol on every parchment within every cylinder?" he questioned.

"Yes, sir. There are no cylinders with information before *The Great Engulfing*. There are also no cylinders with information about the Lake-keepers," Moriel, Lord Rencon's steward said. "Corven must have taken them all."

Raecli's grandfather's face turned the color of the sun rose. Raecli watched the scene from behind the living room wall of their lavish city townhome. She remembered when she first moved there three years ago. It took her months to get used to a house made up of rock that was smoothed out and bound with dyed Sand-shaper glass. The intricate patterns of glass and rock were unnaturally beautiful. It was so different from her Achion tree at Right River Hook which was organic and alive. Now she was accustomed to her new life—the city, the stones, the glass, the servants and her grandfather's rage.

"Where is he going with them? Who knows what's on the other side of the new south ocean!" her grandfather continued to yell.

"My only thought is that he read something in those cylinders that makes him believe there is land and people beyond the south lands and across the new waters."

"The Lake-keepers," her grandfather muttered to himself. "I shouldn't have trusted all my archives to Corven. I was too good to him for his father's sake. Who knows how many of my cylinders he has memorized."

"I believe he has memorized all of them," Moriel said, hesitantly.

Her grandfather quickly turned. "What makes you say that?"

"He came here before his childhood memories shut. He's lame in the foot. He had nothing better to do, and they were all easy to open like they've been read and reread. Plus, he has them all organized not only by dates but by subject matter. It's quite ingenious the way he managed your archives."

Her grandfather paced. "I shouldn't have left Lord Tarmian's lands so quickly. I may need an ally if Corven somehow manages an alliance with these so-called Lake-keepers, which I seriously doubt."

Raecli thought of the farmlands. She hated leaving Lord Tarmian's home, but after her grandfather discovered that Corven, his cylinder archives steward, had been seen on a boat in the new waters of the south, her grandfather had his servants pack them up and they left the following day. She wondered about Sabien. His predicament saddened her. She didn't know what he would choose: life as Lord Sabien over the farmlands or life with the Marsh-landers with the one he loves. She would not be marrying him either way. Her grandfather made it clear he would not let his granddaughter marry into a family of lies and secrets. It didn't matter, though. She had renewed hope from a different source. Just before they left, she received a note from Weston that F'lorna was alive and back with her family.

Her grandfather looked back at Moriel. "Do you remember my last words to Lord Tarmian? Were they enough to sever all ties, or do you think there is still hope for an alliance even without a marriage?"

Moriel spoke instantly. "When it comes to auraium, there is always room for negotiations."

"Send several servants back to his lands. Tell them to not rest until they arrive at his home. Bring enough auraium to entice him but not so much that his thirst for more is quenched. It's spring, and he needs all his servants planting in the fields. Only I have the servants necessary to dig the auraium out of the rockface. We will keep cutting it out with obsidian. It's not efficient but at least it works."

"Once I receive his answer, should I return to the city?" Moriel asked.

Raecli's grandfather shook his head. "No, we have left the land bridge vulnerable. Other merchants from the cities or even some of the landowners may try to stake claim to it. Bring your men and arm them with obsidian blades as well. Make temporary houses. Do everything necessary to establish your presence in the south lands near the bridge. The River-dwellers fear us. They won't attempt any attacks on us. Besides they don't have any use or need for auraium."

"Will you be joining us?" Moriel asked.

"Yes, but not for a few weeks. I have business to attend in the cities. Plus, I need my granddaughter to attend at least some of the many gala invitations we have been receiving. I can't marry her off if she's hidden from high society in the south lands. I was hoping for a landowner connection, but I have several wealthy merchants who have suitable sons. They are all drooling to connect with my family name. Very few of them seem suitable, though."

Raecli felt like someone elbowed her in the gut. She didn't want to stay in the city. It was home for now, but if she lived near her grandfather all her life, he would continue to wield control over her. Plus, she may never see F'lorna again if she lived so far north. F'lorna couldn't possibly make her way up to the cities.

"Let me at least inquire about other landowners who may have sons of marrying age as I travel south again. We only offered an alliance to Lord Tarmian because his lands are further south and closer to the auraium, but it would be ideal in the long run to meet a landowner further north and closer to the cities."

Raecli liked that idea better than marrying a merchant's son and waited, holding her breath for her grandfather's answer.

"I think you are right. The travel to Lord Tarmian's lands does take several weeks. I'll admit that his lands are vast, but his management tactics are completely barbaric. He doesn't keep money ledgers, which is why his servants revolted and left. My guess is that eventually the rest of his servants will do the same. Even his son may leave him. Yes, we will look for wealthy landowners further north. Their lands may be smaller, but an alliance with a family without secrets and deception is preferable."

Raecli's grandfather turned and yelled her name. She waited a moment, so he wouldn't discover she was in the hall listening. He shouted again.

"Yes, Grandfather," she said as she turned the corner of the stone wall.

"Have your lady's maid get you ready. You will be attending a gala at Lord Munchester's home tomorrow evening. I want you to meet his son, Lord Layton. He's a fine-looking young man with violet eyes. He's a bit small, but I believe he will find you suitable."

Raecli looked confused. "I've never heard of that name before. I have invitations from friends here in this city to dine with them. I haven't seen them since we arrived home."

"Ha! Those were simply friends I allowed you to get to know to help teach you to act like a Sand-shaper. Their parents do well enough, but they are by no means rich enough to make an alliance with me. They are upper-middle-class youth who catered to you because of our family name. Oh, how they loved eating our food and having our servants wait on them! Now that your horns have been extracted, I can introduce you to the wealthiest of merchants. Lord Munchester's home is closer to the Northeastern Mountains, so it will take a full day to travel there. We will leave first thing in the morning in a traveling case. Plus, as a special treat, you'll get to see the Sapphire Bridge that crosses over the River just before it breaks off into the Four Horns. They have just reopened it after that damage from those costly earth shakes. So much was lost because of those forceful land shudders!"

Raecli nodded her head. The earth shudders were bad up north, but Raecli was told by Lanie, the housemaid at Lord Tarmian's home, they were much worse in the south.

"Now let us see who will be the first to make the best offer for your hand in marriage. I wanted an alliance with a landowner, but a rich merchant would be just as profitable. Plus, I already have my own lands."

"We have land?" Raecli asked.

Her grandfather's lips warped into a side smirk. "Yes, the lands by the land bridge."

"But that's River-dweller territory!" she cried out, quickly covering her mouth. "I'm sorry. I didn't mean to yell."

"From what I've seen there is a village to the right of the land bridge and to the left, but no one has claimed the land in the middle."

"That's because we consider it shared lands of Rodesh."

"Now it will be mine." He turned back to Moirel. "Set out tomorrow for Lord Tarmian's lands. Inquire if any of the northern landowners have a suitable mate for my granddaughter, but do it discreetly and quickly. I need you to get to the south lands and claim that territory and the land bridge with all the auraium as mine."

Chapter 3

A Divine Reading

All the members of the house including the house servants stood around the grave of Lord Dexarian. The field servants gathered a hundred yards behind the grave to pay their respects. Lord Tarmian held an old parchment and read the words over the grave. The words intrigued his son, Sabien. He had never heard his father speak of a God named Ra'ash and the Indwelling. And where was this Eternal Dwelling that he spoke of that his grandfather was going to? All the words on the parchment seemed important. They spoke of an afterlife once the body died on Rodesh, so why had his mother and father neglected to tell him? He turned to look at Kysha. She stood next to her father, Mr. Barton, his father's steward. She kept her head down. Sabien didn't want her near the grave, but her father insisted she was not a field servant. He had feelings for her, but she wouldn't look at him in the face. He couldn't stand being so close to her while a thick wall of tradition separated them.

Maybe if they waited long enough, he could finally marry her once his father entered his own Eternal Dwelling—wherever that was. His mother would not be happy, but she would have no say in the matter. But could he or she wait that long? It could be twenty years or more before his father died—probably much more since his grandfather had lived so long. Surely, his mother would insist on a grandbaby sooner than twenty-plus years. Then another thought came to him! It was perfect. He could have Kysha and his lands. He would talk to his father after the funeral.

Lord Tarmian ended his speech with the words, *so be it.* His mother, Mr. Barton along with the housemaid, Marva, and the cooks repeated the words. What did they know that he didn't? Kysha finally looked at him and gave him a look of bewilderment. She had never been to a funeral either, and the entire process was foreign to them. Even Lainie, the other housemaid who stood behind Miss Marva, looked baffled by it all.

Lord Tarmian rolled the parchment and placed it back into the cylinder and handed it to Mr. Barton.

"I don't know why my father insisted on me reading this archaic gibberish at his funeral. My father's many travels have exposed him to a bunch of nonsense. Couldn't he have died months ago with the secret of my half-sister and niece buried with him? Lord Rencon was so close to being part of our family's name. His granddaughter, Raecli, was perfect. He himself is aged. He probably has less than ten years left of life. We could have had his city properties, townhomes, businesses and connections incorporated with ours."

Lord Tarmian turned to Sabien. "Do you understand the weight of all this? Do you understand what that alliance would have done for our family and for you? But you had to ruin it just like your grandfather with your infatuation with a servant who can't run a home or work the fields. Besides her beauty, she's useless."

"She's more than that, Father," Sabien said. "She is kind. She loves me for me and not for what I own." He eyed Kysha who was staring at the ground. It was normal for landowners to speak about their servants as if they weren't there.

"You mean what I own," his father corrected.

"Yes, for now. But you too are advanced in years. You'll be in your Eternal Dwelling, whatever that is, soon enough, and I will inherit these lands. And when I do, I will reinstate the money ledger to the servants. And I will not treat them like slaves."

Suddenly, he felt a slap across his face. When he opened his eyes, his mother stood eye-to-eye to him.

"How dare you say that about your father. He has been nothing but benevolent to our servants," she said.

"If that were true, Mother, why did almost a third of them flee? I would like you to live even one week as one of them. You wouldn't last a day."

"I am of highborn birth. They are not. They are accustomed to a way of life that is safe and good but different than my own. Yet, it is still a good life."

"Mother, I don't want to argue with you. I know your disposition can weaken with stress. Why don't you go into the house and finalize our dinner to celebrate my grandfather? Let me talk with Father for a moment."

Lady Rosarian's shoulders relaxed. "You do know me well, Son. Yes, let me focus on the dinner. We have several prestigious families joining us for our dinner to celebrate your grandfather's life. My sister should be here with her traveling case at any moment. We must ensure that everything is perfect." She turned to Marva. "Get the servants and cooks into the house. I want to go over every last detail."

"Yes ma'am," Marva said with a curtsy.

Lord Tarmian faced his steward. "Mr. Barton, get the field hands back to work. The plants won't plant themselves. And take your daughter back to your house. I don't want her outside. She's already caused enough trouble."

Mr. Barton glared at his daughter. "Get to the house and learn to do something of value."

"But my childhood memories are shut," she whispered. "I didn't have a mother to teach me, and you were always gone."

"Then open some of my cylinders and read. You can do that. I, at least, made sure you learned the forty-four symbols. Then follow the instructions word for word and produce something useful."

"Yes, Father," she said, bowing. Then she again glanced briefly at Sabien as she walked past him to her house.

"Now I'll go deal with the field hands," Mr. Barton said, leaving the gravesite.

Finally, Sabien and his father were alone. "Father, can I speak with you for a moment?"

"Yes, I've been meaning to speak with you," his father said. Something in his voice was off like he had a secret he's been holding onto for a while.

"Shall I go first or you?"

His father grinned. "Let me hear what you have to say; though, I'm fairly certain I know what it is."

Now Sabien was beginning to feel insecure. His father had a way of always being one step ahead of him.

"I'm going to marry Kysha and find where the servants who fled are located. I will live with them until you enter your Eternal Dwelling. Then I will come back here and claim my lands. It may take twenty years or more, but I'm willing to wait."

His father appeared indifferent to his statement.

"No, you will not. Now that I know you will be marrying a lowborn, I've already made arrangements to declare F'lorna, my niece, as heir to these lands."

Sabien shirked back. "But she's half highborn and half lowborn, and she's illegitimate. Her grandmother was not my grandfather's wife. Why would you give the lands to a half-breed, but you won't allow my happiness by marrying a servant? Why will you break tradition for her but not for your own son?"

"I had to," Lord Tarmian snapped. "When you decided not to marry the merchant's granddaughter. We have a lot of land, but I'm losing servants. I need an alliance that will continue our family line. And you will not offer that to me, so I must find it elsewhere."

"But F'lorna is half River-dweller and half Sand-shaper born out of wedlock to a mistress. How can she possibly help our family line?"

"I have discovered that she is not River-dweller at all. In fact, she is the daughter and niece of a powerful chieftain of the Lake-keepers."

"That's preposterous! They don't exist!"

"That's where you are wrong. When Lord Rencon's steward of his archives didn't show up, I overheard his servants telling him that Corven had proof that they do exist. They have a material called steel. With this metal, they create weapons that can destroy any of Lord Rencon's knives of obsidian. An alliance with this chieftain will make us the most feared and powerful family of all the landowners. Then, I will turn my sights to the cities. Why shouldn't we have a home here and a townhome in the cities? Or maybe two or three?"

"But isn't that girl, F'lorna, dead? She fell over the land bridge," Sabien said, feeling desperation fill his chest. "If she is my half-cousin, she is no longer alive."

"No. In fact, she's alive and well and living in the south lands. This is where the entire story gets more interesting."

"How do you know she's alive? You've been here, and we haven't sent any servants to the south lands."

Lord Tarmian's smile broadened. "I intercepted a parchment. It was ingenious. This falcon flew to Lord Rencon's granddaughter's room next to the large Achion tree your grandfather planted when I was young. There was a piece of leather wrapped around a thick tree branch near her window. I watched her take the parchment from a cylinder the bird of prey wore around his ankle. Then she left and came back with some meat for him, and he flew off. I waited until she left her room for her morning walk with the maid, and I found the note in her drawer. It told me everything that I needed to know. Not only do Lake-keepers exist, I have a relative with them through that F'lorna girl and my half-sister's husband."

"It's too risky," Sabien said. "You don't know these Lake-keepers. You don't know if they'll even accept her and especially you. And the relations are too distant. You're not related to T'maya's husband."

"I am related to F'lorna! My father's blood is part of that girl through my half-sister."

"Yet, it is a risk," Sabien said with a sigh.

"Yes, you are right. It is a risk. However, I do know the Lake-keeper chieftain does not have an heir to his throne, and he was willing to make F'lorna his heir. An alliance with her and the Lake-keepers would be most beneficial since you won't cooperate."

Sabien felt his life slipping from his hands. Could he really live as a River-dweller in trees like an animal? Like his mother, could he even live one day as a servant? Had he taken his position and lifestyle for granted to the point he would give it all away for a pretty servant girl who did not have grey or violet eyes? And who practically had no talents or abilities?

He looked back at his father who was obviously waiting for a reply. "Okay, I will marry Raecli but on one condition."

"You're in no position to be demanding conditions, Son."

Sabien raised his hands in defeat. "I know. I just want Kysha to be taken care of."

"She's to be married to Lord Steson's Steward, Mr. Beal. His wife passed away, and he needs a new wife. He will be here for dinner tonight to meet her."

"He's almost twenty years older than Kysha!" Lord Sabien yelled.

"Completely normal for a second wife. His first wife gave him no children. Now he has another chance. The deal has already been made. What? Did you think I would let her stay here for you to create more illegitimate children in our family? Our family name has been tarnished enough by my father. It is time for you to do your duty as a lord and heir of these lands. The only thing that girl has to offer Mr. Beal is her youth, beauty and, hopefully, babies."

Sabien felt his quickened heartbeat slow. A numbness spread across his body. "Yes, father. I will do as you say."

"Good. Now let us hope that Lord Rencon will have us back."

Chapter 4

Official Adoption

Lothar didn't like waiting. The Supreme Sage should have been here at least an hour ago. He had to keep his irritation to a minimum, however. Today was important. He paced the dining hall. The food had already gotten cold. No matter. The Supreme Sage would never dine with him. He didn't much like her company anyhow. He looked to his left, expecting to see Garth. He had been his trusted advisor for so many years only to find out he led his mother to her demise in the caves. He ran him through with his sword—maybe a little too hasty since he knew information about his brother surviving. He had a little brother out there on the other side of the waters and his niece, Amorfia—or F'lorna, so the old sage from the Lowland Cliffs told him. He would get her back, and she would be his heir. And unlike himself, she would produce more heirs and continue the bar Haven family line. He just needed the Supreme Sage to finally arrive.

"Has she kept you waiting this long?" he heard the voice of his Aunt Dalia ask. "How dare she keep you lingering."

"I will not let her ruin this day. When she arrives, we will be on our best behavior. She knows this is important to me, so she is simply enjoying making me wait."

Lothar paced the halls impatiently. He had waited his entire adult life for this moment. And the waiting had caused a heaviness in his chest he couldn't shake.

Finally, his Swordmaster, Dagor le Armon, entered the halls. He had taken Garth's place as his advisor, but Lothar still didn't trust him. He would probably never trust another advisor again.

"The Supreme Sage's boat has arrived," Dagor announced.

"Why would she be in a boat? The sages from Atlatl Forest always arrive on their Swarves."

Dagor looked uneasy. His pale face flushed, and his shoulder-length blonde hair and beardless face made him appear almost feminine. Too handsome to be a swordsman, but here he was. He was young and inexperienced, unlike Garth who had a scar to show his battle wounds. However, Dagor had proven himself to be the best swordsmen in his army and one of the tallest and strongest. While the other men at night would drink and seek out the beds of women, Dagor le Armon would practice his sword fighting—most likely to make up for his father's banishment from the bar Haven's swordsmen years ago when Dagor was just a boy.

Lothar's father, Vandar bar Haven, humiliated and dismissed Dagor's father, Cresden, for getting too comfortable meddling in the bar Haven family's personal affairs. Last he'd heard of Cresden was that he demeaned himself to become a farmer on the rocky lands of the Highland Cliffs. However, he taught his sons everything he knew about war and fighting, including the le Armon Swordcraft, which was cunning but not as violent as the bar Haven Swordcraft. Dagor was the first of five sons sired and reared by Cresden and his wife. Lothar had his qualms about taking the boy on, but war was war and a chieftain had to put his or her personal feelings aside to create an unbeatable army. That is how a chieftain's house stayed strong. Besides, Dagor worked harder than the rest, which made up for his fancy looks and family history. Lothar didn't know exactly why his father dismissed Cresden, but in recent months, he had an inkling that it may have to do with his father's treatment of his mother. But that was the past. Now he had a future that included F'lorna at the center.

"We saw her leaving the Lowland Cliffs. She's coming directly here from Rugar bar Hathway's castle."

"How dare she visit my enemy just before coming here!" The frustration Lothar was feeling transformed into anger.

"Lothar, don't jump to conclusions. The Supreme Sage is highly intelligent—" Dalia said quickly. "And she doesn't have favorites. She only uses chieftains to her advantage. We are all equal opportunities in her eyes."

"You mean she's highly cunning," Lothar interrupted.

"My point is that she would never do anything to jeopardize her position as Supreme Sage. If she is coming from the Lowland Cliffs, there must be a reason that will benefit her and us. We are the strongest of the chieftains and have been faithful with our tributes and tithes to the sages. She wants our family line to continue. Now loosen the grip on your sword. You will ruin our family if you even draw the sword in her presence."

Lothar hadn't noticed that he was about to draw his sword. He quickly loosened his fingers. Several swordsmen walked into the dining hall, leading the Supreme Sage and two young sages—a young girl and boy around the age of ten years old.

"Good, you made it," Lothar said, nodding his head slightly.

"I never did like this castle," she said looking around. "It's always so dark with a cold, damp chill from the lake. And those Goliathan heads all over you walls. So barbaric." The Supreme Sage wore her customary gold jewelry with an elaborate scarlet gown and adjoining robe. This dress, however, did not drape along the floor since she would be doing much traveling today.

"As I remember, you didn't mind me killing them when they attacked your Swarves."

"As I remember it, your advisor Garth had a hand in helping you take down those monsters. But, yes, you are right. They need to be managed. They especially enjoy raiding our Swarve stables and taking them one by one for their nighttime snacks. But by the Befores, do you have to display them as trophies?"

"Like the jewels you display around your neck and wrists? Are those not trophies?"

The Supreme Sage held up her bejeweled arm. "These are symbols of my position as Supreme Sage. They are passed down to each consecutive Supreme Sage. It is tradition and a right."

Lothar chuckled. "Well, then, these are symbols of my position as the most powerful chieftain of the Lake-keepers."

"That is still yet to be determined," she said. "I just had a visit with Rugar bar Hathway. It seems he has an interpreter in his family now."

Lothar felt heat rise in his cheeks. "Interpreter of what?"

"Please, Lothar. Do you think you're the only one who knows about the forty-four symbols we keep finding in those translucent cylinders?"

"But how could he have already gotten an interrupter so quickly? He has built no boats large enough to cross the new waters that replaced the desert sands. My boats, however, are almost completed, and nothing like them has ever been built in all of Rodesh."

The Supreme Sage looked unimpressed. "The newest member of the bar Hathway family's name is Corven, and he has proof that he has distant relations to the Hathway lineage. He has a great of great grandmothers who was separated from the Lake-keepers during her travels after the Great Shake. I listened to the symbol reading myself."

"How can one of our people possibly have read them?" Lothar asked. His plan was quickly diminishing. He would need to come up with another way to keep his power over Rugar bar

Hathway. His father had mortally killed Rugar's father long ago over an undisclosed dispute. Again, Lothar regretted killing Garth. He was sure Garth knew why his father had reason to kill Verdan bar Hathway. Rugar had been planning his revenge for decades, but since Lothar was heirless, Rugar bided his time.

"I brought two of my brightest sages to learn the symbols. The symbols themselves are each so beautiful—much like art or a dance on parchment. Parchment—that's what they call the circle scroll they write on. And each symbol has a sound in our language. Forty-four symbols and forty-four sounds. Brilliant, isn't it?"

Lothar sat down at the long wooden table that held his now cold midday meal. "So you have sided with the Lowland Cliffs, have you?"

The Supreme Sage laughed. "I don't side with the bowmen or the swordsmen. Highland Cliffs or Lowland Cliffs make no difference to me. The sages are a unique group. We take no sides. We record history and determine future events from our knowledge of the past."

"But why help Rugar bar Hathway?" Dalia interjected.

"Dear, Dalia. We've known each other for years. Why would I help someone?"

Dalia looked confused. Then her face lightened with clarity. "To help yourself. You fear that these symbols will take the place of the sages, don't you?"

"Indeed, but they shall not," the Supreme Sage said forcefully. "Look around you. One ground shudder and the people beyond the waters have lost their symbols. Centuries of history gone. You need the sages to memorize and pass down information. We can keep your little symbols as a backup, but we are an institution of knowledge. Parchments of symbols cannot and will never take our place as sages of the Lake-keepers."

"You fear losing power? You fear losing your monthly tithes and expected tributes?" Lothar said with a slight growl.

The Supreme Sage walked up to where Lothar sulked at his table. "Would you fear losing Lake-keeper history from the time we came to Domus Lake? From the time your mothers and fathers before you established your castle? I can command all my sages to keep quiet about the history they know. I shall keep researching and recording current events and passing on historical occurrences to my sages but not tell a single soul outside the Temple walls. If that happens, who will really know that you are the rightful heir to the Highland Cliffs?"

"We have our own sages," he yelled, slamming his fist on the table.

"Yes, but yours are biased. They memorize only your family's history the way you want them to remember it. All the chieftains' sages have family histories memorized through the motive of what is best for the family. The sages of Atlatl Forest are the only ones who are indifferent to the chieftain families. You need the objectiveness of my sages. Without us, all Lake-keeper knowledge would be lost. You are no true chieftain without the verification of my sages, not yours."

Lothar stood up, but Dalia quickly grabbed his right hand before he could grab his sword. "We see your point," Dalia said, motioning for her nephew to sit down. "What is it that you want?"

"Nothing. I want nothing but for things to stay the way they are. I will teach my sages to write the symbols and they will write down the history and store them in their youth memories as well. I'm already drawing up plans to build an archives center at the Temple. We will store them in a safer way instead of those floating, translucent cylinders. They will be organized by families and time and easily accessible. Leave the burden of history to the sages, Lothar bar Haven. You have grander things to worry about," the Supreme Sage said.

"What do you mean?" he asked, standing up again but this time without so much anger. Maybe the Supreme Sage was right. Having to write and organize cylinders sounded burdensome. How would he even begin, and who could he trust to do the task? He was a chieftain and led a great army of swordsmen. History was not his concern.

"I just finished the adoption ceremony for Rugar bar Hathway. His distant relative Corven is now part of the Hathway family. The only problem is that he is lame in the foot and does not know how to wield a sword. He doesn't even have his horns, nor does his mute servant. However, he has brought over at least a hundred cylinders and has gifted them to me, and he has memorized thousands of cylinders in his youth memories. He will be reciting them to our sages to add them to our archives."

"How is that possible?" Lothar was skeptical. It all seemed too preposterous to be true.

"His father is an extremely wealthy merchant from the north land cities with thousands of cylinders. But after Corven became lame at twelve years old, his father disowned him, and he became the archives steward for an even wealthier merchant, Lord Rencon. So Corven memorized all of his father's symbols and those belonging to the richer merchant before his youth memories shut. Besides F'lorna, Corven bar Hathway has more in his youth memories than anyone I know. He actually may have more than F'lorna because there are two people groups across the waters: Sand-shapers who extract their horns and River-dwellers who live in large trees."

"Which is my F'lorna?" Lothar asked, intrigued.

The Supreme Sage paused, allowing the anticipation to build. "She is half Lake-keeper and half Sand-shaper, but she grew up as a River-dweller. Her grey eyes are a sign of what Corven called a highborn landowner."

"The healer who rescued my brother, she must have been a River-dweller," Lothar said, trying to put the pieces together. "Then F'lorna must have more than Corven in her youth memories as a River-dweller, especially if she was raised by a healer."

"Yes, you may be right. Who knows what lies in her memories after fifteen years living another life, especially since your brother married a Sand-shaper, which is very uncommon for River-dwellers. And this Sand-shaper's father, Lord Dexarian, is a rich landowner—although he illegitimately sired F'lorna's mother. This landowner and F'lorna's grandmother were unwed. He does, however, have a legitimate son from his wife. His name is…" She looked to one of the young sages. "What was his name? The story is now fading from my memory."

"Lord Tarmian," the young girl said.

"Ah, yes. Lord Tarmian. He's in charge now because his father, Lord Dexarian, is unable to manage the estate."

"The bar Haven family line just became very complex," Lothar said.

"Yes, my nephew, but with complexity comes opportunity," Dalia said, coming up beside him. "You are now tied to wealth and land across the new waters."

Lothar thought. "Does this Lord Tarmian have an heir?"

The Supreme Sage nodded. "His name is Lord Sabien, and he is of marrying age. In fact, he was to wed the daughter of the wealthy merchant Corven worked for. The girl's name is Raecli, but as of now they have not come to an agreement."

"Why are you giving us all this information?" Dalia asked. "I thought you don't take sides."

"My dear, I don't take sides. I performed an adoption ceremony for Rugar bar Hathway's distant relative. He is now part of the Hathway family, but Corven will live in Atlatl Forest as a sage donated by the Hathway family. He's much more prone to study than fighting. In return, Rugar gave me several of these," the Supreme Sage said as she felt through the folds of her ornate robe. She pulled out a shining golden rock.

"They have gold?" Lothar asked in disbelief. "We haven't found gold on our shores for centuries. Only ore to make the steel."

"From what Corven told me, they call it auraium. And they have discovered a great amount of it hidden within a land bridge, but they don't have the steel to mine it well. It takes them hours just to take one tiny piece from the rockface. With your steel swords, you could take it all in a few weeks."

"Again, why are you telling us this?" he asked.

"Corven was steward to the wealthy merchant who is mining it. He knows the exact location of all the gold. You are building boats, are you not?"

"Yes. That is why I wanted you to bring a young sage. I want it on record that Chieftain Lothar bar Haven has built the first of many oar-powered galleys to cross the great waters," he said with obvious pride.

The Supreme Sage said nothing to his grand announcement.

"Please, don't tell me you have already seen the galleys that I have hidden behind my castle," he said irritated with himself. Never underestimate the sages of Atlatl Forest.

"Like I said, we sages crave information, but to answer your question, no. I have not seen them yet, but a few of my young sages have. How are these galleys different from the fishermen's boats docked at the basin? They use oars, as well." The Supreme Sage couldn't hide her interest.

"Boru, the young man who designed them, is a builder by trade, but he grew up around the fishermen in East Basin. In fact, his sister married into one of the most lucrative fishing families in East Basin run by Morgo. He was the fisherman who initially found F'lorna on my shores and took her to the basin. Fitting that his brother designed the boats to bring her back to me. Granted his brother, Boru, is very young, but before his youth memories shut, he envisioned a multi-oared boat that would be bigger and faster than all the fishing boats of the basin fleet. He imagined he would guide it down the Great River to see what was on the other side."

"The Great River has been decimated along with the desert sands. Now all we have is one giant sea before us. Do you think his so-called galleys can prevail over the waves? From what Corven told us, he and his servant barely made it here. It took them weeks."

"Boru did have to make modifications, which is easy for him since he's a builder by trade. He lengthened the boat by ten feet, and now, instead of six benched rows on each side, he has added twelve on each side. Can you believe it? Twenty-four benched rows in all! Three men on each bench with twenty-four benches makes for seventy-two rowers in the galley. And we have space at the back and front of the boat for passengers and supplies, and even more space on the deck."

"Fascinating. I guess there are more stories to be told about the great Highland Cliffs Chieftain, after all. How many are there and when will they be complete?"

"There are six galleys in all. They will be ready to enter the waters soon. I have the best builders working on them from East and South Basin."

"No builders from West Basin, I see. Too close to the Lowland Cliffs?"

"I have who and what I need," Lothar said roughly. "I know who really rules the West Basin, and it is not Laninson bar Hudson. He is too young and inexperienced."

"I will be the judge of Chieftain Laninson." She paused. "I'm surprised you can use the builders from the East and South Basin. Weren't you and Darmin bar Holthen at odds when last you met? Didn't you tell him the marriage between your heir, F'lorna, and his son Rathtar was off?"

Lothar shrugged nonchalantly. "We made peace of sorts. I shall need his fisherman skilled at boating, as well. He knows that F'lorna has learned the bar Haven Swordcraft and that she is my younger brother's daughter, not simply someone found on my shores. He still is hanging onto hope for his son's marriage. I don't know how many people are in the other lands. I may need the bar Holthen family as an ally after all. We'll wait and see once I find my niece and scout out the lands across the waters. A union may be inevitable. He will want the ore hidden in my cliffs no doubt. He knows the sword is a greater weapon than the bow, which is why he wants F'lorna as a daughter-in-law. She knows my swordcraft and can teach others."

"You can have a union between F'lorna and Chieftain Laninson. It will give you land closer to your enemy," the Supreme Sage suggested.

"You forget that his mother is related to Rugar's wife. Besides, their territory is the least of all the Lake Domus Basin."

"Yes, but his lands are very fertile, and the forest behind his lands is rich with animals to be harvested," she countered.

Lothar gave a sinister chuckle. "Yes, and devious nomad woodsmen in their forest who kill and thieve."

The Supreme Sage ignored his comment. "If you can make peace with the bar Holthens, you should be at least willing to make peace with the Lowland Cliffs if you want this plan to work. Chieftain Rugar bar Hathway has an army of swordsmen, not mere bowmen like the basin chieftains. Corven bar Hathway knows how to get to the new lands, and you have the boats."

"I will never side with the bar Hathway family!" Lothar yelled, slamming his fist on the table.

"When I asked Chieftain Rugar to make peace with you, he gave the exact response," she paused, thinking. "Peace was worth a try, but now we must prepare a new plan. I will have Corven dictate all he knows to my young sages. I wish his mute servant could talk because he's the one who rowed the boat here, but maybe I can get him to write down symbols. Then when it is time to make your way across the waters, I will send you several of my sages—ones old enough to hold their own on your galleys but not too old that their youth memories will shut. They will guide you to the gold."

"And I guess you want gold in return?" Lothar asked. He knew there would be a catch.

"I have no need of gold. Rugar bar Hathway gave me enough to build my archives center at the Temple. I'll be using builders from the West Basin since you've taken all the rest of them for your galleys. Let the bowmen and swordsmen fight over the gold and decorate their halls and horns with it. No, what I want is knowledge. I want you to take my sages and let them travel and learn. Let their minds soak up these new lands, people and customs. Give them safe passage and time to gather as much information as possible. And most of all, they need to make it back to the Temple safely."

Lothar looked to his aunt. "What do you think?"

Dalia gave a slight shrug. "Sages desire knowledge above all else. It makes them feel superior."

"Does it give them power, though?"

Dalia shook her head. "Without bow or sword, how much power can one truly wield?"

"And I also want the cylinders that I know you have been saving in your vaults. You have no need for them. Rugar has already given me the ones Corven brought him and the ones he has collected from Domus Lake. I crave stories, not gold," the Supreme Sage said, holding out the golden stone before putting it back into the folds of her robe. "F'lorna in just a few months absorbed almost all of the Lake-keepers' history. My sages need fresh stories to learn and tell, not of mere fisherman and average innkeepers, but of cities made of that translucent—" She looked to one of the young sages next to her. "What did Corven call that material?"

"Glass," the young sage said.

"Yes, cities built of glass and stone and people who live in trees. We sages need to expand our knowledge since Rodesh herself has expanded. The sages of Atlatl Forest must have this new knowledge."

Lothar stood, crossed his arms and began to pace. Finally, he came to a conclusion. "I will have my servants deliver the cylinders. I don't need your sages snooping around my vaults. Then when our galleys are complete, we will bring twelve of your sages with us—two for each galley. We haven't extra room because the oar cabin takes almost all the space below deck. But when I return with my niece and heir, we can plan for another expedition for more of your sages to gain knowledge. But I have two conditions myself."

"Yes?" the Supreme Sage asked.

"Have one of your sages record every detail of my galleys today. I want the names of the designers and builders archived in the Atlatl Forest Temple. No boats this big have ever been built by Lake-keepers. It takes six dozen men to oar just one boat. I want the bar Haven's name in the history of the sages as the first to build

36

giant galleys to cross the new waters. And have them write them in the symbols too."

"I shall have it done. And what is your second request?"

"I want F'lorna bar Haven officially adopted into my family. And if she is heir to lands on the other side of the waters, I shall claim them as well. We haven't adequate land on the cliffs to make enough food. The Befores are finally on my side for once."

"But what of the landowner's son?" the Supreme Sage asked.

"If he gets in my way, I'll kill him."

"Then you better hope he doesn't marry the rich merchant's granddaughter."

Lothar scoffed. "And why is that?"

"That girl, Raecli, is F'lorna's best birth friend. From what Corven has told me, she is the reason F'lorna fell into the river and floated onto your shores. F'lorna was trying to save her on a land bridge, but her Fear of the Cliffs caused her to pass out and fall into the Great River. If Raecli does marry the landowner's son, F'lorna may not forgive you if you kill him."

"That's my niece's lands and therefore my lands. I'll try to reason with them. Her friend—this Raecli—can stay there for all I care, but I will not let what is mine be owned by another." Lothar turned to face his young advisor. "Dagor!"

Dagor jumped when he heard his name shouted. "Sorry, sir. Yes, what would you have me do?"

"Take that young sage and bring her to Boru. He designed the galleys, so he should be the one to explain the details."

"Yes, sir." He nodded and walked to the exit of the hall.

"Follow him and memorize every detail of those galleys," the Supreme Sage commanded. The young sage ran after Dagor and followed closely behind him through the great doors of the hall.

Lothar turned back to the Supreme Sage. "Now I want this other sage to record the adoption of my niece, F'lorna, in front of me and my aunt."

"It is unorthodox that she is not here."

"We had the ceremony already. There were simply no young sages to record it."

"I wonder why," the Supreme Sage said knowingly.

"The Befores meant for it to be this way because now I have her real name. Do as I say. Commence the adoption ceremony before this young sage, and I will make sure to bring your sages on my galleys to the new lands when I fetch my niece and take her back to the Highland Cliffs where she belongs."

"As you wish," the Supreme Sage said. "I will perform it now." She looked to the young sage. "I performed this adoption ceremony already but for unknown reasons, we neglected to bring a young sage. You will remember this adoption ceremony with the understanding that Amorfia—now known as F'lorna—was present. Do you understand me?"

The young sage nodded. "Yes, Supreme Sage. I will make a note of it in my youth memories."

Chapter 5

Sharing Symbols

Boru tested the pine tar with a flattened rock. "It's not hot enough. You need to melt the pine roots until all the sap is boiled and runs to the bottom. Only then can we gather it and waterproof the wood of the galleys."

"Yes, sir," a man twice his age said.

Boru felt uncomfortable being in charge, but he hid his discomfort well. He had an older brother. He grew up learning how to think and act in a maturity that was beyond his years. Plus, it was his galley design explanation to Chieftain Lothar bar Haven that got his attention. Dozens of young and old builders explained their boat designs to Lothar. Some even used a sage with family history of various boat designs. However, out of everyone's boat description, his—Boru of the East Basin—was chosen. And now they were building six of his galleys. He was thirteen years old when he imagined the galley's design as he watched the fishermen's boats oar out into the lake, and now what he imagined in his youth had become a reality.

He looked at the progress. The galley structures were resting on sand that they removed from the east basin shores to and placed behind the Highland Cliffs to keep the eyes of the Lowland Cliff Chieftain from seeing what they were doing. That task took almost a month. Boru wondered how Lothar got Darmin bar Holthen to give him some of the sand from his shores. There was a lot more of it since the desert sands washed away, but he prayed to the Befores that the marriage between Rathtar and Amorfia was still off. Boru shook his head. "Her name is F'lorna, you goof. And she is from across the waters. If you want to get her back, you will have to accept her true identity."

Word of Amorfia's true identity spread quickly. Not just from the swordsmen who watched the exchange between Lothar bar Haven and his advisor, Garth, which ended in his death, but also from the old sage from the Lowland Cliffs who came to live in East Basin. He told the story to Voddie about how the *Chants of Jeyshen* helped Amorfia remember who she really was—F'lorna, a daughter of the River-dwellers. Voddie repeated the story to her husband, Morgo, but it was their son, Range, who passed on the story to every ear—young and old—willing to listen.

"Excuse me, Boru," Dagor said, coming up from behind. Dagor was a few years older than Boru, and they had become close friends.

"Did you hear me talking to myself again?" Boru asked in jest.

"Yes, but nothing of interest. Just stuff about that Amorfia girl again," he said with a smile. Then he pointed to the young girl standing just behind him. "This is the young sage that will be memorizing your galley constructions and all the details. She needs the names of all the builders and the designer—meaning you. And of course, Chieftain Lothar bar Haven gets credit for the entire undertaking."

Boru looked at Dagor in disbelief. "Are you serious? Is my galley design going to be archived in Atlatl Forest Temple by the sages?"

"Yes. Not only that, but it will also be written down with the symbols."

Boru looked at the young sage. "What is your name?"

"Kolie," she answered shyly.

"Do you have all the symbols memorized?"

She nodded her head. "I know how to write them and read them. Corven bar Hathway taught me. He was very instructive and not mean like the Supreme Sage." She quickly covered her mouth. "Please don't tell her I said that."

"Of course not. I've met her, and she definitely is not pleasant—although, she did do what was right according to the customs of the sages. It was my great uncle, Shardon, who designed the Temple in Atlatl Forest. She finally paid off that debt to my family."

The young girl's eyes opened wide. "Your family must be very prestigious indeed. Your uncle designed the Temple and now you have designed these galleys for Lothar bar Haven. I am honored to have your work in my youth memories," she said with a deep bow.

Boru didn't want to disappoint the young sage and let her know that his family has built and now runs the Fishermen's Inn in East Basin. But her words did ring true. Though his family was humble at heart, they did have their moments of brilliance.

Boru then looked back at Dagor. "Can you do me a favor? Tell the Supreme Sage that she has no need to wait for me. Get her a Swarve from the stables and send her back to the Temple. I'm sure she has lots to do. The galleys are very detailed, and there are a lot of people involved. I live near the Temple. I'll make sure to take her home this evening."

Dagor grinned. "What are you planning?"

"Nothing," Boru said, giving a mischievous grin. "I just know this will take a long time, and the Supreme Sage and Lothar bar Haven aren't the best of friends."

41

Dagor thought. "This is true. It was difficult watching their discourse just now. Okay, I will let her know. I believe she will be more than relieved to return to the Temple."

"Thank you, Dagor," Boru said. "And please don't let on to any ulterior motives."

"Believe me, the last thing I want is to walk in my predecessor's footsteps and be slain by Lothar bar Haven. Taking Garth's position was a decision I did not take lightly. The less I know, the better."

"I hope to the Befores that your path leads another direction than Garth's."

Dagor nodded and turned to walk back to the castle.

Boru knelt and smiled at the girl. She had hair dark like the waters at night, yet the blue eyes of many of the Highland Cliff people. Her unsunned skin indicated she was a sage. They rarely went outside, and when they did, the trees of Atlatl Forest shaded them. "I will show you everything there is about the galleys. Then we will ride a Swarve to make a quick stop at East Basin. As we ride, I will give you the names of the builders and other details you don't necessarily have to visualize."

"Why do you want to take me to East Basin?" Kolie asked. "All your beautiful work is here."

"I have family there. My nephew, Range, I want him to learn the symbols that Corven taught you. In exchange, we have a sage from the Lowland Cliffs living with us. His name is Kragel, and he has information from before the Great Shaking about the Creator of Rodesh and the Forty-four *Chants of Jeyshen*. Yet, he is very old, and I fear he won't make it another week or two."

"Ahh, there are Forty-four *Chants* just like the forty-four symbols?" the young sage inquired.

Boru nodded his head. "I know my galley designs are intricate and fascinating, but I think you will find the chants even more so. Will you do it? Will you teach Range the symbols and learn the Forty-four *Chants*? Range already knows them and sings them all day long."

The young girl enthusiastically nodded her head. "I would love to learn new stories."

"Then we had best hurry. Let me take you to one of the galleys and go over all the details. Be ready. There is a lot to learn, and I will talk very fast. But I do believe, Kolie, you being here is not an accident."

The young sage gave a determined look. "I'm ready to memorize."

Voddie watched as Paxton grabbed hold of one of the wooden chairs and wobbled his way to a standing position. His smile spread as his squeals of laughter bounced off the walls of the Fishermen's Inn.

"He'll be running soon. Just you wait and see," Vexi said. "Then you'll have two boys on your hands getting into mischief."

"Aye, at least I'm finally done nursing him," Voddie said as she dried the wooden mug Vexi had washed and handed her. "I wouldn't be able to help run the inn if he were still attached to me day in and day out." She looked out of the window toward the waters. "We'll have to open the restaurant soon for the evening meal. Spring has brought the fish to our shores, and the fishermen are going to be hungry after a long day of fishing."

"Too true, and the last thing these fishermen want to eat is more fish. I'm glad Chappell traded some fish at the market for red-hoofed deer meat. I have a large pot of soup simmering with fresh baked bread waiting for hungry mouths."

"Isn't Chappel your oldest daughter? I always get their names confused. Plus, they look so much alike," Voddie said.

Vexi nodded. "Chappell is the oldest. She's working your husband's stand in the market more and more lately. The other two are complaining because they want to be where all the people are. To be honest, Chappell is scouting for a husband. She pretties herself up every morning before she heads off to work the fish stand."

"That's how I found Morgo," Voddie reflected. "I worked my father's stand of small wooden goods. Just simple things like mugs, plates, keepsake boxes and a few things my brothers would make out of their imaginative whimsy. I got good at selling their wooden creations because they'd give me fifty percent of the proceeds. Though, my dad only gave me ten percent. Then one day, Morgo came to my stand, wanting to trade some fish for a few kitchen items. I could have given him any price, and he would have paid it. I could tell he was smitten with me right away."

"Aye, and a good pair you two make," Vexi said. "And now you have built this inn and brought more business to East Basin. Which reminds me, my other two girls, Francell and Glandell, are washing the bedding and kitchen towels and napkins for the inn. They should be dry by now. They'll have them here before dinner time, but we have more than enough for now."

Voddie turned to face Vexi. "I don't know what we would have done without your family. The Fisherman's Inn takes more work than I could have anticipated."

Vexi set down the plate she was washing. "No, no. It is I who should be grateful. Once my dear Toren died in that fishing accident, Morgo gave me a job right away at the fish stand. I had three young girls and no way to provide for them."

"I was very pregnant with Range at the time. I'm glad I got to be home with him and then Paxton. You gave me that ability when you took over the fish stand."

There was a knock at the inn door.

"We will be opened in just a few minutes," Vexi called out.

"How about for one of the inn's builders? Are you opened for him?" the voice rang out.

"It's Boru!" Voddie yelled.

"Go get the door. I'll finish up here."

Voddie ran around the counter of the bar and quickly grabbed Paxton who was now sitting on the ground rubbing his eyes. His bedtime would come soon after he ate his evening meal.

She put him on her right hip and opened the door with her free hand. "Boru! I can't believe you are here." She gave him a side hug with her left arm. "Everyone is talking about the galleys you are building for Lothar bar Haven! You are famous all over the basin shores."

Boru squeezed his sister's side and then pinched Paxton's chubby cheek. "Once he starts walking, those chubby cheeks will soon disappear."

"Just like I remember yours doing," Voddie laughed. "Who do we have here?"

"This is Kolie," Range said, coming up from behind Boru. "She's a sage from the Atlatl Forest Temple. She's putting Uncle Boru's galley design into her youth memories. And guess what else?"

"Range," Voddie said sternly, "I thought I told you to check on Kragel for me."

"And I did exactly that," Range said. "I was bringing water to the old sage's room and that's when Uncle Boru came in. And guess what else?"

"What?" Voddie asked enthralled. She couldn't believe how much Range talked these days. She believed she finally found her match in words per minute.

"Kragel and I taught the *Forty-four Chants of Jeyshen* to Kolie. We sang several of them on the way over here!"

"Fascinating," Voddie said, looking confused at her little brother. "Does the Supreme Sage know? You can get in big trouble."

Boru leaned to whisper in her ear. "Look if Amorfia, I mean F'lorna, thought they were important, then they should be added to the Temple of Atlatl Forest. Right?"

Voddie thought and nodded. "I guess you are right, but what if she finds out?"

"I truly love the chants," Kolie said. "I'm honored to have them in my youth memories. The Supreme Sage doesn't control all of our memories. There are things we learn before entering the

Temple. I'll just make a note that I learned them before I came to Atlatl Forest."

"Are you sure that's okay?" Voddie asked still unconvinced.

"Completely," the young sage said. "The older sages have us put notes in our memories all the time. When we add a note, we don't mention it when we repeat the memory. We simply skip over it like skipping over a rock in the road."

"I have something to ask of you," Boru said. He stared into his sister's eyes with earnest.

"Aye, it looks that way. You seem to be on some sort of mission."

"You know those symbols the chieftains have been collecting. They've discovered there are forty-four symbols in all. And now we know there are Forty-four *Chants*. There must be some kind of connection, and I want Range to learn them. I can't explain it all because it's getting dark and I need to get Kolie back to the Temple, but she is only one of three people of all the Lake-keepers who know the symbols so far. I don't know why I feel its importance on me like an anchor made of steel, but Range needs to learn them. It won't take long, but I wanted to ask you first."

"But shouldn't we wait for Morgo?" Voddie asked. "I'm sure he won't mind, but he'll want to be involved."

"If we wait any longer, the Supreme Sage will ask questions."

"I know the connection," Kolie's voice said softly.

Both Voddie and Boru stared at the little girl.

"What connection? The connection between the chants and the symbols?" Range asked.

The girl nodded. "Each chant starts with a different sound of our language. Did you know that there are forty-four sounds in how we speak?" she asked.

Everyone shook their heads.

"Corven taught me how to write the forty-four symbols and how to pronounce the sound for each one. So now if you tell me a word, I can write it down in symbols. The connection is that the sound of each symbol is in the exact order of the beginning sound of each chant."

"So somehow these symbols that represent our language come from these chants?" Voddie asked.

"Mother, let her teach me, please! I want to know how to write our language!"

Voddie bit her lip. "Okay, but how will she teach you to write each one?"

"I learned by writing them in the sand," Kolie said. "But Corven said they usually write on something called parchment using smokestone."

Voddie looked behind Boru. The fishermen were docking and putting up their lines. "Okay, go to the shores and learn the symbols, but you will explain everything to your father when he gets home, do you hear?"

Range nodded his head and grabbed Kolie's hand. "Come on! Let's go before it gets too dark!"

Voddie watched the two kids run through the door and toward the sand.

She shook her head. "What's Morgo going to think?"

"It's his fault after all," Boru said, giving another one of his mischievous smiles.

"What do you mean?"

"He's the one who brought F'lorna to your doorstep and into our lives. He started this entire thing by looking for your favorite fish, and the Sukio fish led him to the shores of the Highland Cliffs."

"Aye, indeed. All of this fuss because of a fish."

"Or maybe a husband's love for his wife," Boru countered.

Voddie gave Boru a little nudge with her shoulder. "You're right, little brother. I think this all did start with love, so I shouldn't fear."

Chapter 6

The Sapphire Bridge

T he sound of rushing water reached Raecli's ears and woke her
from her slumber. Traveling in one of her grandfather's
carrying cases tended to put her asleep. She could travel and
sleep all day without worry of galas and meeting future intended
husbands. However, her grandfather's words about the Sapphire
Bridge stretching from the west of the River to the east woke her
even further. He was not a very descriptive man, and for him to
describe the bridge specifically caused her to recognize that the
bridge had to be a spectacular sight.

She reached her hand up and pulled open the fabric
covering a small opening to the carrying case. A bright translucent
blue light shined into her case. They had left very early that
morning, and it looked to be midday now. They had finally begun
their travel across the bridge. Raecli couldn't help but exhale. The
bridge was made of solid, vibrant blue glass bricks and natural

stones from the Northeastern Mountains with a hard resin poured in between the two materials, holding the manmade and the natural together. It was a beautiful display of the intermingling design of Sand-shaper artistry and the naturally ornate stones of the mountains. She glanced ahead of her and could see her grandfather's hand holding his window curtain open as well.

She looked beyond the bridge and the Four Horns of the River split in four directions and then emptied into the Great Expanse, or ocean, as the Sand-shapers call it. She wondered if there were other Rodeshians on the other side of the waters. Rodesh was growing all around her, and her Achion tree in Right River Hook seemed so small in comparison. If Lake-keepers could live across the waters to the south, who could be dwelling across the waters to the north?

She crawled across the many pillows and blankets in her carrying case to the other opening facing the River. She had only seen the River once as a youngling when her mother decided to take her on a journey to visit old friends who lived in the northern tributaries along the River. It was safer to walk the open rocky shores of the River than through the dense shrubs and trees of the wild woodlands. She saw it again when her grandfather discovered there was auraium on the land bridge that was exposed after the earth shakes.

When she drew up the fabric even more, the majesty of the River greeted her. Somehow the greatness of the River's mass and abundant flow made the intimidation of her grandfather lessen. He could not make something so wonderful. He could sell and trade goods on a massive scale and boss servants around, but this beauty and mastery was beyond him. He was a mere man. Only Ra'ash could have scraped the River's depths down the spine of Rodesh with the slightest touch of His finger. And to think she grew up on a tributary just off this force of nature.

As the traveling case continued, the River and Four Horns moved out of sight behind her. They must have made it to the other side and were making their way to Lord Munchester's townhome, so she could meet his son, Lord Layton. Raecli thought of her grandfather's words. All the friends she had made after he took her from F'lorna were fake. They were only there to enjoy the luxuries of their family's social status and wealth. They ignored her turban-wrapped horns only because she was the granddaughter of Lord Rencon. She thought of the farmlands in the south at Lord Tarmian's estate. She should have fought harder for Lord Sabien. He was young. She was young. They were both bound to not know what was right for their family lineage. They needed to listen to the wise counsel of their elders—or so she told herself.

She closed the fabric of the window and straightened her shoulders. She would not let that happen again. She probably would not marry Lord Layton because her grandfather wanted an alliance with landowners, but she would make an appearance that would let every highborn Sand-shaper know that she was more valuable than any auraium her grandfather could offer.

Finally, the carrying case stopped and the servants holding the poles gently placed the case on the ground. She waited as was customary for her grandfather to come and give her directions.

He opened the curtain. "We are here, my granddaughter, and Lord Munchester's estate is more impressive than I had initially been told. It is not merely a townhome in the city. His home hugs the most eastern horn of the River. Spectacular views of the River to the left of him and the mountains to the right, yet his home is not so close to the smoke of the mountains. Choice location, truly. I'm impressed, and I'm glad we made the trip."

"Yes, Grandfather. I enjoyed the view of the Sapphire Bridge and the Four Horns. Really breathtaking. Thank you for mentioning them to me."

Her grandfather seemed pleased by her compliment. "Didn't I tell you?" he laughed. He was in a good mood. She hoped he would stay that way during their visit. No more knocking over vases and yelling at servants for at least a day or two. She would do almost anything to keep his rage from baring its sharp teeth.

"Now, there are several families invited to dinner tonight. Most with sons and daughters around your age. I want you to get to know the young ladies, but don't be so eager that you seem lowly. And make sure that Lord Layton catches sight of you. He will most definitely want to become acquainted with you. You will be a new, intriguing possibility to court. All the other young ladies have dined with him before."

"Yes, Grandfather. I will do everything I have been taught."

"And now that your grotesque horns have been extracted, you will surely be the highlight of the dinner this evening." Her grandfather looked at the sun as it was beginning its descent. "Have your lady's maid put on your finest gown for dinner this evening. Everything most go perfectly. I want every rich merchant on this side of the River to not only know my name but know my power, riches and accomplishments. You will be my greatest jewel of them all."

"Yes, Grandfather," she said. He called her a *jewel*. Maybe she meant more to him than a mere girl to be traded like merchandise. She might have finally found a way to win his favor if not his affection. She had to perform and be the *jewel* he expected her to be.

Raecli's white gloved hand slid across the satin lavender gown, which made her eyes an even more vibrant shade of violet. Along with the violet moon streaming in through the windows of the large riverside estate, her eyes would appear to glow to the other guests.

"Are you ready, Lady Raecli?" her maid, Cecil, asked.

Raecli felt the thick braids of her dark hair circling the crown of her head. Cecil had left the lower half of her hair to flow with curls draping her shoulders.

"What gave you the idea to do my hair in this manner?" Raecli asked. She didn't want to hurt Cecil's feelings but tonight had to be perfect. When they arrived at the riverside estate, the servants sent them straight to their chosen rooms. This would be her first time to meet the rich merchant families, and she needed to make a good impression.

"Did you not see them?" Cecil asked. Her skin was a few shades darker than Raecli's, and she was about four inches taller. She had the golden eyes that the hunting twins of Right River Hook had. They were older than she and F'lorna, but their brother Lemmeck was their birth friend and in many of their lessons of the different Adorations. Raecli wondered if Cecil had family related to any of the River-dwellers. She had a suspicion that all the people of Rodesh were related somehow in the distant past.

"See whom?" Raecli asked.

"When we arrived, I made sure to look around. I wanted to see how the ladies here were dressed and how their hair was done up. I wouldn't let my lady be outside of the local trends on this side of the River. I peeked into many doors as we walked the halls and saw several lady's maids doing the hair of their ladies. Your hair is very similar to theirs, but I didn't want it to be exactly the same. I made your braid much more intricate. They used a basic four-twist braid, but I did a six-twist braid, which very few lady's maids know."

Raecli stared into Cecil's golden eyes. "Thank you for thinking of me and looking out for my best interests. I never asked you when you arrived after we got back from the farmlands, how is it that my grandfather found you for me?" Raecli's grandfather had simply presented Cecil to her and told her she would now be her lady's maid.

"My mother was a lady's maid, but her lady died, and the new wife had her own maid."

"What's the difference between a housemaid and a lady's maid?" Raecli asked, thinking of Lainie, a housemaid for Lord Tarmian's estate.

"A housemaid has many duties, which can include attending to the lady of the house. But a lady's maid is specifically for one lady. It is a sign that a family is more prosperous than most."

"Oh," Raecli said. Her grandfather must have hired Cecil as a sign to other Sand-shapers of his wealth.

"What happened to your mother? Did she find another lady to attend?"

Cecil shook her head. "No, she decided to leave the cities for a time and on her travels south she met my father. He was a glass brick maker. They married and had me. We were so happy until he got the Smoke Sickness a few months ago. Once he died, my mom set about finding me a permanent residence as a lady's maid. She taught me everything she knew, and I learned a lot from my father. I can create many things with glass, like jewelry and sipping cups, but I stay away from the bricks. They create too much smoke. Lord Rencon knew my mother's old master before his first wife died, so he hired me. My mom moved back south and lives with another widow friend of hers. They will be happy. I will try to visit her when I can. But now I want to be the best lady's maid of all the northern cities. My Lady! Why are you crying?" Cecil said, wiping Raecli's tears with the handkerchief she always held in case of emergencies.

"It's just that my mother died of Smoke Sickness too. That is why I was brought here. I grew up as a River-dweller. I've only been a Sand-shaper for a few years, and it's been a difficult transition for me."

Cecil wiped the tears dry. "There, your tears didn't do much damage. I think you and I are going to get along just fine. Ra'ash has His reasons for everything. We must trust in Him."

"How do you know about Ra'ash?" Raecli exclaimed.

"I had many River-dweller friends growing up. We lived just under the mountains and close to the lands of the tributaries. They taught me several of the *Chants of Jeyshen* and a few of the *Sacred Songs of the Prophets*. My mom saw no harm in it. I can even do some of the Images of Jeyshen—though, I'm not much of a dancer."

Raecli embraced Cecil. "Thank you so much. I needed someone I could trust. I do believe what you've said. Ra'ash did send you to me."

Cecil squeezed back after a moment's surprise. "Now, my lady. You are going to dazzle at the dinner party. Just remember that Ra'ash has you here for a reason, and you just need to simply step boldly into His plan. He will make everything come together just fine for you. And I promise that I will be here for you, and I'll be offering those silent words the River-dwellers say."

"You mean V*oiceless Words,*" Raecli said pleased. She hadn't felt a real smile spread across her cheeks in a long while.

"Yes, that's it. Voiceless Words. I'll be offering those up for you to be confident and graceful."

"Thank you, Cecil," Raecli said, squeezing one of her hands. "I am ready." Raecli faced the door of her guest quarters. Cecil opened the door wide, and Raecli walked through with her shoulders back, chin up and a confident glow.

Her grandfather was at her door with his servant looking irritated having waited so long, but when his focus fell upon Raecli, his irritated expression turned into one of pride—an expression she had rarely seen on him in regards to her.

"My granddaughter, you will be a stunning adornment to Lord Munchester's dinner party this evening. No doubt you'll have the eyes and ears of every suitor at the table. I hope you have prepared yourself. There will be much scrutiny."

Raecli didn't want to marry into city life, but she was determined to practice her social skills on the sons and daughters of these merchants. If Ra'ash was watching over her, she would help Him by commanding her own actions. She did not have to be like a leaf in a river tossed around in currents wherever the wind and rocks decided.

"Yes, Grandfather. I am ready. You have taught me well and thank you for my lady's maid, Cecil. She has given me wise counsel. I am much comforted by her presence."

Her grandfather puffed out his chest from the compliment and presented his arm to Raecli. She placed her hand on the crook of his elbow, and he led her to where a servant would announce their names before being led into the dining hall.

"You are welcome. Her mother was an excellent lady's maid, and she assured me that she taught her daughter all she knew plus more, which by the look of you tonight, I now believe."

Raecli nodded and gave her grandfather a delicate smile. Then she fixed that same polite smile upon her face. This evening, she would transform herself into a young lady not torn by two worlds and not conflicted by her own thoughts but into a young woman who had enough wealth to hide away all her fears, insecurities and pain. She would prove her value to herself and to all the Sand-shapers she met.

Chapter 7

Establishing a Village

F'lorna walked through the marshlands behind her parents. Jaquarn and T'maya listened intently to Merriton's words about all that the Marsh-landers had accomplished in their new lands since they defected from Lord Tarmian's lands. Weston walked leisurely beside her. F'lorna noticed that his grin hadn't left his face since they arrived before the Heat Source touched its zenith in the sky. He was content to let his brother ramble on about their newly built structures and planted crops as he kept eyeing her.

F'lorna was indeed impressed with the Marsh-land Village. They had found a large swath of dry land right in the center of the marshlands—though, they did have to clear it of shrubs and other harsh plants. They constructed wooden paths that lead into the village from the west, south and east but not the north. If anyone escaped from the northern farmlands, they would have to walk around the marshlands and find the path coming in either from the east or the west. It was best to leave the marshlands separating the farmlands and their village to the north alone to keep invaders out.

Each family had a small piece of land usually next to several trees where they could hang their hammocks. They used their land wisely and planted patches of various crops. River-dwellers had Planting Elders who would provide produce for the entire village, but this plan worked for the Marsh-landers since most of them used to be fieldhands. As Merriton explained earlier, each family would trade some crops for others they lacked. It was a good system. Also, many of the Marsh-landers knew how to make their own clothes, eating utensils and even toys. They were an extremely resourceful group because they had to be innovative as servants who received less than the bare minimum to survive.

"Can you tell how proud he is?" Weston finally whispered into her ear.

"You all have accomplished much," F'lorna said. "I can see others have joined your community." She motioned to an adult with horns. "Is he a River-dweller, or is he a Marsh-lander who has learned to replace his horns with the bulbs of another?"

"He's a River-dweller," Weston said. "We Marsh-landers are content to be hornless, but our children will have horns. It's a sign to the Sand-shapers that we are now a different group of Rodeshians," he said proudly. "Besides, I wouldn't know what to do with horns on my head." He laughed. "But, yes, some of the Marsh-landers have already joined with River-dwellers. Our community is extremely diverse. We have even received Sand-shapers from the Northeastern Mountains. I don't know how they heard of us, but they made their way to our lands."

"It is good to be diverse," F'lorna encouraged. "Marsh-landers know how to creatively survive in the marsh. River-dwellers know the *Divine Oracle*. Those from the Northeastern Mountains bring Sand-shaper skills. The more variety of information your village gains, the more opportunities you'll have access to."

"After we escaped Lord Tarmian's estate, Merriton and I traveled through River-dweller territory to gain knowledge. We were impressed by the unique way your villagers teach skills to their younglings. You call the skills *Adorations*, correct?"

F'lorna nodded. "We learn Adorations to please Ra'ash and live our life with a purpose that will serve Him and our village."

"How many Adorations do you have now, F'lorna? Let me see—Dancing and Singing. Remember that night we danced? That was a fun night," he reflected. "And I see you dabble in Healing." He pointed to her medical pouch. "Now you bring us a new Adoration—Swordcraft and the ability to make weapons of steel. I can't wait to see the process of making swords like the one you carry. How long will you and your parents be with us?"

F'lorna noticed Weston's grin deepened as he leaned closer to her. Then he flickered his eyelids in jest. He wasn't being shy about his excitement that she was there, but somehow his relaxed demeanor made his obvious advances easy to deflect. On the other hand, Lemmeck had a very serious countenance. She did admire him, but she was not ready to court anyone yet. She wondered how he and her friends were doing. They were all back home at Right and Left River Hook, but her family would be travelers. For how long? She did not know, but she enjoyed the feeling of not being weaved into a community.

"I think we will be here longer than the other villages. My father wants to teach one or two of your older younglings who still have an opened Eternal Memory all he knows about healing. That will take a while. I will be teaching the Swordcraft. Somehow my singing and dancing Adorations don't seem as important, but if anyone wants to learn, I will teach them. My mother will be teaching her Cooking Adoration. There are many plants here that she knows how to utilize that the Marsh-landers may have never seen. We will also be making swords for many of the villagers. My father and his team finally found the rock ore we need to make steel at the bottom of the waters of the land bridge, but we don't have much left. I believe we can only make five or six for now."

Suddenly, Weston's laidback countenance became serious. "That won't be enough, F'lorna. Lord Tarmian is sure to find us somehow. And Raecli's grandfather will be back to get the golden rocks from the rockface. We will be the first they intercept as they come south."

"But you all are hidden in the marshlands," F'lorna countered.

Weston shook his head. "Do you really think our home will stay hidden long? It will be only a matter of time until the word of our village is spread by servants and then heard by the highborns. When Lord Rencon and his servants come back for their auraium, which they will, we will be the first line of defense."

By now Merriton and F'lorna's parents were listening to Weston's words.

"Weston, don't burden our guests with our fears right when they get here," Merriton said.

"Look at the scar on my brother's face. The mark that Barton gave him is proof that their obsidian blades will give the Sand-shapers an edge over us. Weapons of wood will not work. We need these swords. Our kids need to learn the Swordcraft, and I have no doubt that Merriton and I and the other adults of our village can use the swords well enough to defeat our enemy."

T'maya put her hand on Weston's shoulder. Her horns were fully developed and F'lorna couldn't help but see how beautiful she looked with them. All F'lorna's life her mother braided sticks into her hair. Now her mother's head held grown bulbs from F'lorna's own horn. F'lorna understood that one of the reasons Ra'ash sent her to the Lake-keepers may have been to finally give her mother a tangible sign that she was assuredly a Child of Ra'ash. The years she had to believe by faith had come to an end. She now had her horns, and F'lorna was determined to give her all of the *Divine Oracle* no matter how long it took her to write the symbols of every *Chant of Jeyshan* and every *Song of the Prophets*.

"Believe me, Weston," T'maya began. "We share your concern. Not only do we have an enemy coming to the south from the north, but now the Lake-keepers surely know there are others across the waters that Ra'ash unleashed across the Desert Plains.

They may come to find us, especially if Jaquarn's older brother finds out that he indeed has an heir in F'lorna."

"The chieftain wouldn't try to take you, F'lorna, would he?" Weston asked with a hint of fear in his voice.

"No," Jaquarn asserted. "That is why we are trying to prepare all the River-dwellers with knowledge of the sword and of healing."

"Do you think there is more of those ores in the rocky water of the land bridge?" Weston asked.

"I do," Jaquarn admitted. "We had gotten so many that we believed it would make many swords, but much of the rock is taken away in the melting process. There is very little ore that makes the steel in each rock. I can take you back to get more, but I will need many hands to help me."

"There is much to do," Merriton added. "But we don't need to rush. Let us enjoy an evening meal tonight. Let us introduce our friends to the village. Let us share stories. Let us play music and dance. Let the Marsh-landers show the River-dwellers how we enjoy our freedom. Tomorrow we can worry about rocks with ore and thoughts of enemies."

"I am very hungry," Jaquarn said. "We have walked two rises of the Heat Source to get here, and we have eaten all the leftovers given to us from the South Village."

"Let us show our friends where the guest plot is, so they can get comfortable. Then we will feast tonight before the sun or what the River-dwellers call the Heat Source goes down," Merriton added.

"I must attend to someone while you show my parents where we are staying," F'lorna said, feeling a little uneasy. She never knew how each village would react to her Swarve, Croga.

"Is this the famous Swarve we have heard about?" Weston asked, not hiding his enthusiasm. "I will help you with Croga. We can find a nice, shady spot for him near the guest plots."

"I will be grateful for your help. As we walked the wooden planks to the Marsh-land Village, I surveyed the best place to bring him in with the fewest trees. He will get wet, but he is big enough that his head will stay above water. If he gets stuck, I believe he can use his wings to pull himself up from the marsh. There weren't many Achion trees to the south, and he eats their leaves. Are there Achion trees across the planks to the east or west?"

"The east marshlands are rimmed with Achion trees. They are the closest to River-dweller territory. I will send out several Marsh-landers with our nets to retrieve some for you," Merriton said.

F'lorna hesitated. She hated to add extra burden to the Marsh-land Villagers already difficult predicament. "Croga eats a lot. I'm reluctant to ask this, but I think they will have to be sent out every day we are here. I won't be able to get Croga in and out of the marsh each day to eat. It will be too difficult for him. Once he arrives, he will have to stay until we leave."

Merriton came up to F'lorna and placed his hand on her shoulder. Then he stared into her eyes for several seconds before speaking. She was embarrassed by the gravity of his stance and the intensity of his dark brown eyes. "We are indebted to you and your family for all you are doing for us. To send out young helpers each day to pluck leaves for your Swarve is a very small task compared to all that you have come to offer us. You are willing to teach us how to heal, how to fight and how to cook the plants indigenous to our new home. And the truth is," Merriton said, giving a grin that turned his scar into a side smile, "we are all very eager to meet your Swarve. Whispers of him have reached our village, and the anticipation has been growing each day. The children will be eager to fetch Achion leaves for him."

F'lorna reached out and squeezed Merriton's opposite shoulder. "I will introduce Croga on one condition," she said with a playful expression.

"Anything."

"I would like to sing the *Chant of Jeyshen's Arrival* to your people tonight, so they know how important the Swarve is to the River-dwellers."

Merriton nodded. "Yes, we would be pleased. In fact, I didn't want to burden you, but we would very much like for you to teach our younglings some of your *Divine Oracle.*"

The Indwelling deep within F'lorna burst with what felt like warm flames. She realized that she had been so consumed with writing the symbols of the *Divine Oracle* for her mother, but here was her chance to teach every word to the next generation of the Marsh-landers—villagers who had only heard rumors of Ra'ash and His Son, Jeyshen. She felt the importance of this opportunity. This knowledge was more important than cooking, healing and fighting. "I will not only teach them some of it, but I will teach them all of it. I will not leave your village until I know that every Eternal Memory yet opened has the *Divine Oracle* locked securely within."

"Thank you," Merriton said. "During my brother and my travels to the different River-dwellers' villages, we saw first-hand the hope and security you have. And as Marsh-landers, we want that as well."

"Then it is settled," Weston said. "Brother, you take Jaquarn and T'maya to the guest plot, and I will help F'lorna bring Croga into our village. I already know a spot that will be perfect for him to the east of the guest plot. That way he will be close to F'lorna and close to his beloved Achion leaves."

"I have a suspicion you want to see the Swarve first," Merriton quipped.

Weston looked at F'lorna and then back to his brother. "I can tell you in all honesty, you are wrong on that suspicion."

Chapter 8

Saving Croga

W eston watched F'lorna as she rode atop the enormous golden animal. She tried to stay close to the walking plank, but sometimes she had to move out of the way of large shrubs or trees. The Swarve was so much bigger than he had imagined—even bigger than the dead River Monster that Lemmeck had killed. No wonder she wanted him away from the village. The villagers would get nothing done with the Swarve visible. They would stare in wonderment at him all day. F'lorna sat upright with her hands on his back and her knees and legs bent behind her. The golden Swarve's fur was wrapped around F'lorna's legs and arms. Weston though it interesting that F'lorna would sit upon her animal while his falcon would sit upon his arm.

He looked down at the thick worn piece around his left tunic sleeve. He hadn't seen Banthem all day. He shouldn't be far since Raecli had gone back to the Northwestern Cities and F'lorna was now at his village. The letters from Right River Hook had stopped for a time. He wondered if they had gotten caught or if there was just nothing to write about. He would send them a letter soon about Raecli going north, F'lorna coming to his village and about the threats concerning the land bridge's auraium. He looked back at F'lorna. Her hair almost matched that of the Swarve's except hers had more of the color of fire just before it turned to red from yellow. It had grown longer while she was away, and he noticed that she no longer braided the front part of her hair around the base of her horns. He liked her better this way. Different, like him. He wasn't a Sand-shaper anymore. He was a Marsh-lander, and F'lorna—she was half Sand-shaper and half Lake-keeper who grew up as a River-dweller. He figured she was the only one of her kind in all of Rodesh.

If his excitement to receive her letters were a single tree, then his excitement to have her staying in his village for a time was like a giant forest of trees. He thought of Raecli for some time after she freed him from Tarmian's estate. She was a beauty, and her violet eyes beheld a color he had never seen up close. They matched the violet moon that kissed them goodnight from the night sky. But Raecli could never overshadow how he felt for F'lorna. The first time he saw F'lorna in the woods with her friends, a force inside of him was drawn to her.

A loud flapping noise sounded next to him, and he wondered momentarily if Banthem had finally come home, but the noise was too loud for a single bird of prey. "What is he doing?" Weston yelled, almost falling from the walking planks lining the marsh when he looked toward F'lorna.

"He's stuck," she called out. "I brought him too close to this large clump of shrubs. I didn't realize the shrubs had so many thorns! He can't flap his right wing. He's sinking!"

Weston thought quickly. An animal that size could sink deeply into the muddy depths below. "I have an idea." He looked around. The Marsh-landers had made a habit of putting long sticks into the marsh beside the walking planks in case someone fell off. He glanced behind him and saw an extremely long one several planks back. He carefully walked backward to retrieve it. It took him numerous tugs, but the mud finally relinquished the long stick.

"I'm going to swim to you and hand you the stick. Don't worry. I will swim above the mud. It is deep here. Take the stick and dig it into the shrubbery next to you. Maybe that will give him enough leverage to pull out."

F'lorna tried to say something but sprays of mud began to splash across her face as the Swarve beneath her flapped his left wing, desperately trying to stay afloat. He was going deeper into the mud and his large, flat face was just above water level. Weston used the stick to catapult himself above the water from the walking planks. Before he landed, he made sure to pull the stick out from the mud behind him. Muddy water covered his face, and he opened his eyes, ignoring the sting. He treaded the water with one arm, holding the stick with the other. It didn't take him long to come to the right side of the Swarve next to the large pile of shrubs.

"Here!" he called out. As he pushed the stick up toward F'lorna, his own body sank. He pushed the stick further up with his hands, hoping it would reach F'lorna. Finally, he felt the stick break from his grip, and he came up for air. Instantly, he made his way up the shrubbery. The coarse plants cut through the palms of his hands as he climbed, but he didn't notice. By the time he got to the top, F'lorna was looking at him.

"The stick only sinks when I place it on the marsh's muddy floor. It's not helping Croga get out!"

"Here, hand me the stick and jump off Croga and swim to the walking planks."

"No! I must help him!"

Weston hesitated. His new idea to help the Swarve would cause him a lot of pain. He didn't want her to get hurt too. Before he could tell her no, she jumped off the Swarve and onto the shrubs next to him. The spines of the dense plant could not penetrate the leather of her feet coverings.

"Hurry! He can't breathe!" she screamed.

He sat down on the edge of the shrubs and grabbed the long stick. "Sit next to me. This is going to be painful."

She quickly sat down next to him, giving no voice to the thorns digging into the back of her legs.

He reached the stick under the belly of the Swarve. The right wing of the animal was too close to the shrubs and folded helplessly at the Swarve's side. Then Weston placed the other end of the stick across their thighs. "Hold the stick firmly on your legs, so your Swarve has some leverage to lift up!"

Weston's legs dug deeper into the shrubs as the Swarve pressed his belly against the stick and flapped his left wing. He laid back keeping his head up to spread out the weight of his body. The spines of the shrubs under his back began to rip against his skin, but at least his legs weren't sinking anymore. He grabbed the stick close to the Swarve with his left hand and lifted while holding the stick firmly against his thigh with his right hand. His left shoulder scraped against the spiny shrubs, but maybe the added lift would help the Swarve wiggle free from the mud. However, the added pressure pushed him harder into the thorns.

F'lorna also laid back, and he could hear her breathless cries as the spines of the shrubs dug into her back.

"Keep your head up, so the thorns don't touch your neck!"

She instantly lifted her head.

Now the thorns were going into her back. His only solace was that most of the pressure was being put on him since he was closer to the animal. The stick continued to try to rip out of their hands as the Swarve frantically pushed his belly against it. F'lorna began calling out to Ra'ash for help. Suddenly, the pressure on the stick lessened. They tried to keep the stick still, but the back legs of the swimming Swarve kicked it from their grip. The stick splashed into the water several feet away from the shrubs. Then all was still, and a loud moaning sound echoed through the marshlands.

Weston got up and looked at F'lorna. She was covered in mud to the point he could not see one inch of her skin.

"Is he out?" she asked, breathlessly.

He looked straight where the muddied Swarve now stood. He was almost completely out of the water except for his feet. "Yes, he's out, and he's as muddy as you are."

F'lorna didn't move. Then he could see the whites of her teeth as she began to laugh. Some mud got into her mouth, and she got up wiping the muck with a muddied arm, which made her laugh more. "I really need to stop letting him eat so much. He's much too fat. Maybe I will keep his rations low while we are here, so this won't happen when we leave."

"Yes," Weston said, catching his breath. The urgency to help F'lorna's Swarve abated as his desire to protect her increased. "Are you hurt badly?

She finally sat up. "It does hurt, but nothing I can't handle. Believe me, I got many more painful blows learning bar Haven Swordcraft. How's Croga?"

Weston pointed. "He looks fine, but he doesn't seem very happy."

F'lorna looked to where her Swarve was standing covered in mud and moaning. "Oh, poor, Croga! You need Ra'ash to bring the rains. We can't introduce you to the Marsh-land Village looking like this!"

Croga took that moment to shake the mud from his body and fur. He jolted with such velocity that mud drops hit Weston and F'lorna.

Once the shaking and mud flying ceased, Weston looked back at F'lorna. "This is going to make a great story for this evening's meal."

She leaned to the right and spit out mud from her mouth. "I agree," she finally said. "Hopefully, I'll still be able to sing."

Weston realized that they were still sitting on sharp shrubbery, and he needed to get F'lorna down safely without more damage. "Come on. Let's jump into the water and swim to your moaning Swarve. The water is shallow from here on out. We are almost to the village."

F'lorna nodded her head and looked around, trying to figure out how to get to the edge of the shrubs. Without asking, Weston grabbed her under her arms and legs and scooped her onto his body and rolled back. "Here, I'm right on the edge. Sit on me and then you can jump in. Just be careful." His back burned as she sat up and positioned her feet, but he wouldn't show it. He didn't want F'lorna to know that the weight of her hurt him. She pressed against his chest and placed her booted feet next to him on the very edge of the shrubs. Then she pushed off with her feet and sprung into the water. He sat up and watched her swim to her Swarve. She moved quickly and within seconds was stroking the animal's muddy face. Finally, he positioned his feet on the edge and stood up. Then he too jumped off the shrub edge and splashed into the water. Every part of him stung. He swam toward F'lorna and made it to the harder vine-laden mud of the shallow end. When he rose from the water, he felt a kiss on his cheek.

"Thank you, Weston. We wouldn't have made it without you," F'lorna whispered into his ear.

The pain Weston felt disappeared and again a deep urge to protect F'lorna seared his chest like the light that scorched the skies at night when the rains fell and thunder roared. Then the urge dug itself so deeply and brazenly into his soul that he knew nothing could ever pull his desire to protect her out.

Chapter 9

Secret Pain Revealed

F'lorna and Weston left Croga in his new temporary home. After the day's adventure, he was content to eat the pile of Achion leaves already left for him and then fall into a long nap under one of only a few larger trees in the marshlands. His fur was still damp from the water and a little muddy. Swarves did not clean themselves, so F'lorna would have to send silent words for the rains or bring several water containers from the River, which would take many trips. He was already twice the size of the Swarves owned by the Lake-keepers. She may have to ask the Marsh-landers for help. Then the thought came to her. That would be a great way to introduce small groups to Croga. They would help bring water and each get a turn at washing him. She turned to Weston who was also deep in thought. She noticed that his usual lighthearted demeanor was now pensive.

"Do you think the villagers will take turns helping me bring water in from the River to Croga, so we can wash him? If we divide everyone in small groups, we can have him cleaned before his fur begins to become matted."

Weston didn't answer her.

"Weston, can you hear me?"

He turned to her startled. "Yes, I'm sorry. I was just thinking about what happened today."

"It will make quite a story. Croga's first official experience with the Marsh-landers comes with a little adventure and a lot of danger," she said.

"And an epic ending," Weston added, offering his usual grin once more. "With a kiss."

F'lorna's normally pale cheeks flushed. She had been so scared to lose Croga that when he was saved, she was overcome with both relief and joy. "I believe your younglings will soak up the story in their Eternal Memories and tell it by firelight when they are Twofolds."

"I'm sure you are right. What was it that you asked me?" he asked.

"Croga isn't able to clean himself on his own. I thought a good way to introduce the villagers to him was for us to take small groups from the River with jugs of water, and they can each take a turn washing him."

Weston thought. "I think that is a perfect idea. I'll ask Merriton tonight if he would bring it up with the other families. We can start early tomorrow morning."

F'lorna nodded. She liked that his Marsh-lander accent had returned. When she met him, he sounded almost like a River-dweller, but their village was the last one that he and Merriton had visited, and they had picked up their accent after visiting so many River-dwellers. The accent disappeared once they returned home. Even his letters were written in his natural way of speaking. She knew how it felt now to be part of two worlds. Her words sometimes came out like a Lake-keeper. Her parents and friends had noticed but said nothing. She had great difficulty separating her two Eternal Memories. It felt like a burden. Raecli must feel the same way. She left before her Eternal Memories shut, so she too had two accents and two worldviews that warred against each other. F'lorna wondered how she was coping.

"F'lorna," Weston said. "Did you hear me?"

"Oh, I offer you my apology of healing," she said. "I guess we both lapsed into deep thought." As she watched him laugh, she noticed how he had grown more mature since she last saw him. He had an honorable strength that belied his servant birth and which he concealed with laughter and light-heartedness. Life as a field-hand for a cruel landowner gave him an understanding that most lacked—that she once lacked. It was nice to see him again. He brought her memories of simpler times before she fell off the land bridge. She reached over and pressed her head against his shoulder and reached her arm around his back. Her back burned a little from the scrapes of the shrubbery, but it wasn't anything a little ointment couldn't fix.

"F'lorna, don't!" he yelled out. His body tensed with pain.

She looked at her arm, and there was blood on her tunic sleeve from his back. She stopped. "Let me see your back."

He sighed. "Don't worry about it. It's nothing."

She didn't listen and walked behind him to look. "Your tunic is soaked in blood, and there are tears and holes in the fabric." She didn't ask. She carefully lifted the back of his tunic. He had deep scrapes all over his back and arms except the one with the worn piece of leather wrapped around it for Banthem. She looked down at his leg-coverings. "I will not ask you to show me your legs, but I assume they are just as injured." She turned to face him. "Weston, you helped me down all the while I was hurting you!"

"I would rather take the hurt than allow you to experience more scrapes from that shrubbery. It was my idea to go up there. F'lorna, you've been through enough, and now I can see the scrapes through the back of your tunic too."

She grabbed his hand and gently pulled him toward the village. "Mine are minimal. Your back, however, is very angry with red, heated gashes."

"Where are you taking me? You're not thinking about tending to me, are you?"

Her cheeks flushed. "No, my eyes will see much of your backside if I do, but my father has everything you need. You are very hurt, Weston, and those scrapes can easily become infected. I've seen it happen before with an injury like yours. If not properly tended, your body will become hot and sweaty, and you will sleep for days or even weeks until your body can fight off the infection. It is best to stop the damage before it starts."

"You are right. I didn't want you to know and carry any weight of guilt, but…" He stopped. "You are going the wrong way. The guest plots are this way. Maybe I should lead."

He tightened his grip on her hand and led her in the opposite direction. Once they came into view of the guest plots, F'lorna let go of Weston's hand and ran to her father who was setting up their temporary lodging. She ignored the slight pain in her back from the swing of her arms while she ran. She could already see concern on her mother's face.

"Do not fret, Mother. I am only a little hurt, but Weston is badly wounded. He helped me save Croga, but the thorny shrubbery in the marshlands damaged his backside considerably."

Jaquarn walked up to her. "Turn around. Let me see your back first."

She turned and held down the front of her tunic while her father lifted the back. "You have many scrapes, as well. You will have to be treated too."

"Yes, Father, but please look at Weston first."

By then, Weston was by their side. He couldn't run.

"Can you take off your tunic?" Jaquarn asked.

Weston shook his head in embarrassment. "The excitement of our adventure is gone, and now the pain is preventing me from moving my arms much."

"Use your mother's dagger," T'maya suggested. "You can cut the tunic off. It is badly damaged and cannot be salvaged."

Jaquarn nodded. He went to one of his leather travel bags and brought out his mother's metal dagger. "Hold very still. This dagger is incredibly sharp." Jaquarn carefully cut down the fabric of the tunic.

"Here, let me take off your leather swatch from your arm," F'lorna said.

Once the tunic was cut, T'maya helped peel it off his skin. "I'm glad you are still wet from whatever happened to you both or else the dried blood would have made taking off your tunic difficult and painful."

"His leg coverings are also damaged, so he will need tending there, as well, but his back is worse off," F'lorna added.

"F'lorna, Merriton left us three jugs of drinking water. Can you fetch one along with some of my fabric wraps? Also, bring me my medicine pouch."

"I can get the ointment out of your medicine bag, Father, and bring it to you. I know where it is."

"No," he said, looking at her with a sternness that surprised her. "I will get it out. Just bring it here. Then I will give your mother some of it, and she can tend to your wounds on the other side of those bushes. Just direct her on how to wash the wounds and apply the anointment."

He turned to look at his wife. "She will need a new tunic and possibly leg coverings. I will let Weston borrow a tunic of mine."

"I will get them," T'maya said, and quickly walked to where they placed F'lorna's traveling bags.

F'lorna stared at her father for a moment, willing him to look at her, but he continued to investigate Weston's wounds. Finally, she stared at the ground and walked toward the water jug. The pain in her back numbed as a feeling of dread came over her. Had her father discovered that he was missing some of his sleeping herbs? She told herself she would not take anymore, but her dreams had only gotten worse with time and the thought of sleeping gripped her with fear that stole her appetite at evening meal. Lothar and her father had the same blue eyes, and every time she looked at her father's face, great guilt began to surpass the love that once came so easily. During the waking hours, she could keep the negative thoughts silent—or at least ignore them; but once the Heat Source hid under the horizon, horrible images and thoughts created an atmosphere of chaos in her mind. Even Croga couldn't penetrate this fear with his feelings of well-being. She was no longer Amorfia or F'lorna. She was an abomination of the two, and Lemmeck's words of her overcoming this struggle felt like a lie.

She retrieved the jug of water, ignoring the weight of it that pulled her arm and stretched the wounds in her back. She brought it along with the strips of fabric to her father and set them down. He still wouldn't look at her. Then she went back to where his medicine bag was located on his hammock. She grabbed the strap and walked back to her father.

"Here, Father," was all she could say. He was washing Weston's wounds with a strip of fabric dipped in water.

"Set it next to me and open it up. Get some of the ointment out for your wounds and nothing else. Then go to your mother, so she can treat you," he said, again, not looking at her.

"Yes, Father," she whispered. She opened the bag. First thing she noticed was that the pocket where the sleeping herbs were located was now empty. Her father must have moved them. Her hands trembled, but she was able to open the treated animal intestine that held the ointment. She untied the top and squeezed some of the ointment into her hand. Then she left the unopened pouch on the bag, so her father could use it. With as many wounds as Weston had, she believed they would be making more ointment soon. She took a handful of fabric strips, as well. She walked to where her mother was waiting for her with a change of clothes and a jug of water.

"Follow me," T'maya said. She didn't have the stern look of her father, but she did appear worried. Lately, her mother looked at her with a concerned expression often. F'lorna was too thin. She wasn't eating enough. She got easily distracted. Her mother knew something was wrong, but she couldn't pinpoint it. They walked behind the tall bushes of the guest plot. F'lorna took off her shirt and pants and held them across the front of her body. Her mother soaked a strip of fabric and gently rubbed it across F'lorna's wounds.

"Father is mad at me," she finally said.

"He's not mad," T'maya said. "He's worried."

"He wouldn't look at me," F'lorna said, feeling hot tears wetting her face.

"He knows what you have been doing," T'maya said quietly. "I knew something was wrong. You've lost so much weight. And it's more than that. You have a heaviness about you. I can feel it. And you stay so very busy. I never see you rest anymore."

"There's lots to do," F'lorna said lamely.

"I know you have your reasons, but now it is time you confide in us. Let us help you. I know you have been through a very difficult time, and your situation is different from mine, but when I first met your father at the Pillar, I looked much like you. I wasn't eating. I had a heaviness after losing my mother. I felt lost and alone, but your father helped me. He introduced me to Ra'ash, and I slowly healed."

T'maya took the ointment from F'lorna's hands and began rubbing it over the scratches on her backside.

"But he's so mad," F'lorna said. "I'm scared."

T'maya turned F'lorna around to face her. She placed her hand gently on her daughter's cheek. "I will talk with him. He takes your unhappiness personally, like he has failed you. Let me calm his fears, and we will have a family discussion tonight after the evening meal. I promise you that once you let us in and let us help you, you will heal. It may take time, but Ra'ash will replace your sorrow with joy."

All F'lorna could do was nod.

"Now, you better get ready. You are singing tonight for the village. I'll take the jug and these strips back. Your fresh clothes are right there on the stone. Bring me those torn ones when you're finished changing. I'll repurpose the fabric."

"Yes, Mother. Thank you for understanding."

F'lorna watched her mother walk back to their guest plot. She knew her mother experienced many pains in life, and the fact that she heard no disappointment in her mother's voice gave her hope that maybe things could get better.

Chapter 10

Merging Two Worlds

Jaquarn watched his beautiful daughter sing the *Holy Chant for the Peace of Jeyshen*. The Marsh-landers listened so intently that the evening birds could be heard mixing their sweet song with F'lorna's full-bodied voice. She had been gone less than a full turn of the moon, yet she had changed so much. Her unbraided hair fell almost to her waist and her normally rounded face like his had become more angular like her mother's. He didn't know if her transformed face shape was due to her maturing or to her loss of weight. He offered to try to take off the golden cuff of the Highland Cliffs from her horn, but she insisted on keeping it. He sensed great pain behind her grey eyes. Something was wrong, and the missing sleeping herbs proved that his instincts were correct. His daughter was hurting, and he couldn't help her unless she talked to him. Both their worlds had dramatically altered when they discovered they were born of Lake-keeper lineage, not River-dwellers. He was still struggling with the fact that his elderly parents were not related to him. Maybe that was why they didn't look at him like the other parents of Right River Hook looked at their younglings. And maybe that was why he looked to his community for affirmation and connectivity. If his parents were still alive, he would most likely look at them differently. But why was F'lorna looking at him so strangely? It was like he wasn't her same father. Instead of love in her eyes for him, he saw unease—and something else, like guilt or shame. His wife had told him to give her time, but when a big portion of the sleeping herbs went missing from his deceased sister's medicine bag, he knew he couldn't wait any longer. Those herbs taken without care could cause someone to sleep through storms, animal attacks and even earth shudders.

He looked to his wife. She was holding his arm while tears streamed down her tan face. She had both horns and her hair braided traditionally around them in River-dweller style. When F'lorna was only thirteen turns of the moon, she had argued with her mother about choosing Dance instead of Singing as her Adoration, and here she was singing with boldness before Marsh-landers eager to learn more about Ra'ash, Jeyshen and the Indwelling. He sighed. F'lorna was intense and stubborn and felt things very deeply. She was difficult when things didn't go the way she expected and falling from the land bridge, waking up with no memory and becoming a chieftain's daughter for a time must have inflicted confusion on her young mind. He learned long ago that medicines could help heal a body, but only words and time could help heal the mind. She needed healing, and he gave silent words to Ra'ash to help him and T'maya with the right words because it seemed that time was only making things worse. He was upset when he found the missing herbs, but T'maya correctly admonished him. F'lorna needed love and understanding not a lecture on stealing and lying, which was something she never struggled with before.

When F'lorna finished her song, the first one to stand was Weston. He clapped and cheered so enthusiastically that those around him snickered. His clap was limited, though, because of his bandaged wounds on his back. The others quickly rose after him to applaud the gift of Singing that Ra'ash had given F'lorna. She smiled and gave a bow that Jaquarn didn't recognize. Her cheeks flushed when she realized what she had done was not a River-dweller tradition, but there were very few River-dwellers in the audience to notice. The Marsh-landers wouldn't know the gesture was most likely of the Lake-keeper tradition. She briefly glanced toward him and T'maya, and he smiled back nodding in encouragement. He knew she was having trouble uniting both worlds that she had inherited. He had heard of Rodeshians losing their Eternal Memory after an accident and forging a new one with the support of family and friends. But to have two Eternal Memories was unheard of—at least he had never heard of such a thing until his daughter saved him from the ground shudders with a giant, golden Swarve, which he also didn't know still existed. *The Great Engulfing* had indeed not swallowed up all the Lake-keepers, and he wondered if there were more Rodeshians across the north and south waters. His view of Rodesh was enlarging quickly.

"Ra'ash," he whispered while the Marsh-landers continued to clap, "why have you chosen my daughter for so much difficulty at such a young age?" He pondered. He hadn't made her life any easier by marrying a Sand-shaper and by putting the community of Right River Hook above his duties as husband and father. That was one regret he wanted to redeem, which is why he decided they would not be going back. Even though T'maya had her horns, she still did not have the *Divine Oracle* in her Eternal Memory and that was considered an abomination by many River-dwellers, especially the ones in the north who lived closer to the Sand-shapers.

He noticed his daughter coming to sit with them. She sat next to her mother, avoiding his gaze. T'maya pulled F'lorna into her arms. At least she would receive tenderness from her mother—though it still hurt him that her view of him had morphed into something he would have to untangle and make right.

"You sang very well, my daughter," he said.

She didn't look up from her mother's shoulders. "I offer you my apology of healing for performing the curtsy of the Lake-keepers."

"I'm sure Ra'ash enjoyed your curtsy. You honored Him with your song and your bow. I know He is pleased. All Rodeshians are His children."

He noticed tears began to stream down her face. He would say nothing more until they returned to the Marsh-landers guest plot of land. After the evening meal, they would need to discuss the situation as a family: F'lorna, T'maya and himself. He felt the need to reach out to his daughter fiercely in his spirit.

F'lorna trudged behind her parents. She looked down at her feet. She remembered when she was following behind them just before her Doublemoon Ceremony. The size of her feet felt like a horrible weight. Now feet seemed inconsequential to the heaviness she carried daily. Bodily features meant very little when fear ravished the mind. She knew her father had discovered that she was stealing the sleep herbs, but the sternness she saw earlier that day had transformed into concern. She doubted it was a trick to get her to confess. Her mother must have talked with him. Though she and her mother didn't always agree, she did defend her any chance she could. And her father was always honest in his dealings with others and usually thoughtful and understanding. So different from the fierce sternness of Chieftain Lothar whom she had called *Father*. Her chest tightened as her mind tried to make sense of her memory loss. Would her father be pained to know that she had discarded him for another father? Why couldn't she remember her own family and friends? So many things she didn't understand, and Ra'ash was giving her no help with clarity.

When they finally entered their sleeping quarters, she panicked. "Can I go visit Croga please?" she begged.

"Yes, you may," her father said, "but only after we chat for a while."

F'lorna froze. Fear gripped her throat so tightly that she could no longer breathe.

"F'lorna," her father said, soothingly, "no one is angry. We love you and want to help you."

She began to cry and fell to the grassy floor. "I'm so sorry I've been using the sleeping herbs. I have nightmares every night. My thoughts attack me with shame and these negative thoughts of disloyalty. I can handle it during the day, but the nights are becoming crueler. Even the sleeping herbs are not helping me much anymore. Croga can't help me. He seems just as confused and scared as I am."

Jaquarn and T'maya both sat on the ground and embraced their daughter.

"Why would you have feelings of shame and betrayal?" T'maya asked. "You betrayed no one."

"You don't understand, Mother. I accepted Chieftain Lothar as my father." She looked toward her dad. "I offer you all the apologies of healing that I have to give, Father. He looked so much like you. I recognized him like a shadow that I couldn't grasp, and I feel like I transferred the love I have for you to him. Every time I look into your eyes, I feel so much remorse for betraying you."

He picked up his daughter's chin and stared at her face until she returned his gaze. "He is my brother, F'lorna. I am glad you saw me in him. It gives me hope that I may meet him someday."

F'lorna couldn't hide her surprise. "You want to meet him?"

"Yes, I have lost all my family besides you and your mother, and to find out I have a brother who knows my true family history and what it is to be a Lake-keeper is an exciting new prospect for me."

"You're not sad to find out Aunt Eline and your parents weren't really related to you?"

Jaquarn thought. "It's like you and I are next to the same river but on opposite shores. I lived with parents who, albeit were older, genuinely tried to care for me and protect my identity as a Lake-keeper—all the while knowing I wasn't biologically theirs. Eline also cared for me—saved my life as an infant, and she taught me many things. But all this time, I had a brother and an aunt that I have never met."

F'lorna nodded. "Yes, Aunt Dalia. She is the one who taught me the bar Haven Swordcraft. She was the nicest to me besides Garth and of course Morgo, Voddie and their younglings— Range and baby Paxton."

"You see!" her father exclaimed. "You were given a gift. You had your mother and I for fifteen turns of the moon, and then Ra'ash sent you to meet my family and your family along with new friends. We are in the same situation but in reverse. There is nothing wrong with loving your uncle, but now you can place that love to both the F'lorna and the Amorfia sides of you. Those two sides don't have to be at war. They can walk hand in hand in this new adventure that Ra'ash has for you, for your mother and for me. And look at all the good that came from it. You sent that sage who knew some of the *Divine Oracle* to live with the fishing family who found you. You grew your horn back and brought those bulbs for your mother. You learned how to make metal and a way of fighting that is awe-inspiring. You know all the Sand-shaper symbols without having to translate them through the *Forty-four Chants of Jeyshen*."

"Yes, but the Supreme Sage made me memorize so much history of the Lake-keepers. The information overwhelms me. I don't know what to do with it all."

"Share it! I want to know all about my lineage—the good and the bad. Talk to me. Tell me everything you know. And if we ever do meet our Lake-keeper family, you can use what you know to forge new relationships with a people group we believed to be exterminated long ago."

F'lorna laughed. "I think that would take many turns of the moon, Father, for me to tell you all I know. I've learned about

Highland Cliffs families and Lowland Cliffs families from centuries back. They are the swordsmen because they can extract metal from the rocky cliffs. Then there is East Basin Bowmen. That's where Morgo and Voddie live. And there is South Basin and Atlatl Forest where the Sage Temple is located. There are so many stories and songs I have memorized. It is difficult to know what to do with the information. I try to shut them down, but they are imprinted inside of me."

"I am here with you. Talk with me. Tell your mother and me the Lake-keeper stories. Tell anyone who is curious about these people we thought we lost in *The Great Engulfing*. They are part of our identity now. You don't have to keep repressing something that is part of you. And look how Ra'ash trusts you. He has given you another Adoration to your growing list."

"Which one?" she asked, curiously.

"Storytelling," he said. "And it sounds like Ra'ash has given you plenty of stories to share. Don't be ashamed by what you have learned. Instead, embrace and share it with others. I have a feeling that the world of Rodesh is about to become bigger than we ever expected, so prepare us with what you know!"

For the first time since her Swarve scaled the rock wall and saved her and her father from the great waters that took over the Desert Plains, F'lorna felt lighter than a leaf floating in the wind. She gently grabbed her father's cheeks with both hands and stared into his eyes. "Thank you, Father. I feel much better."

"May I add something, as well?" her mother chimed in.

"Yes, Mother?" F'lorna asked, turning to her mother. Her grey eyes matched her own and now her horns were fully grown. The same horns that came from the bulbs of F'lorna's brokenness. When it came to matters of the mind and heart, her mother normally kept quiet, but she knew her mother to be wise because life had been difficult for her.

"When you lost Raecli, you were deeply saddened so much so you became almost despondent. Why is that?"

F'lorna realized that the pain of Raecli's leaving didn't hurt as much, so she could look at the loss more objectively. "Because I think it was unfair that she had to leave. It wasn't supposed to happen that way."

Her mother nodded. "Just like my mother shouldn't have died, but her death led me to your father. Just like you shouldn't have fallen off the land bridge, but that led to the discovery of yours and your father's family. Can I be honest with you, my daughter?"

F'lorna hesitated. "Yes," she answered. They might as well get all the ingredients of her pain out in the open.

"You want to control the elements of your life, and when bad or unfair things happen, you can't understand them. You want to understand it all, but you can't. There are many things in life that only Ra'ash will understand. I believe we will see the full environment of what He is creating some day, but we only see in part now. You are going to have to learn to let go of control and let Ra'ash lead. And you must trust Him that though life can be unfair, He has a plan. You fell and you forgot, but now you are here. It's time to celebrate and take everything you have experienced and memorized and make it part of your greater story. Don't be ashamed of Amorfia. Your father and I are so proud of her. She remembered, and she returned. That is one strong young lady."

F'lorna couldn't stop the tears from streaming, and she felt her voice cry out in moans of relief. Finally, when she could talk, she wiped her tears on the back of her tunic sleeve. "Thank you, Mother. Thank you, Father. This is the beginning. I can feel it. I will be healed like Lemmeck said. I will be stronger. I will overcome."

"Of course, you will. You are our F'lorna, and Ra'ash has a special plan for you, or He wouldn't have allowed so much difficulty into your life. It is the hardship that makes us stronger if we don't give up and trust Ra'ash," her father said.

F'lorna hugged both her parents once again. She wasn't alone. They understood. Not only did they understand, but they were proud of her. "May I go to Croga before the Heat Source goes down? I want to lay with him and see if I can bring F'lorna and Amorfia together as one."

"Yes, he's probably tired of all the visitors he's had today washing him," Jaquarn said.

"F'lorna," T'maya said, "replace your shame with joy. Replace your need for control with a fervent anticipation of what's to come. Let Croga sense in you a renewed love for yourself—all the parts of you—not separated but united."

"Yes, Mother," F'lorna said, getting up. "Croga is about to meet his complete companion, and I think he'll like me even more."

F'lorna carefully walked through the cleared marshlands to where Croga was carefully hidden from outsiders. Her back pained her a little, but she knew that Weston's wounds were at least triple her own. She gave silent words that he would heal quickly. Finally, she saw Croga stretched out on his back with his belly up. The Marsh-landers took turns washing him. His golden fur looked exceptionally fluffy. He smelled her coming before he saw her, and he rolled on his side. He began to grumble low moans when she came into view.

"Croga, you miss me?"

He moaned even louder, and his wings flapped gently in anticipation. She crawled up next to his belly and unbuckled her tunic belt and laid it on the ground beside them. Then she took off her tunic, leaving her under garment on. Finally, she rolled her body alongside his belly, and he covered her with his wing. His fur wrapped gently around her wounded back and shoulders.

F'lorna began whispering stories of her life as a River-dweller. Then she whispered stories of the Lake-keepers. She continued to share every story and song that came to her mind. It felt like Croga was listening and receiving. At first it was difficult, flipping from a River-dweller to a Lake-keeper story, but as she continued whispering what was stored inside her two Eternal Memories, a peace began to gently flow in. The more she shared, the more feelings of well-being flooded her spirit. She kept whispering as the Heat Source hid behind the horizon and the Violet Moon brightened the darkened Upper Realm. At one point, it seemed that her two Eternal Memories touched in what felt like a greeting of hello. She must have fallen asleep because she awoke to Croga's rhythmic breathing and darkness surrounding them. Complete tranquility had overcome her as the two warring factions in her mind made peace. They weren't two separate identities. They were both F'lorna. Like her father was a Healing Elder and a Spiritual Elder, F'lorna's identity hadn't fractured; rather, it had expanded. She loved her mother and father. She loved Voddie and Morgo and their younglings. She loved her friends from Right River Hook. She even loved Chieftain Lothar and Aunt Dalia—though, in somewhat of a guarded way.

F'lorna rolled away from Croga's grip. He didn't budge. When he was asleep, his fur slept as well, and she easily slipped away from the golden strands. She put on her tunic and grabbed her tunic belt. She knew the way back to the guest plot. When she thought of falling asleep, she sighed with relief. The anxiety was gone. She hadn't let anyone down or been disloyal. In fact, her father said she was strong. Her failure had become a victory, and now it was time to sleep in peace as F'lorna—the singer, the dancer, the writer, the healer, the sword heiress and now the storyteller.

Chapter 11

The Protégé

The Supreme Sage dined at the table with Corven bar Hathway, the newest member of the Temple at Atlatl Forest and one she had been waiting for. The Befores had finally answered her request. Servants around them held trays of food awaiting a signal for more. She thought Amorfia was the answer, but she was only the catalyst. Of course, the Befores knew better than she. She was glad that she allowed the bar Haven family to take her away. It became obvious that the task of being her protégé and future Second Supreme Sage would not fall into the girl's hands, and she needed to have faith and be patient. She looked at Corven at the other end of the table. Though he was lame in the foot, it was obvious he had come from wealth and prestige. When he wasn't trying to please her or his newly adopted bar Hathway family, he walked in confidence with his servant around the Temple grounds. He was reared until the age of twelve to be a master and that was taken from him, but it would be to her benefit. He would someday assume her role as Supreme Sage, but she had to move delicately with him. She could feel his desire for power, which needed to be harnessed and not let out of control.

Although she had many years left of being Supreme Sage, she had to look to the future and the longevity of the Temple of Atlatl Forest and the line of the sages, like every Supreme Sage before her. She would not disappoint the Supreme Sages of old by not ensuring a consistent future in the expanding world of Rodesh. The Befores had seen fit to bestow upon her a momentous purpose: to ensure the sages' presence beyond the Lake-keepers. Corven would be that bridge to both worlds. She looked at Corven's servant, Reece. He did not eat. He only stood by Corven's side about a foot back from his chair. He was a well-trained servant. Only Corven could have commanded the young, mute man in this manner. Corven and Reece had been at the Temple for long enough, getting to know the landscape of life as a sage. It was now time for her to implement the first part of her plan.

Corven motioned for one of the servants to bring her tray to where he sat. He selected a delicate sweet sap tart.

"Good choice, Corven. Those are my favorite sweets. How do you like our Temple food?"

Corven slowly took a small bite. He did not chew for several seconds, analyzing the taste. Finally, he chewed and swallowed the small portion. He set the tart down and stared at the Supreme Sage with sureness. "Supreme Sage, I have dined with the greatest of all merchants in the Northwestern Cities, and none of their delicacies compare to yours here at the Atlatl Temple, and I say that with the utmost honesty."

She smiled, pleased by his answer. She knew when a sage was merely trying to cater to her vanity, which she loathed but tolerated.

"On the topic of our Temple, I would like to know your initial thoughts of our systems and procedures. I know it has only been a few weeks, but I would value a second opinion from one who has organized and categorized information of those cylinders of the Sand-shapers."

Corven pushed the delicate plate with his tart on the table several inches away from him. Then he held out his hand to his servant, Reece. Reece instantly pulled Corven's chair and helped him up. Together they walked up to the Supreme Sage.

Corven took his time before speaking. The Supreme Sage could tell he was organizing his thoughts.

"I do not say this lightly," he began. "I visited every sage from the youngest to the oldest. I examined the information they know and how they have been grouped in streamlined forums. Even their living quarters are arranged by the information they hold and the historical era in which they have been assigned. And lacking the knowledge of the Lake-keepers, I know I come at a disadvantage. However, I have read, categorized and arranged thousands of cylinders each containing historical and current documents of all kinds—leasing agreements, betrothal agreements, money ledgers, land and business mergers, Sand-shaping methods and even recipes. And I confess, to my detriment if I am no longer needed, that your organization is pristine, accurate and flawless. There is not one thing I would change. Believe me, I thought over several different organizational patterns, but nothing will be as efficient and effective as what you have done with the sages. The structure quite moved me."

The Supreme Sage said not a word, but Corven's words were what she had hoped he would say. "You flatter me, Corven, but I did not create the precedences we have now. I merely steward them."

He clasped his hands. "Yet, even that task is difficult. It is no mystery that chaos is always trying to overrun perfection. And you have kept the snags of disorganization at bay."

She stood up gracefully. "Then it is settled. You will be my protégé and the next Supreme Sage. We will have you confirmed as the Second Supreme Sage, and I shall send out sages to the swordsmen and bowmen chieftains with my announcement."

Corven tried to hide his stunned expression, but she knew her words would surprise him.

He bowed slightly. "I am honored Supreme Sage, but I do not have the day-to-day procedures of the sages in my youth memories."

"Don't you worry about simple logistics like that. We've had Supreme Sages from the mighty chieftains who did not grow up as sages but were donated by chieftain families to appease the Befores. My great-grandfather, Larsian bar Hathway, was donated by his father, the Lowland Cliff Chieftain a century and a half ago after his Youth Memories closed, and he is recorded as one of the most versatile and accomplished Supreme Sage of all time. He is the one who instituted the structure of our Temple that so moved you."

"Do you think your great-grandfather could have been a descendent of my grandmother before *The Great Engulfing*?" Corven asked. "To have such blood—even a drop—running in my veins would be a great honor. All my life I knew I was destined for greatness, which is why I memorized every scroll I could get my hands on. When Lord Rencon visited other merchants and thought to bring me, I would ask to see their cylinders and make suggestions for organization. I would then go in and memorize as many as possible, and many times I memorized them all."

The Supreme Sage lifted an eyebrow. "Then you have a wealth of the Sand-shapers and River-dwellers."

He shook his head. "Sadly, the River-dwellers do not use the symbols. They consider them an abomination. They have passed down what they call the *Divine Oracle* from generation to generation, and they choose what are called Adorations to their God, Ra'ash, as their purpose and to fulfill a need to their village."

"Their *Divine Oracle* is not written on parchment?" the Supreme Sage asked. "We must have this information in our Temple if we are to understand them. F'lorna must know the *Divine Oracle*, and she has learned the symbols. Can she not write it for us?"

Corven shook his head. "No, she is valued by many. Chieftain Lothar wants her, and she has a mother and father and friends who did everything to find her. You don't need her. You simply need a River-dweller willing to come on one of Lothar's galleys or have one of the sages listen to the *Divine Oracle* when they arrive. They will meet River-dwellers first since they live close to the new waters that overtook the Desert Plains. I will have to add a forum to the structure of the sages once they return. I've already added the Sand-shapers. It is small but growing. Though I know information about the River-dwellers, there are too many missing parts. I won't add a forum until I have a greater understanding of their history, culture and tradition."

The Supreme Sage thought for a moment. She would command her sages going on the galleys to the new lands to learn as much as possible about the River-dwellers since Corven had brought over so much information about the Sand-shapers. Lothar would be deploying his galleys headed north across the waters very soon. She needed to implement the next part of her plan, and this would be a test to see if Corven would truly devote himself to her as the Second Supreme Sage.

"Corven, take me to where you have stored and organized the cylinders you brought along with the ones the chieftains gave us."

He instantly reached out his arm for Reece to take. "I have made plans for an excellent vault to keep them fortified by rocks and locks of steel."

Reece didn't need to be told what to do. He gave a simple nod and gently grabbed Corven's arm. The Supreme Sage followed Corven and his servant and said nothing.

"Right now, they are in the two extra bungalows for sage families which are empty. I have them crudely organized in baskets. It will take time, but once we get the cylinder vault built, we can start adding cylinders of the Lake-keepers. Several of the sages know the symbols now. We can start writing them out and have all the Lake-keeper's history and culture documented."

The Supreme Sage simply nodded. They left the Temple and made their way past the Swarve stables. The unwed sages who were young or who chose to remain unmarried stayed at the quarters flanking the main Temple. However, some sages chose to marry and moved to the small bungalows deeper in Atlatl Forest. Corven was having difficulty with the incline of the hill, so Reece picked him up and carried him on his back. The Supreme Sage noticed they moved with ease. Each reading each other's minds— or at least, Reece instinctively knew what his master needed. When they finally got to the two side-by-side bungalows, Reece squatted to let Corven down on the ground.

"Here they are," he said, opening one door. "We had to organize them from the back of the bungalow to the front. There is no way to enter in now, but I will have Reece move them in such a way that they will be organized once they arrive to their new home."

Corven wobbled to the other bungalow and opened the door. "You see. Just as full as the other, and this is only the beginning."

"Corven, as the Supreme Sage one day, would you have these cylinders replace the sages?" the Supreme Sage began, eyeing the rows of cylinders dubiously.

Corven initially looked confused at the Supreme Sage's new line of questioning. "No, the sages should always be the main source of information. These, as you have said, are merely backups."

"I said that to appease Lothar and to get his scrolls, but do you really think I would want to risk these parchments replacing the position and the power of the sages?"

"They wouldn't replace them, Supreme Sage. They would only serve as a safeguard."

"Or a threat," she added. "Think about it, Corven. The sages are not warriors. Though many of us have swordcraft and bowcraft in our memories, we will not be able to defend the cylinders if a chieftain wants to break in and steal them. And once they have the cylinders and the ability to read and write them, they will no longer have need for us. They will stop paying their tithes and tributes, and the sages will become obsolete in the expanding world of Rodesh. I chose you to prevent that from happening and to get us ready for a level of rapid growth, so we can establish our prestige with all of Rodesh and her people."

Corven leaned against the door of the bungalow pondering.

The Supreme Sage knew that his mastermind was going through every scenario of keeping or destroying the scrolls in his mind.

He started to speak his thoughts aloud. "Keeping the scrolls updated does take work. They become old and need to be rewritten. We would be adding a redundant system to an already perfect system of storing and stewarding information." He looked at the Supreme Sage. "But I have been a steward of scrolls my entire life. Would you want me to leave that behind?"

"The scrolls were merely a stepping-stone on your path to become who you were truly meant to be—a Supreme Sage. You once stewarded pieces of parchments, but now I'm asking you to steward the sages. You were kept in those archive vaults alone for years, but now you will be Second Sage of the Temple of Atlatl Forest. You will be surrounded by sages and servants. Never alone, walking with honor with your servant. And I will assign you a personal sage who will help you with the day-to-day activities of the Temple. My great-grandfather had a personal sage to help him since he didn't grow up in the Temple. You will be as great as he, but even greater because you will establish the sages to all Rodesh."

"What would you have me do?" he asked. "I cannot memorize the scrolls from Chieftains Lothar bar Haven and Rugar bar Hathway. Only the ones I brought are in my youth memories."

"It looks like your work has begun. I will use the gold given to me by Chieftain Rugar to build additional quarters for our Lake-keeper and River-dweller sages and additional ones for future encounters with other unknowns of Rodesh. Read them the scrolls and have the sages memorize them."

"And once I am done?" Corven asked.

"You burn every one of those reprehensible parchments and any new ones that come our way. Have them memorized and then licked up by the flames. The sages will never compete with symbols."

"But the Sand-shapers—both the landowners and the merchants—have thousands and thousands. We will never get them all."

"And that will be your burden to bear, Corven. When I have passed and joined the Befores, and the Lake-keeper chieftains begin to secure lands and dominate their inhabitants, you will take the scrolls of all the conquered and have them memorized by our sages and burned. The sages will become the most powerful group of all Rodesh. We will have leaders from every corner of our world coming to us for information and guidance. You will be highly honored—not because of your physical strength but because of the mass of information at your fingertips."

"Yes," Corven said, lost in his imagination. "The scrolls will only be a burden and a threat. They must be assimilated into the sages' memories and then destroyed. I see the greater width of what you are wanting to achieve."

"And one last thing, and it is extremely important," the Supreme Sage said. "And this includes you, Reece."

Reece instantly came up beside Corven ready for instruction.

"You will both need your horns back. We have saved many bulbs over the years. The process can be simple as one set of bulbs being implanted and the horns instantly sprout; but sometimes, the bulbs aren't a match, and the process needs to be done again until we find the correct pair."

"Horns are considered lowly in my culture," Corven said.

"You are not a Sand-shaper, Corven. You were never destined to be one. The Befores sent you to the north lands in order to prepare you for your place here with the sages. Horns in our culture are a sign of strength and honor. Once you have them, you will see that you will command the respect of all who meet you. Your family line was taken from the Lake-keepers because of *The*

Great Engulfing, as you call it. It is now time for your family line to return to its rightful place here."

Corven looked at his mute servant. Reece gave an innocent shrug. He turned back to face the Supreme Sage. "Let's get the bulbs implanted today. I have a lot of work to do before Lothar bar Haven sends out his boats and our sages with him."

Chapter 12

Shot Through the Heart

C hieftain Laninson bar Hudson stared at his mother a moment longer to ensure he was taking the correct action. His light brown skin and golden eyes made a nice contrast like that of dusk and dawn. He was tall and thin and not yet twenty years of age—though he had been the Chieftain of South Basin for almost six years since his father and many of his father's men were killed by nomadic woodsmen during a bow hunt in the forest. The nomads hid in trees and used netted stockpiles of stones hanging from thick limbs to throw at the men. Laninson's father died from a severe blow to the back of the neck. It was a coward's way of killing someone—not even allowing their horns to protect them. Laninson did not have enough power now, but one day, he would take his revenge—even against his mother's wishes. He wore the golden crest of West Basin proudly on his left horn and kept his long, dark brown hair braided and tied together at the nape of his neck. Flying strands of hair could force a bowman to lose his shot.

"Yes, my dear," Sarina, Laninson's mother, said. "Now, take the mallet and hit the gong as hard as you can."

She had darker skin than her son's, and her black hair caressed her horns like curly vines. Her emerald eyes matched those of the Lowland Cliffs. Her cousin, Panela bar Hathway, was married to Rugar bar Hathway, Chieftain of the Lowland Cliffs, which is why their small wooden fortress in West Basin has been protected since her husband died. Her cousin requested her husband, Chieftain Rugar, to protect West Basin from Chieftain Darmin bar Holthen who now commanded over both East and South Basin. They did stay protected but at a costly price. Much of their crops and harvested animals went to Lowland Cliffs where they had little farmable land and even fewer animals.

If her husband had not died so young, she was hoping to give birth to a daughter who could one day marry into a chieftain family, merging families and expanding lands. However, she delivered another baby boy only weeks after burying her dead husband's body with woodchips to become compost for the Crested Tea Field. This fenced and guarded field slept quietly near the wooden fortress of West Basin, preserving the memory of the chieftains and their families who walked with the Befores. The Crested Tea that grew from their nutrients would be served to family and guests to honor the dead.

"Brother, you can do it! You are better than all our bowmen. You are the best bowman in all of Rodesh!"

"Hush, Valor!" Laninson said to his younger brother. The lad looked just like their mother; though, his curly, thick hair was braided like his. He did not have the golden crest on his horn yet. They were still bound to allow them to grow back and down, not like the woodsmen who grew theirs straight up. He was only six years old and wouldn't get his crest until his horns were set.

"I'm sorry, Brother," Valor whispered. "I will watch everything and keep every moment in my youth memories and share it with our sages just like you told me. I am so excited! You are going to be celebrated. Maybe Mother will let us appoint a festival on your behalf!"

"Yes, that will be fine," Laninson said, kneeling to face his little brother. "But remember, you must keep very quiet. You need to be like the sages and act like you are not part of the action. Do you understand?"

The little boy pursed his lips together and nodded fervently.

Laninson stood up and stretched his fingers and hands. "It is time."

The three of them stood at the stairs of the Atlatl Temple. They did not bring their Swarves because they wanted to make their way through the forest inconspicuously. They were now near Chieftain Darmin bar Holthen's lands. Though the forest around the Temple was property of the sages and considered unconquerable land, it could still be dangerous for them. Laninson moved his bow further up on his left shoulder and grabbed the handle of the mallet. Then with all his might, he smashed the golden disk, and a loud clashing sound rang out for several seconds and faded to a shimmering sound of rain that hummed across the forest for several seconds.

The double doors of the great Temple opened, and the Supreme Sage herself came down the stairs slowly to meet them. "I do believe young Chieftain Laninson bar Hudson that was the loudest I've heard our welcome gong ring out."

Laninson and his mother did not bow to the Supreme Sage because they were of Chieftain blood. Valor stood like a statue giving no reaction like the sages would do. However, Laninson did lower his head briefly with respect. "I apologize. When I do something, I tend to do it with all my strength."

The Supreme Sage smiled. She wore gold around her wrists and neck. Her long white wool dress was made thin and breathable, paralleling the hue of her silver hair. The skirt of her dress fluttered along the ground, already stained from the day's walk. Laninson knew, though, that the Supreme Sage didn't bother herself with little things like stains. She had servants who would make the dress white again by the next day.

"Yes, I too give every effort to do the best I can do with the mundane and the magnificent. Before we go into the Temple to talk about building our new quarters and other business, I want to know if the rumors are true."

"What rumors, Supreme Sage?" he asked.

"Are you really the greatest bowman of all the Lake-keepers? I can believe of West Basin since your village is so small, but to be best of all the bowman from South and East Basin seems hardly possible since you are still so young."

"I've had reason to practice harder than the others," he said. He didn't mention his father's death and him becoming chieftain so young because the Supreme Sage already knew his predicament. He had to work harder to prove himself a capable leader and the bow was his main source of accomplishment.

Sounds of footsteps came up from behind him. "Ah, Corven. Let me introduce you to the Chieftain of West Basin and his mother. They will be witnesses to your acceptance as my protégé as Second Supreme Sage."

"We would be honored," Laninson repeated his mother's words. He stared at the hornless man who had bandages on his hairline. He was being carried on the back by another man also with bandages on his hairline. The Supreme Sage must have had horn bulbs planted in them. The man carrying the other finally set him down once they got to the forest floor. He was an odd choice to become the Supreme Sage, but the sages were often unusual in their ways.

"Let me introduce my protégé, Corven, and his servant, Reece."

"Honored to be introduced," Laninson said.

Corven gave a slight bow as his servant held his arm. "The honor is mine."

Laninson knew right away that Corven was not a Lake-keeper. The rumors from the Lowland Cliffs must be true. There were lands across the great waters that took over the deserts.

"Now that introductions have been made. I have a slight dilemma, Corven. I have heard rumor that Chieftain Laninson here

99

is the best bowman of all Domus Lake Basin. How can we test this rumor to see if it is true?"

Laninson watched Corven think. "I listened to a story from a young sage just this morning that is still in my memory about an ancient test for the bowmen. They had a bow demonstration called the *Shots of the Tree Heart Fruits* long ago that would prove a bowman's skill. I will need five large fruits. Weren't the ones served at breakfast Tree Heart Fruits?"

The Supreme Sage nodded. "Yes, and I do know this test. I believe you have found us the solution." She turned to one of the sages. "Go fetch me five of the Tree Heart Fruits."

"Do you have five arrows in your quiver?" Corven asked.

"I never leave home without at least twenty of them," he responded.

The Supreme Sage turned to the young sage next to her. "Please make a special note of this in your memories if Laninson shall fail or if he shall prove himself and his place as the youngest chieftain. I do believe you were the youngest when you stepped into your father's position." She looked at Laninson. "You were only thirteen when your father died at the hands of those monstrous woodland nomads, correct?"

Laninson felt anger rise at the mention of his father's death by the nomads, but he harnessed the anger. This was his moment as the chieftain of the smallest territory to prove himself. "Yes, I was thirteen."

"Then there it is. Make note he was the youngest chieftain to take his command in the history of the Lake-keepers."

The young sage she tasked to get the fruit came up to her with a basket filled with them.

"Reece is the strongest one here. He will throw them. Laninson," Corven said, turning to the young chieftain, "my servant will throw with all his might five of these fruits in all different directions into the forest. Keeping your arrows in your quiver, you must pierce the heart of each one when I give the command. Then you will pass the test of being counted as one of the best bowmen."

"Do not throw five," Laninson said. "Throw six, for my father has been dead these six years. I don't want to be counted as one of the best. I want it to be known that I am the best."

Corven looked at the Supreme Sage for approval. She slowly nodded her head.

"Hand the basket to me," Corven said to the young sage. "Reece, I will hold the basket here next to you. When I shout, *throw,* begin to heave each of the six Tree Heart Fruits in different directions one at a time. Do not hold back. Grab each one as fast as you can. I want to warn you, Chieftain Laninson. My servant, Reece, has extremely quick reflexes."

Laninson walked several feet away from the Temple where the crowd of sages and his mother and brother stood. He gave a quick wink to his brother who gave a slight smile but then resumed his indifferent stance as a sage. Laninson readied his bow. "I am ready."

"Ready your bow!" Corven shouted. "Throw!"

Reece grabbed the Tree Heart Fruits swiftly and slung them in all directions into the forest. Instinctively, Laninson's right hand reached for an arrow from his quiver and by the time the arrow took flight his hand had already grabbed another arrow, launching it onto a different course. Once Laninson shot all six arrows, he took two more shots and slung his bow back over his shoulder.

"What were the other two shots you took?" the Supreme Sage demanded.

"You will find I have shot two gifts for you, Supreme Sage. I have shot a Mud Piglet that was sniffing around the large tree in front of the Swarve stables with the seventh arrow, and I have shot a Large Lady Dove resting on one of the steeples of your Temple with the eighth. It has fallen right there," he said and pointed. "And if you send out your sages, you will see that every Tree Heart Fruits has been pierced in the center, hopefully with my arrow still plunged within. I tried to gauge the strength of the wind while shooting, so my arrows would not fly too short and pierce only half, but not too far and pierce all the way through. Either way, the hearts of all six fruits have been pierced."

Laninson returned to the group and stood next to his mother and brother, who was grinning broadly now, and they all waited as the sages hurried to find the missing fruit and the harvested animals.

"Place everything before us," Corven ordered.

When the final young sage came and set down the last of the Tree Heart Fruits, they all looked at the pile in awe. There were six fruits each with an arrow stuck through the center with the nock and the point of the arrow equal distance from either side of the fruit's skin. A plump Mud Piglet was pierced through the neck and a Large Lady Dove was pierced through the chest.

The Supreme Sage laid her right hand upon her chest. "Let it be known," she began in a stately tone, "that Lake-keeper history has been made here today before our very eyes. Laninson bar Hudson, Chieftain of West Basin, becoming the youngest Chieftain of all the Lake-keepers at the age of thirteen years old, has shot his arrows through the center of six Tree Heart Fruits thrown quickly and with force in all directions into the forest along with a seventh shot to a Mud Piglet and the final one to a Large Lady Dove as gifts to me, DeEldra Le Actelion, the Supreme Sage of the Atlatl Forest Temple. The test was conducted by Corven bar Hathway, soon to be Second Supreme Sage and his servant, Reece. The test finished in mere seconds. Therefore, I make the declarations that Chieftain Laninson bar Hudson is the best bowman of all the bowmen of Domus Lake Basin."

Then she turned to Laninson and his mother. "I chose correctly when I chose the chieftain from West Basin to join us today. You are our valued guests, including you, young Valor bar Hudson. You may talk now. Your work as Sage of West Basin is now complete," she said, giving a slight smile. Then she turned to a sage. "Please show our guests into the Temple and have the dove and piglet prepared for dinner."

"Yes, Supreme Sage," a young sage said.

She turned to another sage. "Please send out sages to all the chieftains' sages with the story of Chieftain Laninson's victory."

"Yes, Supreme Sage," an older sage answered.

Laninson suppressed his excitement. Finally, he would be the chieftain the Lake-keepers would be talking about. His story would be told in the wooden fortresses of the basin chieftains and in the castle walls of the cliff chieftains. His victory would be repeated and memorized in the taverns, inns, homes and boats of all Domus Lake. Already the Supreme Sage herself has insisted it be memorized by the sages at the prestigious Temple of Atlatl Forest and for their memories to be shared with the other chieftain families. Finally, his family line would have a triumph to compensate for the fact that his father was killed by a rock in the back of the neck by a nomad of the forest.

"You did it, Brother! You did it! Now those filthy woodsmen nomads will fear the day they killed our father!" Valor yelled. Instantly, his mother knelt to quiet the young boy.

Laninson turned away to hide the anger that flashed across his face. His hatred for those spiny-horned thieves had become his sole motivator for six years. He had been secretly training his bowmen and adding to his army. Every young boy and girl from his territory of West Basin learned the skill of the bow along with their family trade of farming, hunting, fishing and building. He started training everyone at the age of thirteen with their youth memories still open the bar Hudson Bowcraft—an intricate blend of speed and accuracy. He now had a bowmen army of youth from the ages of thirteen to nineteen who could work the bow almost as well as he did. He also had the expertise and experience of his Master Bowman, Barronne le Sharon, the only survivor of the attack on his father and his men, to guide him. He kept his growing army a secret for the right moment to strike.

"Chieftain Laninson," the Supreme Sage said.

He tucked his anger away and turned back to face her.

She handed him a bag and pointed to it as an indication to open it.

"What is in it?" he asked.

"Why, it is your payment of gold in advance. I hope my sage was able to reach you with the information."

"Yes, he did, but normally the sages don't pay until the job is finished," he said, staring at the bag.

"Normally, we do. However, like you said, you do everything with all your strength. You have demonstrated that what you say is true. And I believe the money will come in useful since so much of your territory's resources go to the Lowland Cliffs. Now, please follow Corven and Reece. Corven will go over all the plans he is envisioning for the additions to the Temple. When you are satisfied, we will have the ceremony to establish Corven as the Second Supreme Sage. Then we shall dine on the meat you have harvested along with the other delicacies the sages are renowned for." She turned to face his mother. "Sarina, why don't you and Valor join me, and I will give you both a tour of the Temple? You are blessed by the Befores to have such a son as Chieftain Laninson. I believe he will surprise us all as he has already done."

"I believe you are right," his mother said, squeezing his hand before she and Valor followed the Supreme Sage up the stairs to the Temple doors.

Chapter 13

Messages in the Sand

Jayston jumped onto the dock as Morgo eased the boat into the slip with his oars. He waited by the dock piling for Morgo to throw him the line. He quickly grabbed the line and wrapped it around the piling several times before tying the knot that Morgo taught him. He had been living with his sister, Voddie, and Morgo for several weeks now. After Kragel, the old Sage from the Lowland Cliffs, died, Jayston took over his room. He had lied to his sister and brother-in-law. He said he didn't have building work to do because Lothar bar Haven's galleys were complete, but that wasn't the full truth. He could easily go back to work. There were always house additions, boats and other construction work available, but he told his brother-in-law that he needed work and asked if he could fish with him. The skill of fishing wasn't in his youth memories; though, he had memories of watching and even helping fisherman while they worked which helped. His father also built boats and their construction was in his youth memories. If he fished and boated every day for several weeks, he would be ready.

Once the line was secure, Morgo placed the oars inside the boat and jumped onto the dock. He patted his brother-in-law's shoulder. "I could swear that if I didn't know better, you were meant to be a fisherman not a builder."

"You doubt my building skills?" Jayston jested. "Do you not see that grand Fisherman's Inn just near the shoreline that I constructed? Your wife, my sister, has her very own source of income now coming in from all of the Lake-keepers. And she has employed many who otherwise would not have work."

"If memory serves right, Boru also helped with the design."

"Yes." He thought of his little brother commanding all the construction workers on the galleys he designed for Chieftain Lothar. He was not jealous of what his brother had achieved. Rather, he wanted to go with him. He wanted to sail the new waters and explore distant lands. There was nothing for him at East Basin, nor on any basin or cliff. He was not married and had found no one he deemed worthy to settle down with. That is why he needed to practice boating with his brother-in-law. He would request an assignment on one of the galleys, and he needed to prove his value. Plus, someone had to look after his lovesick brother. Jayston knew that Boru had his eyes set on getting Amorfia, or F'lorna as she was really known, back. The fact that Chieftain Lothar also had his eyes set on the girl did not phase his little brother. She was to be a chieftess, and there was no room for a lowly construction worker in her future—even if he did build the galleys that will eventually find her."

"You are lost in thought, Brother," Morgo said.

"Sorry, I was thinking of the great galleys that Boru designed. He always had an imagination. While I worked with our father, he'd be off watching the boats and the fisherman. Now I can see that dreaming is just as important as building. You can't imagine new ways of constructing if you are too busy building what's already been designed."

"Aye," Morgo said. "So when are you going to tell your sister?"

"Now what would I be telling her?" Jayston asked, knowing the answer.

"You will be headed to the Highland Cliffs tomorrow, won't you? Now that the construction is done, they will be collecting as many oarsmen as possible. Chieftain Darmin bar Holthen will not be happy. He is leader over both East and South Basin. If he loses his fisherman to Lothar to oar his galleys across the new waters, his command may weaken."

"How did you know I would be going?"

Morgo laughed and nudged Jayston's shoulder. "You are an excellent builder. You can find work anywhere in East or South Basin. I even heard that the Supreme Sage is summoning builders from West Basin to add additions to their Temple. You could always join them. Nay, you came to me not because you couldn't find work, but you want to learn to man a boat."

"Aye, you are right, Brother. I've been tying every knot you taught me each night, so I do not forget. I don't want to be stuck in the bottom with oars. I want to be at the top with the lines."

"Let us pray to the Befores that Lothar pays the fishermen well. They still need to pay their twenty percent taxes to Chieftain Darmin."

"Chieftain Lothar and Darmin have come to some kind of arrangement, and I believe it is concerning Amorfia—I mean F'lorna."

"Ah, I sense a war brewing if Chieftain Lothar does not keep with the end of his bargain. Now that F'lorna knows the bar Haven Swordcraft, Chieftain Darmin wants her for his son."

"That's what concerns me," Jayston said. "Boru."

"Does he know?" Morgo asked. "I fear he's in love with the F'lorna lass. I never thought that when I found her on the shores of the Highland Cliffs that she would go from our home to the sages and back to the cliffs. Then when she escaped Chieftain Lothar, she unleashed the waters to cover her tracks. She has slipped through everyone's fingers and now Boru is trying to bring her back."

Jayston sighed. "I don't think he has thought his plan all the way through."

"I guess that's what love does—causes a young man to think only of his aching heart," Morgo said.

Jayston's little brother almost never spoke his mind, but his actions would speak for him. "Boru has promised me a position on the top deck of the galley if I can learn the knots and work the lines. Once I'm on the galley, I am sure the daily work will keep the skills intact in my memories."

"You are going to protect your little brother, aren't you? He's going after a girl he can't have," Morgo said.

"I doubt Chieftain Lothar will allow F'lorna to marry Rathtar either. He is a disgrace to his family. He robs innocent innkeepers, and he is not discrete about his relationship with women. I even heard he isn't the best warrior also. He surrounds himself with bowmen to stay protected."

"His father spoiled him," Morgo added. "Yet, F'lorna is a chieftess herself. She doesn't have to marry a chieftain. She can marry a Swordmaster. I hear Durstin le Guyel of the Lowland Cliffs is unattached and only a few years older than she."

Morgo looked around to ensure no one was around to overhear their words. "Chieftain Lothar would never allow his heir to marry into the bar Hathway family. Do you think the rumors we heard as children were true?" he whispered. "Were they really fighting over who had the best bar Swordcraft at family dinner? It is a petty reason to fight to the death. Each swordcraft is unique in its own way with its own strengths and weaknesses."

"Who knows what rumors be false or true. All that we know for sure is that Lothar's father gave the fatal blow, and the Highland and Lowland Cliffs have been enemies ever since. The bar Haven Swordcraft is ruthless, but for a dinner with friends to end in bloodshed goes to show how brutal Lothar's father was, which is why many believed his pregnant wife left him, disappearing into the tunnels."

Both men stood quietly, lost in the drama of the Lake-keeper chieftains as the water of the basin lapped up against the wooden dock.

"Best not to dwell on speculation. The more we think, the more we talk, and the more people hear," Jayston said. "The only chieftain other than Rathtar is Laninson bar Hudson of West Basin, he is of the right age, but his territory is small, and his rule is weak. Everyone knows that the Lowland Cliffs control him. Chieftain Laninson's father died when he was just a lad, and his mother raised him with the help of their Master Bowman, Barronne le Sharon." Jayston paused, thinking of his brother. "Couldn't F'lorna marry a commoner? Lothar married Tarsha, and she was a commoner from South Basin."

"True, but she had some relations—though very distant—to the bar Heston family of South Basin before it merged with East Basin, and she was known for her beauty and her singing voice," Morgo said. "Unless your family finds a sage from the Temple with claim of your family's connection to the chieftains, I believe that Boru will have to ignore his aching heart."

"Unless," Jayston said and then stopped.

"Unless what?" Morgo questioned.

Jayston sighed. "Unless she is unwilling to go with Chieftain Lothar and chooses to stay in her homelands."

"Do you think Boru would be willing to leave Domus Lake for a new life with her?" Morgo asked.

"I don't know what his heart would choose. He is a very quiet young man who keeps his thoughts hidden."

Morgo gave a chuckle. "Maybe because Voddie and you talked so much while he was a lad that he learned to stay quiet. Speaking of Voddie," he said looking back up to the Fisherman's Inn, "let us head to the inn. I could use some supper."

The two began to make their way from the dock to the sandy shores. Much of the sand had been given to Chieftain Lothar for his galleys to set upon, but there was still plenty of sand left to cause the scuffing sound of the beach underneath their leather boots.

"Wait," Morgo said stopping. "The sands haven't been brushed."

"Brushed?" Jayston looked to where Morgo was pointing. "Those are the symbols Boru's sage taught to Range." He continued to gape at the shoreline. "They're everywhere. How come I've not seen them?"

"Aye, this is going to cause some trouble with the sages," Morgo said. "I've been having my men brush over them by putting rocks in our fishing nets and dragging the nets over the sand, but every day the lads and lasses come to the shores to practice their symbols and to teach others. It's like a new game for them. Now they are even writing them with ash from the fire onto rocks. I just hope Boru knew what he was doing when he taught our son those symbols. I can try to hide them as long as I can, but the fact is that soon all the children of East and South Basin will know the symbols, and I have a feeling that the Supreme Sage will not approve."

"Why?" Jayston asked.

Morgo turned his gaze beyond the shore to Atlatl Forest. "Because we see the fires from the Temple at night and see the ash scattered by the wind at day. Smells different. Seems to me that the Supreme Sage is burning the scrolls that the chieftains have donated to the Temple."

"Why would she want to burn the scrolls?" Jayston asked, matching his brother-in-law's gaze.

"Voddie says because the symbols create words and words create stories. The Supreme Sage doesn't want competition for the Temple's knowledge. If we can document history and knowledge with symbols, there is no need for the sages."

Chieftain Lothar sat at the second most prestigious place at the long, wooden table in the great halls of the wooden fortress of East

Basin. He was at the head of the table sitting left of the entrance. His aunt sat on the long section of the table to his right and next to her sat Dagor le Armon, his Swordmaster. The rest of Lothar's men stood guard outside of the entrance to the fortress. Chieftain Darmin bar Holthen sat at the first most prestigious seat—at the head of the table to the right of the entrance of the great halls. To his right sat his wife, Chieftess Yaunda bar Holthen and next to her sat their daughters, Zuana and Claraun. To the left of Chieftain Darmin sat their only son, Rathtar bar Holthen. All the bar Holthen family wore the golden crest of the East Basin on their left horn except for Chieftess Yaunda who kept the golden crest of the South Basin—the last of its kind—visible in all Domus Lake. The marriage of chieftain and chieftess had merged the two territories into one.

Chieftain Lothar stared at Rathtar having his fifth tankard of ale and conversing red-faced to his bowmen. He was a young, careless son of a chieftain whose reputation of indiscretions, like stealing from the South Basin innkeeper, preceded him. *Spoiled*, Lothar thought. He can't be trusted. Lothar would only offer F'lorna as his wife if the situation was dire. Yet, F'lorna—when she did return to the Highland Cliffs and take her rightful place as his heir—would be a chieftess not by marriage but by birth. She did not have to marry a chieftain—though, the bar Holthen lands were vast. Too bad they were wasted on a rotten chieftain.

The wooden halls of East Basin were lit with torches lining the wall and servants stood holding smooth, wooden trays from every angle. Greenery looped on hooks under each torch and stretched along the walls. Green sprouts stuck in small wooden vases spread across the table. The great dining hall mimicked Atlatl Forest with all the brown and green accents. A few of the bar Holthen sages sat on chairs against the back wall. Close enough to be summoned if something needed to be recorded but not close enough to record anything personal. The rest of the seats at the table were occupied by bowmen. Lothar didn't recognize many of them, but he certainly knew Evander le Remy who sat next to his wife, Avyan, and their son, Truston. Evander was Master Bowman and advisor to Darmin. His son, Truston, was the best of all the young bowmen in Darmin's army and best friends with Rathtar. He was the one who made up for Rathtar's inadequacies. Lothar felt sweat trickling under his warfighting leathers. He loathed the heat and humidity of the basin. His castle built into the Highland Cliffs kept the atmosphere cooler and dryer. Yet, the trays of food adorning the table's surface made the uncomfortable atmosphere almost bearable.

"How are you enjoying your meal in our East Basin Fortress?" Darmin asked, flushed from his third glass of mead.

Lothar wanted to laugh, but he put his tankard of ale to his lips instead. A chieftain did not drink a lady's drink. Once he finished swallowing his brew and silenced his chuckle, he answered. "Your fruits and vegetables have no match. And your meat taste fresh of animals beginning their mating age." He hated giving flattery, but he needed to ensure Darmin believed that he would soon join lands with him, which he would not. Darmin acquired South Basin from his wife, Chieftess Yaunda of the bar Heston family. After she married Darmin, the lands were promised to the Holthen family once her parents passed away. They were aged parents and had no other relatives besides their one daughter. A merger meant more to their parents than keeping the bar Heston family name alive because it guaranteed their daughter's safety from the stronger, swordsmen chieftains of the high and low cliffs.

"Did you receive one of the sages from Atlatl Forest today? The Supreme Sage sent them to all the chieftains to put on record what happened at the Temple," Truston said.

"If one was sent, I missed it because I and my men were atop our Swarves enroute to the wooden fortress at Chieftain Darmin's request for dinner," Lothar said irritably. He hated when one of the sages from Atlatl Forest came to his castle while he was gone. He only hoped that the swordsman Dagor left in charge remembered to fetch one of the bar Haven sages to hear the information the Supreme Sage was sharing with the chieftains.

Darmin pounded the table with his fist, knocking over his empty wooden wine goblet. One of his servants instantly stood it up and filled it with more mead. "No doubt, Lothar, you will enjoy this story from the Supreme Sage. I know you think the bowmen are weaker, but after you hear what happened just this morning, you will think differently of us!" He looked to Truston. "Do you still remember the story or do you need the sages that heard it?"

"I still remember," Truston said, nodding his head. His dark blonde hair fell across his forehead. His brown eyes shone with anticipation.

"Father, why did you not summon me to get the sages for the story?" Rathtar asked almost whining. "I would have liked to hear the sage's first-person account."

Darmin's face reddened. "Because when I summon you, I must wait. When I summon Truston, I do not wait. I needed our sages fetched quickly without delay. Now silence, so Truston can tell the story."

Rathtar opened his mouth to say more, but he quickly closed it after a stern look from his mother.

"Proceed, Truston. Tell us what news comes from the Temple of Atlatl Forest," Chieftess Yaunda said.

Truston set down his ale. "Chieftain Laninson bar Hudson achieved a victory of an ancient bow demonstration called *Shots of the Tree Heart Fruit.*"

"That's impossible," Rathtar yelled. "No one can pass that test anymore because the Tree Heart Fruits has gotten too small!"

"I know. I didn't believe it myself when the little sage began the story, but it is obvious to me now that Chieftain Laninson might be the best bowman of all the Lake-keepers. I too am one of the best with the bow, and I tried the demonstration several times after hearing the sage. However, I came not even close to achieving the demonstration and the difficulty level he added to it," Truston said with obvious admiration.

Lothar was intrigued. To him, Laninson was yet a small boy being helped by his father's Master Bowman, Barronne le Sharon. Yet, Truston, an already accomplished bowman at such a young age agrees with the Supreme Sage's declaration that

Laninson was the best. "What is this young chieftain's age?" he inquired.

"His father died—five or six years ago—and Laninson still had his youth memories, so he's either eighteen or nineteen years. Perfect marrying age for one of my daughters," Darmin said, winking at the girls sitting next to their mother.

"I would like to hear more of this Chieftain Laninson," Dagor said. "My father taught me our le Armon Swordcraft, but I learned the bow during my stay at East Basin with my aunt and uncle."

"I did not know you knew the art of the bow," Lothar said, looking at his Swordmaster skeptically.

"Ah," Dagor said uncomfortably. "My father always said it was best to learn the craft of all war weapons. I also know how to throw a spear and dagger with precision."

"Interesting," Lothar said. He wouldn't admit it, but knowing more than wielding a sword would be an asset, especially being surrounded by armies who use various weapons. Only the Befores knew what weapons the people in the new lands across the waters used. He was glad to know Dagor had a variety of fighting skills.

Silence permeated the dining hall, so Lothar took a drink of his ale. He would not be talking the rest of the evening. He needed time to absorb the latest information and formulate a new plan to get his niece back. He knew now that he would not be leaving the Highland Cliffs. His weak alliance with the East Basin was merely a ploy by Chieftain Darmin to claim the Highland Cliffs. He wanted his swordcraft and his ore found in the mountains to make swords. Dagor would be capable enough to lead the galleys to the new lands and find his heir. F'lorna was a chieftess by birth. She did not have to marry a chieftain to keep her rank. She had the bar Haven name. Now all she needed was a formidable mate to continue that name. Maybe he had underestimated Chieftain Laninson of West Basin.

"Why so much silence when we have an ancient demonstration relived? Go ahead, Truston. Finish your story,"

Chieftain Darmin demanded. "No one is to talk until he is finished."

Lothar listened to the story told by Truston about the young chieftain's accomplishment, but his eyes stayed locked on Chieftain Darmin. Anger rose from the gut of his belly, permeating his entire body. Darmin was Chieftain of East and South Basin. He was eager to marry his son to F'lorna, future Chieftess of the Highland Cliffs, and now he was eager to marry one of his daughters to Chieftain Laninson of the West Basin. The realization of Darmin's plan unfolded like the scrolls found in the translucent canisters. Though Darmin drank the wine of a female, his mind thought like a cunning chieftain craving power and control. Then another scheme pronounced itself to Lothar's mind. Since Laninson's mother, Sarina, was related to the Chieftess Panela of the Lowland Cliffs, Darmin was angling to become Chieftain of the Lowland Cliffs, as well. He wanted control over all the Lake-keepers, and Lothar would never let that happen.

Chapter 14

The Informant

It was the cool of the early evening, and the three women sat on wooden chairs made by the West Basin builders which rested on the long, smooth rock patio of the Lowland Cliffs Castle. The castle had many such patios, but this one faced away from Domus Lake to the new waters that took over the desert. A spot that once garnered only heat from the desert now had the best breeze and view. The River that snaked its way through sands and split off into different directions was now an endless sea. Panela bar Hathway held her wiggly grandson. He kept reaching for her thick, curly black hair that was ornately braided in the front to expose her horns, especially the left one with the golden crest of the Lowland Cliffs. The hair behind her horns hung robustly around her shoulders. Her emerald eyes were highlighted by her dark skin. "Here, take him, Karthia," Panela said to her daughter-in-law. "He's restless."

Karthia got up from her chair and picked up her baby. "I think his horns may be breaking the skin. He's been agitated lately. I'll swab the tender areas with numbing ointment." Karthia's skin was a lighter brown than her mother-in-law's, and she had oval blue eyes that matched the new waters around their castle. Her glossy, straight black hair flowed under her horns to the small of her back. Her left horn also had the crest of the Lowland Cliffs. Her baby son instantly grabbed for it. She looked at the servant who stood near the patio entrance of the castle. "Get me some ointment for his skin." Though she didn't grow up a chieftess, the role suited her well. Her childhood was one of prestige being the daughter of the Master Bowman of West Basin. Her father, Barronne le Sharon, served under Chieftain Dontonion bar Hudson until his death. Now he served his son, Chieftain Laninson bar Hudson. She sat back onto her chair and pulled a large square of fabric from a wooden box next to her. "Let me feed him. Then I'll have the servant put him down for his nap." She held the baby to her breast and covered her son, so he could nurse.

Chieftess Panela turned to her daughter. "My Izzy, did you hear the story from our sages about Chieftain Laninson's victory of the ancient bow test? I forgot the name of it, but the Supreme Sage has declared him the best bowman of all the Lake-keepers."

Izziatan (Izzy II) bar Hathway slouched in her chair. She was named after her grandmother, Izziatan (Izzy I) bar Hathway because she inherited her light brown skin and golden eyes—an eye color that was extremely rare for Lake-keepers. However, her hair was thick and curly like her mother's and had to be braided in the front so not to cover her horns, so the chieftess crest could be visible. "Yes, I heard the story. I am proud of him, but that will not change my mind about marriage. We are more like siblings, Mother. We grew up together. His mother is your cousin. It would be like marrying my brother."

"It's been done before," Panela pressed.

"You and father don't need me. You have my brother, Jorran, and Karthia to pass on the family name. Look, your next chieftain after my brother has already been born. You have secured two generations of chieftains," she said, pointing to the nursing baby. "I am sure my sister-in-law will have more babies. I am not needed."

Karthia gave an exhausted look. "Let me get this one weaned before we start talking about another one."

Chieftess Panela continued. "Yes, but you can merge the Lowland Cliffs with West Basin. Our family can finally have access to suitable farmlands and forest animals to harvest."

"Father already controls the lands. Laninson pays great tribute to Father for his protection from Chieftain Darmin."

"But the tributes won't last long once Laninson marries. What if he chooses to marry one of Chieftain Darmin's daughters? Then all Domus Basin will be united under the bar Holthen name, and he will stop West Basin's tributes of crops and animals to us."

"This is all speculation, Mother. Has anyone spoken to Laninson himself? Unlike other chieftains, I doubt he has intentions beyond protecting his own lands and people. His mother raised him to have a good heart and to work with excellence. Chieftain Darmin spoils his children. Laninson may not desire his daughters. He is chieftain by birth, so he can marry anyone he pleases. Jorran married Karthia, and she is not of chieftain blood."

"Yes, but her father is a Master Bowman of South Basin. It is acceptable for a chieftain or chieftess to marry the sons and daughter of the Masters of Bow or Sword."

"Precisely, Mother. I am a chieftess by birth. I don't have to marry a chieftain. I can marry whom I want."

"You won't have your own lands. And do you have no concern if Rathtar takes over the entire basin once his father passes to the Befores?" her mother asked.

Izzy gave an exaggerated exhale. "I bore of this conversation."

Karthia switched her baby to the other side to feed. Then she engaged in the conversation. "I've noticed that Durstin le Guyel stares at you, Izzy. He's handsome with his golden-brown hair that almost matches the color of your eyes, and he is the Swordmaster of the Lowland Cliffs. If you two were to marry, you could have a baby with golden eyes and hair. That would be extremely rare!"

"He doesn't stare at me because he likes me. Karthia, you know he is continuing my training in the bar Hathway Swordcraft. That is all I am to him. His student. And—" she paused. "He has given me no indication that he is interested."

"That's because you intimidate him." Karthia laughed. "You intimidate all the swordsmen. You fight almost as well as they do."

"I fight just as well and even sometimes better. I may not have their strength, but I do not tire easily. I just wear them down until I can make my final blow."

"You and your sword fighting," Chieftess Panela said, irritably. "There are more important matters a chieftess should focus on. I really think your time with the sword needs to stop."

Izzy stood and walked to the stone ledge of the patio. The cool air from the choppy waves below felt good against her skin. She had practiced her swordcraft after breakfast until she was summoned by a servant to meet her mother on her new favorite cliff patio. Her swordcraft was the only excuse she could give for leaving the confinement of the castle walls. She didn't want the responsibilities of a chieftess. She wanted to experience life beyond the cliffs. She had been sheltered all her life. Her only journeys were to West Basin to visit her mother's cousin and her son, Laninson. She needed an adequate argument to continue her training—though Durstin has already explained to her that there was nothing more he could teach her.

"Chieftess Dalia taught that girl with the colorless eyes the bar Haven Swordcraft. I want to be able to defend myself, Mother, and not rely on others to protect me."

"How dare you bring up that family—" Chieftess Panela said, stopping when a servant came onto the patio.

"He's done nursing. Take him for his nap after you apply the anointment," Karthia said, removing the fabric and holding up her son.

The servant bowed. "Yes," Chieftess Karthia. "Would you be needing anything else?"

"Where are my husband and father-in-law?"

"They left after dinner."

Karthia looked annoyed. "Did they say where they were going?"

"No, Chieftess Karthia."

"No matter," Chieftess Panela said. "We will take our dinner now. Have the cooks and servants prepare for our arrival at the dining hall when the sun starts to set."

"Yes, Chieftess Panela," the servant said, taking the baby from Karthia. "I will let them know and take this little one for his nap." The servant held the baby who was now sleepy from nursing and exited the patio.

"You have no right to compare us to the bar Haven family! We are nothing like them. Lothar is desperate for an heir. They don't even know if that girl is related."

"They have proof," Izzy said, sitting back down. "I talked to Corven myself. He said that a dagger was found hidden in the tunnels next to the spine of a Swarve."

"It's all so preposterous! Who are these people? Sand-shapers and Tree-dwellers. They sound like a fairytale," Panela said, shaking her head. "Not one word can be believed until evidence is shown."

"They are called River-dwellers, Mother. Do you not believe the information given to us by our kin, Corven bar Hathway? Father did adopt him."

"Only because your father wanted information on those cylinders we have found. Who knows if what this Corven says is true. No matter. He has become a sage and rightfully so. We can't have a lame bar Hathway being led around our castle by the arm. And it's to our advantage. The bar Hathways haven't bequeathed a family member to the Temple of Atlatl Forest for several generations. Corven has given us that ability."

"If I remember correctly, Mother, I volunteered to be a sage," Izzy said.

"Never! Chieftains do not make a habit of donating their children to the Temple, especially since the Befores only gave me two. They donate distant relatives, which is what Corven claims to be. By the Befores, Izzy, you are more stubborn than the stories our sages say about your grandmother."

There was silence for a moment as the three women lost themselves in thought. Finally, Karthia spoke. "But why would Chieftain Lothar be building those large boats? He has allotted a lot of gold to build them, using up most of the builders from East and South Basin. Now I hear he is paying fisherman to oar them. I doubt Chieftain Lothar would give so much if he didn't believe there were people across the waters, one of them being his niece and heir. This Amorfia girl has captured Chieftain Lothar's interest. More than that. She is extremely valuable to him."

"Her real name is F'lorna. I envy her. She is several years younger than I and already has had two lifetimes of experiences," Izzy said. She peered over the rocky edge to glimpse the Highland Cliffs. She could barely make out a section of the castle. "Durstin told me this afternoon the sea boats are almost ready to launch. How wonderful it would be to go with them."

"You talk nonsense, Izzy. The bar Havens are our enemies since Chieftain Lothar's father killed your grandfather with a fatal wound," Panela said.

Izzy turned to face her mother. "Why did they fight? Our families were once friends."

"It was a battle of ridiculous pride aggravated by too much ale. They wanted to prove one swordcraft was better than the other," Panela said. "Look how blood-thirsty the bar Haven family is. First Lothar's father kills your grandfather. Then Lothar himself killed his own Swordmaster with a fatal blow too. There is a madness in the bar Haven family. Garth le Cienten had been the bar Hathway Swordmaster and trusted advisor for two generations. There is no reasoning with Lothar. He is as crazy as his father before him. Besides, we already have an important informant on the boat. We don't need you snooping around the Highland Cliffs. You belong here where it is safe."

Izzy sighed for the third time that evening. She felt the cold stone underneath her hands as the sun began to touch the horizon. The Lowland Cliffs Castle would always be her prison if she didn't find a way out. She needed to find this informant her mother spoke about. Maybe he could get her on one of the large boats before they set out for the new lands.

Dagor le Armon stood on the Highland Cliffs behind the castle facing the rocky farmland his father and his brothers toiled to harvest crops that almost all went to Chieftain Lothar's castle. He could see the six piers leading from the rocky shoreline out onto the new waters covering what once was desert land. Lines led from the metal cleats upon the galleys to the metal cleats on the piers, keeping the boats secure until they set off. There was enough room between each galley to allow the thirty-six long oars to be set in place on either side and ready to power the galleys away from the shore to new lands. The six galleys Boru designed were complete. The sight of them almost made him proud to be from the Highland Cliffs… almost.

"Which boat will you lead?" his father, Cresden, asked. He stood next to Dagor on a large, flat look-out rock.

"Chieftain Lothar has placed me in charge of the entire fleet," Dagor said.

"Then he will not be going to the new lands after all," Cresden said. "His younger brother and niece are no longer worth his time."

"He feels the heat of Chieftain Darmin's lust for his land. Darmin rules both East and South Basin. Now he looks to the left and the right to make the bar Holthen name ruler of all Domus Lake. His son, Rathtar, is an embarrassment. He must surround himself with skilled bowman to look like an adequate leader. It will be a terrible day if Rathtar becomes chieftain over all the Lake-keepers."

"I agree," his father said and remained quiet for several seconds. "Chieftain Rugar wants his daughter, Izziatan, to marry Chieftain Laninson of the West Basin, but she refuses to marry. She says she will never be anyone's wife. He too wants to expand his territory. Now he fears one of Chieftain Darmin's daughters will marry Laninson, and the bar Holthen family will have claim to all Domus Lake Basin."

Dagor turned to his father. "Can we really trust any of the chieftains? We have made an alliance with the Lowland Cliffs. I have become a spy in my own territory. I am leading the very first Highland Cliffs' fleet that I will one day defy. It is difficult to become close to my men knowing that they will soon despise me as a traitor."

"Listen to me, Son," Cresden said, taking Dagor's shoulder and turning his body to face him. "The bar Haven family turned on us when I was dismissed from being Swordmaster of the Highland Cliffs because Chieftain Vandar enjoyed beating his pregnant wife. I was not the only one who saw what he was doing to her and intervened. When Garth replaced me, he became aware of the beatings too and helped Chieftess Tarsha to escape with her Swarve and unborn child, and now we know that the baby survived."

Dagor shrugged his father's hand from his shoulder. "And Swordmaster Garth was killed for his betrayal. Now I have taken his place only to do the same. The Swordmasters of the Highland Cliffs are cursed by the Befores."

"You speak incorrectly, Son. It is the bar Havens who are cursed, and we must endure the consequences. That is why I made the agreement with Chieftain Rugar bar Hathway of the Lowland Cliffs. He has promised you position as Second to the Swordmaster, and he has promised our family land in the South Basin. You only need to oar the boats on your return to the Lowland Cliffs. They will have the piers built before your return. He has promised us protection, prestige and position, and you will give him all the gold and information gained from the new lands. The le Armon family will no longer serve the bar Havens. Their family line will end with Lothar."

"But what if I do find his niece? She is the heir to his throne."

His father thought for several seconds. "She left the Highland Cliffs for a reason. Garth risked his life to help her escape. If you find her, leave her alone. Then Garth's death won't be in vain. Get the gold. Let the sages gain information about the new lands. Then come back to Domus Lake. And make sure you oar the boats to the west part of our shores where the cliffs are low. We will have the lines ready to dock the galleys and end your journey. Then our family will be welcomed to the Lowland Cliffs with celebration and honor."

"Indeed," Dagor said. "And I fear we will also be welcoming war to our shores, as well."

Chapter 15

The Stowaway

Chieftess Izzy gave the South Basin innkeeper a gold coin. She shielded her eyes and the golden crest on her left horn with the hood from her cloak. "Thank you for the stay and the breakfast. I need to get to the Temple at Atlatl Forest. Are you able to direct me?" She awoke several hours before sunrise and ate breakfast quickly. No other guests were up yet, but she could hear movement from upstairs.

The innkeeper eyed the gold coin sitting on his counter. "Aye, but you have paid too much. I don't have enough steel coins to give you for such a surplus in payment. The breakfast is included with your stay."

She slid the gold coin further toward the innkeeper. "The coin is also for directions to the Temple and for your discretion. If anyone comes looking for a young lady with my description, I will hope that you have seen nothing out of the ordinary." She made

125

sure to choose coins that were from West Basin from her stash of money, not from the Lowland Cliffs.

The innkeeper picked up the gold coin and hurriedly placed it into the pocket of his apron, looking around to ensure no one saw them. "I haven't seen anything unusual. Just a fisherman's daughter heading back to East Basin from visiting relatives. I guess you'll be needing directions to the Temple going into the forest and not walking the shoreline?"

She nodded.

He gave her directions. She wasn't far. Less than half a day's walk from the Temple. She would use the excuse that she was visiting her relative, Corven bar Hathway, which was true. However, her visit wasn't a social one. She needed information and a sage. She couldn't use a sage from her castle because they obeyed only her father, but one from Atlatl Temple would be more objective. She thanked the innkeeper and left just as she heard footsteps coming down the stairs into the main dining hall.

She walked away from the shore and to the forest. She'd be safer and less likely seen and recognized in the woods. When she finally made it into the shade of the trees, she pulled off the hood of her cloak. "Confounded horn crest," she said, touching the golden metal clamped to her left horn. "I can't go anywhere with you." She knew she couldn't take off the crest, but maybe her thick, curly hair would cover it. She unwound the tight braids underneath her horns. When every braid was undone, she used her fingers to lift and separate her tight curls until her horns were completely hidden underneath her thick hair. "At least my mother gave me something useful: thick, curly hair," she said with a mischievous smile. "Now, I better get moving. I need to persuade my distant relative to help me."

As she walked, she went over in her mind the possible outcomes of her visit. She hoped she wouldn't have to confront the Supreme Sage. She enjoyed the walk over the mossy forest floor much more than the hard stones of her family's castle. When she passed through West Basin the day before, she stayed at an inn where the local farmers were conversing about the new addition to the Temple. Many of the West Basin builders were working for the Supreme Sage constructing additional quarters for new sages that would be memorizing the symbols found in the translucent cylinders. Maybe with all the construction and workers, she could make it to the Temple unseen.

Finally, she could hear the noise of construction just ahead. She wanted to skirt around the front and skip the Temple entrance. She didn't know where Corven would be, and she reprimanded herself for coming so hastily without enough information. Then again, she knew from hints from her father at the dinner table that the boats were finished. They would be setting off any day now. She also knew who the bar Hathway family informant was on the boats. She shook her head. She still had trouble believing that Swordmaster Dagor le Armon would betray his people of the Highland Cliffs. The le Armon family were renowned Swordmasters. Something happened many years ago that caused Dagor's father, Cresden, to be relieved from his position. Her family was involved somehow, but none of their family sages were there during the quarrel of the High and Lowland Cliffs Chieftains that ended her grandfather's life. "Lothar has barely an heir. The le Armon family has been disgraced by the bar Haven family. They are a family of farmers now, not swordsmen," she said to herself. "But Dagor is Swordmaster now of the Highland Cliffs. Why would he compromise that position? Unless what Mother said is true. Chieftain Lothar has been lost to insanity."

Suddenly, she heard the rustling of leaves to her right. "Why would a builder be over here when the work was on the other side of the Temple?" she asked herself. She crept slowly along the soft forest floor, making sure not to step on a crunchy leaf or piece of twig. When she saw blonde shaggy hair just above the bushes, she knew who it was. It was Corven's servant, Reece. This was her chance. If she could intercept him, he would bring her straight to Corven. She wouldn't have to face the Supreme Sage after all.

She took a few more steps closer to the bushes and then knelt. "Reece, it is I—Izzy Hathway of the Lowland Cliffs. Corven's relative."

Reece's head instantly froze. Though, he couldn't talk. She knew that his sense of hearing was keen. He was hidden behind dense bushes that surrounded a large, old tree stump. From what she remembered of him, he was a dutiful servant—one who would easily be overlooked if it wasn't for his lame master. She heard clinking noises. She recognized the noise when her father gave the Supreme Sage the translucent cylinders.

"What are doing with the symbols?" she asked.

Finally, Reece popped out from the bushes squatting, and he looked to his left and right. He had the starting of horns poking out from his skin along his hairline. Then he stared at her and gave a concerned facial expression. He pointed to her and gave a smile. Then he gave her a frown. Next, he stayed still watching as if waiting for her to answer.

"I don't understand," she whispered, thinking of what he might be indicating. Then the answer came to her, and she smiled and nodded her head. "I am a friend. I'm here to ask a favor from Corven, but I don't want the Supreme Sage to see me."

Reece nodded enthusiastically and pointed to himself.

"You don't want to be seen by the Supreme Sage either. You are hiding those containers with the symbols."

He gave no facial expression and looked down.

"I won't say anything. Promise," she said, placing both palms out and up in a stance of surrender.

Reece looked up and smiled again.

"Will you take me to Corven without being seen by the others? I need his help."

He held his hand over his mouth again.

"I told you I wouldn't tell the Supreme Sage about the cylinders."

He kept his hand over his mouth and pointed to his foot.

She stared for a moment. "Oh, you don't want Corven to know about the cylinders either?"

He dropped his hand and nodded again.

"I promise that I will tell no one. I've already forgotten."

He stood and walked up to her. She noticed he now wore the apparel of a sage. He took her hand and pulled her up. She was surprised by how much strength he had. He gently clasped her elbow and began to walk, leading her through the woods around the Temple.

"This is curious," she whispered to Reece. "I never thought I would be the one being led around by the arm. My mother would be in an uproar."

He looked at her and covered his mouth with his free hand.

"I know you won't say anything. You can't talk," she said.

Reece stopped and lifted his head in silent laughter. His green eyes illuminated with amusement, and she couldn't help but giggle herself. "You are much smarter than you seem. Can you read those symbols?"

He nodded and then covered his mouth again.

"Does Corven know you can read them?"

Again, his face went expressionless, and he looked at the ground.

She bent down, so he could see her face. "Don't worry. That will be our little secret too. Why don't we do this: You keep my secrets, and I will keep yours."

He nodded his head enthusiastically again and began to lead her through the forest.

Izzy wouldn't show it, but she felt exhilarated by her chance meeting with Reece. She was away from the confines of her parents' castle. She found an ally deep within the Atlatl Forest. Now she would finish her plan by insisting that Corven help her. She needed to be free from family expectations and fulfill the passions deep within her, which she couldn't quite figure out but knew they were there waiting to burst forth. However, the process of discovery would only be possible if she got aboard one of Chieftain Lothar's galleys.

Dagor le Armon stood next to Boru on the pier of the first galley. He could sense the excitement of the other men—swordsmen, bowmen and fishermen combined. Never in the history of the Lake-keepers, as far as he knew, was there a journey across waters of this magnitude to unknown lands. He tried to set his hesitation aside about docking at the Lowland Cliffs when he returned. That was most likely several months away, depending on how fast the men oared and how far the new lands were. He looked up at the Highland Cliffs Castle. He could see Chieftain Lothar looking down on them. That morning Chieftain Lothar made it very clear what he needed to do. Get the gold, get the information for the sages and find his niece and maybe his little brother. If his brother refused to come, Dagor was to use force to take Lothar's niece and heir back to Domus Lake, which was the exact opposite of what his father told him to do. His conviction would tear him apart if he didn't stop mulling over the possibilities in his mind. He needed to stay focused on leading six galleys with more than eighty Lake-keepers aboard each one.

"Do you think the provisions will last?" Dagor asked, turning to Boru.

Boru looked uneasy. "We have a lot of room for the oarsmen, which leaves less room for supplies. The best I can say is that if the men oar fast and for long hours, we should have enough to last us a month. Maybe two. But the oarsmen will be hungry. Most of the food must go to them. The men doing the lines above can survive with less food."

"And so can we," Dagor said in agreement. "Corven has given our borrowed sages directions to the new lands?"

"Yes, but the directions are vague. He didn't oar the boat. Reece did, and Reece can't speak, so there was no getting directions from him. He simply nodded to what Corven said," Boru said. "But if they can make it over the waters in a boat, we should have no problem in our galleys."

"I hope you are right." Dagor sighed. "So many unknowns."

"I wonder," Boru started. "I wanted to introduce you to my older brother. I would like him to be on my galley."

"Is he a fisherman? I thought you were a family of builders."

"Yes, he is a builder—one of the best in East and South Basin, but our brother-in-law is a fisherman, and he's been teaching Jayston the lines daily. He knows how to tie knots, pull lines and dock up any boat. I've already gone over every inch of the galley with him. As long as he continues pulling up the lines and tying the knots, he will not forget. We grew up around fishermen."

"Yes, but can he fish? We need the men tending the lines to also fish every chance they get to replenish our food storage."

Boru cleared his throat. "Yes, I was thinking about that. We have plenty of fishermen, but I will be the only builder aboard the fleet. It would be good to have at least two of us, so if anything goes wrong, we will be better prepared to identify problems and fix them, especially if more than one galley finds itself in trouble. I may be the designer of these galleys, but I am not ashamed to admit my brother is a better builder than I. He is also an engaging leader. Those around him are drawn to him. He's just like my sister, Voddie."

Dagor grinned. "I've heard of this Voddie. A beauty with wavy scarlet hair and the gift of gab from East Basin. I always wondered what happened to her. Many of my fellow swordsmen I knew growing up fawned over her. Some even made advances only to be rejected."

"She married my brother-in-law, Morgo. His family owns one of the biggest fleets of fishing boats in East Basin and probably South Basin, as well."

Dagor stopped. "Morgo, the fisherman. He is the one who found Chieftain Lothar's niece. F'lorna lived with them before she went to live with the sages."

Boru's cheeks reddened. "Yes, it is my sister who planted the new horn bulb into her scalp and taught her how to speak."

"Interesting. I didn't know that you knew her. That will help me when I find her. You know what this F'lorna looks like?"

Boru fidgeted under Dagor's inquiry. "Yes, I could pick her out of a crowd of many."

Dagor could already tell the boy was smitten with the girl. That may cause a problem in the future. He hoped the boy's galley design wasn't a fruitless attempt to find her for himself. "Yes, I believe it is a good idea to have another builder as part of the fleet. And I would like to meet your brother, Jayston. It seems he wants to look after his little brother. Why don't you both board my galley tonight for dinner once the galleys are anchored for the night? Use the smaller attached fishing boat. I'll let my men know to expect you."

Boru couldn't hide his smile. "Thank you, sir. You will appreciate his charisma. I dare say he will be the entertainment for most of our voyage. I will go let him know, so he can find his place on my galley."

"Go ahead," Dagor said. He watched the young man walk briskly to his galley—most likely where his brother waited packed and ready for his journey. The boy blushed when he mentioned F'lorna's name. He looked at the sun. It was just peaking over the horizon. They had only a short time before they needed to set off. Chieftain Lothar made it very clear that he wanted the galleys on the waters before the sun rose completely above the horizon.

Right as he began to walk toward his galley, he felt a tap on his shoulder. The figure wore a cape with the hood covering most of the face. A small sage stood close by.

"Who are you?" Dagor asked.

When the figure spoke, he knew she was female.

"I am Chieftess Izziatan."

Dagor looked up uneasily at the Highland Cliffs castle. "Do you know what Chieftain Lothar will do if he knows you are here? He thinks the Lowland Cliffs know nothing of what he's doing."

"He's delusional then," Izzy said. "Everyone knows what he's doing. You can't hire most of the builders of the basin and then the fisherman and expect people not to speculate."

"You are going to get us both in trouble. Does your father know you are here?"

"Yes," she said too confidently.

"You lie. Your father and mother are very protective over you. Everyone knows they keep you locked up in their castle. The Chieftain and Chieftess of the Lowland Cliffs would never let their daughter cross Domus Lake to the Highland Cliffs, and they would definitely not want you stowing away in one of Chieftain Lothar's galleys."

"It doesn't matter. I have been sent by Corven, the Second Supreme Sage. He has decided that the young sages should not be unchaperoned on your boats. I have been chosen to oversee them. This is my personal sage, Remni. She will be assisting me. She has details of the new lands from Corven himself," Izzy said pointing to the young sage next to her.

"Our sages have already been told how to get there," Dagor said.

"No, Remni has details about the River-dwellers and the Sand-shapers and what you can expect when we meet them, including who we will meet first."

Dagor stared at the young sage. She wore the garb of the Atlatl Forest Sages. She had umber skin and hazel eyes. Her hair was tightly braided and wound in a bun at the nape of her neck. He looked back at Izzy. "Even if I could find a place for you on my galley, your gold crest on your horn will give you away."

Izzy uncovered her head. "You see? My thick hair covers it. Also, I am wearing the clothes of the sages. The Atlatl Forest sages are highly secretive. No one would think I was anything other than a sage. The only ones from the basin who would recognize me are from West Basin, and I know that you have no fisherman from there on your boats."

"If I take you, I would be compromising my position," he said. "I can't take that risk."

"You have already compromised your position by choosing to be a spy for my father. Either you take me with you, or I will go to Chieftain Lothar right now and tell him you are committing treason by aligning with my father."

"You wouldn't do that. Then the entire voyage would be compromised."

She leaned in and whispered in Dagor's ear. "Don't test me. This is my chance to get out of that castle, and I will not take no for an answer. Either I go or no one goes."

Dagor rubbed his face. Another unknown had just presented itself. "Fine. But if anyone asks, I believe you were sent from Atlatl Forest by the Supreme Sage herself. You will stay in the sages' quarters. Why didn't you just lie to me? Why tell me who you really are?" he asked. The entire arrangement would be easier if she hadn't said her real name.

She gave a sly smile. "Because I may be disguised as a sage, but I do not want to be treated like one."

"You expect me to treat you like a chieftess?"

"No," she said. Then she grabbed the hilt of her sword and pulled it from the scabbard at her hip with one sharp move. "I want to be treated like a master of the sword."

Chapter 16

Scar of Sacrifice

Weston stopped tending his crops of papyrus plants when he heard a wrestling noise coming into his living plot behind him. He turned and smiled.

"We have become quite the popular village," Weston said to his brother. Merriton had come to his living plot, as he frequently did to find quiet from family and village life. Weston didn't envy his brother. Every villager came to him with their problems and requests. He enjoyed their brotherly visits, though. It gave him a reprieve from his constant thoughts of F'lorna.

Merriton gave his usual grave look. "Yes, but we must be careful. We don't want the landowners discovering our location."

"Merriton, my brother, I know you are both wise and strong, and I am honored to help lead the Marsh-landers. But if we are to become a true and free people group, you are going to have to realize that we can no longer hide. We will have to establish our presence."

Merriton sighed. "I know. And it seems we have no choice now. We have Sand-shapers to the north of us. River-dwellers to the south and east of us. Now we have a land bridge with auraium and a new south ocean that leads to these so-called Lake-keepers. It seems that we are surrounded, and people seek us out daily."

"Yes, and look at all the relationships we have now. Because of F'lorna and the ore we have discovered, Rodeshians are coming to learn the new swordcraft. F'lorna isn't teaching anymore. She has her Novice Elders teaching it now. And we are giving each village several of the swords we are making. We are creating an entirely new way of life!"

Merriton nodded. Then he looked around his brother's plot of land like he was seeing it for the first time. "By the name of Ra'ash of the River-dwellers! Why do you have so many papyrus plants growing on your land? Where is your food source or do you expect to be dining by my wife's hand? Are you still drawing pictures of F'lorna? I see you two together quite frequently."

Weston chuckled with embarrassment. "I cleared some land next to Croga to grow food. I am sharing my crop with F'lorna and her family. I even planted several Achion saplings. Although T'maya can cook and scavenge for wild fruits, vegetables and herbs, none of them know how to plant and tend plants, so I offered to help."

"Of course, you did," Merriton said. "F'lorna has been with us for many months now. Her father and mother are invaluable to our village. I don't think we would have thrived as well as we have without them," Merriton said, eyeing his brother's love-sick awkwardness.

"I don't see plans of them leaving anytime soon," Weston added.

"Which I am sure pleases you, my brother. And about F'lorna. Why don't we see her very often? She is with that Swarve of hers all day except for mealtime—even then she misses many meals."

"I bring her food when she is occupied."

"Occupied doing what?" Merriton wondered.

Weston looked side to side, making sure no one was coming close to his land. "I can't say, but I promise you that it will benefit all of us. In fact, it will benefit anyone who will receive it. I built her a small table and chair—that is all I can say."

"I can probably offer some conjectures of what she is doing, but I will leave that in your capable hands. I am busy with non-stop visitors. Luckily, Jaquarn loves people and genuinely enjoys their company, but I'm thinking of F'lorna being so isolated. What more can she offer us? She has already given us so much. Is there no end to her talents?"

Weston felt a sudden surge of worry. "Do you think she won't like me now that she's so gifted and renowned? Everyone knows about F'lorna and her Swarve who escaped the Lake-keepers just before the Desert Plains were covered with the south ocean."

"Weston, F'lorna is not petty or snobbish. She likes you for you."

"I know. I know. But I grew up a servant. A field hand. All I know how to do is farm and play music, and the only reason I know how to write the Sand-shaper symbols is because Lord Sabien taught me behind his mother's back when we were boys. Why would she want me? I'm not good enough for her. No matter what I do, I will never be good enough to win her heart. Her grey eyes are a testament to that!"

Merriton grabbed his younger brother's shoulders. "Never say that! You are the most selfless person I know. When you learned those symbols, you taught every servant who could learn including me. You have always thought of others first. You got captured and beaten to help F'lorna's father down the land bridge to the Desert Plains, so he could find his daughter. You have written letters and sent Banthem to warn others of what's to come and catch them up on the news. And turn around."

"What?" Weston asked confused.

"Turn around. Let me see your back."

Weston reluctantly turned around and untucked his shirt from his tunic belt. Merriton lifted the fabric almost to his neck.

"Look at your back. Your scars have healed, but you will always have them—layers upon layers of scars that prove you care for F'lorna. You told everyone that the scars were nothing, but I saw you wincing in pain as Jaquarn rebandaged them. You helped save Croga while taking the brunt of the damage."

"F'lorna has scars too," Weston argued.

"Yes, but not nearly as bad as yours. You saved her from getting too harmed. You always put other people first. Even when Lord Sabien was banned from seeing you by Lady Rosarian, you risked your life to say goodbye to him one last time. You are a protector. If I had to give you one of those Adorations of the River-dwellers, I would give you that: Weston the Protector."

Weston laughed. "Brother, you always know how to see the best in me."

"Because your qualities are very apparent. F'lorna is of courting age. Why don't you ask if you can court her?" Merriton asked.

"She's not at the place of courting. She's just found some sort of peace, and I don't want to add another element for her to deal with. Also, she's focused on her many tasks. I'm happy that she'll let me bring her the papyrus paper and sit with her and Croga while she works. I'm patient. She's here in our village. Something I would have never imagined. I wake up every day excited. No more working the fields. No more working our own minuscule crops at night just to barely get enough to eat. We have a flourishing village, and we are adding to our numbers daily. Others want to be a part of the village we are creating."

"Yes, they do, and I better get back to the village center. I'm sure there will be plenty of people waiting for me."

Just then they heard the screech of a bird of prey. It was Banthem.

"Now where has that scoundrel been? He's been gone for almost a week. I see a scroll in the cylinder around his ankle. Who could possibly be writing us? Right River Hook is too far away for less than a week's flight."

Finally, Banthem landed on the piece of worn leather tied around a thick branch of one of Weston's small trees. Weston grabbed one of the dried critters he kept in reserve for Banthem and threw it at his beak. Banthem instantly swallowed it and screeched for more.

"Okay, one more," Weston said, already prepared with another critter. Banthem gobbled it down and allowed Weston to pull the rolled parchment from the cylinder around his ankle. "The only other place this could come from is Lord Tarmian's estate, but no one other than Raecli knows about Banthem."

Weston examined the parchment as Merriton leaned in. "It's from Raecli. I can tell right off. It's her handwriting!"

"What's it read? Is she back at the estate?"

Weston read quickly. Then he turned the parchment over and read the backside. Raecli had a lot to write because she wrote in small letters and thinly spaced lines. It took Weston almost a full three minutes to read it all. Merriton's reading was slower, so he waited for Weston to explain it all.

When Weston finished reading, he fell back against the tree. "I guess I can't hide the truth any longer."

"What do you mean, Brother?"

"I haven't said anything yet. I didn't know if it would shame F'lorna's family or confuse things a bit. When she came back, I kept it a secret until she got settled, but then I didn't want to tell her. She already has a Lake-keeper Chieftain wanting to claim her. I hope he is not going to look for her since the waters covered the Desert Plains, but who knows what a childless chieftain will do to finally have an heir? From what F'lorna told me recently, her father wants to meet his older brother."

"What are you talking about, Brother? You are speaking in riddles."

"This letter affirms what I discovered when I was imprisoned at Lord Tarmian's estate, and Raecli wants F'lorna and her mother to know. T'maya is the illegitimate daughter of Lord Dexarian and sister of Lord Tarmian."

"So that makes F'lorna…" Merriton said stunned.

"His niece by way of his father."

"That is definitely surprising news."

"There is more. Lord Tarmian threatened to give the entire estate to F'lorna if Sabien did not marry Raecli. So Raecli has returned to the estate. She and Sabien are to be engaged for a year, and then they will marry next spring."

"Anything else?" Merriton asked.

"Yes, two more things. Raecli's grandfather, Lord Rencon, is uniting families with Lord Tarmian, and they are aiming to come back to build a working village right in front of the land bridge. She writes that her grandfather is looking for the steel of the Lake-keepers, but the steward of the archives, his name is—let me look," Weston said skimming the parchment. "Here it is. Corven. Raecli's grandfather thinks that this Corven must have found valuable information about the Lake-keepers in his cylinder archives because he never showed up at the estate. A boat was seen with him and his servant floating off into the new waters to the south from the village on the east side of the land bridge."

"Once Lord Rencon and Lord Tarmian realize that we have not only discovered steel but are making weapons, they are going to want to take them," Merriton said. "What is the second thing?"

"Lord Dexarian has passed to the next life."

Merriton exhaled slowly. "We all knew he was aged, but it seemed he would be with us forever."

"They had the funeral before Raecli arrived," Weston said deep in thought. "That's that then. We are left with only one course of action," Weston concluded.

"What?"

"We must come together and extract all the auraium before they do."

"But we have no use for it?"

"It doesn't matter. We take away the auraium, and we take away their reason for coming. I don't care what we do with it. Hide it, bury it, send it on a boat down the south sea to sink to the bottom. We need to get it all out, and we can do it fast with steel."

"We need to make small daggers like the one Jaquarn has."

"We will start right away. I can examine the knife and make a mold."

"Did she say when they are coming?"

"A few are coming to survey, so we need to keep our eye out for them, but the rest of the servants can't join until the harvest is complete in several weeks."

Merriton scratched his chin. "That doesn't give us much time, but we have many villages who have vowed their allegiance to us. If Jaquarn and I can gather them, will you assemble and create the supplies we will need to harvest the auraium?"

Weston nodded. "I will draw up plans now. I have an idea of how to make the extraction easier using ropes and planks."

"Like our plank pathway through the marshes."

"Precisely."

"Are you going to write her back and tell her our plan?" Merriton asked.

Weston shook his head. "No, she knows her grandfather or Lord Tarmian has read one of the letters. She noticed it had dirt smudges on it, and it was moved from its original spot in her drawer. She said she will find a way to visit us. She wants to see F'lorna."

"How?"

"She didn't say, but from what I've seen of her, she is highly creative at finding a way."

"I guess it's time for you to tell F'lorna and her family what you know. Don't worry, my brother. If she truly cares for you, none of this new information will deter her feelings."

"That can't be true," T'maya said. "My mother would have told me." T'maya held the letter that Raecli had written. Her hand trembled and the parchment fluttered. "My mother rarely spoke of my father except that he was a traveler. Never did she mention he was a wealthy landowner. I always assumed he died long ago. And to think he was only a course of the Heat Source's walk from us." She stood next to her hammock in their guest plot. Weston and Merriton had only just arrived with the letter while she cooked the midday meal.

"Maybe even she didn't know," Jaqaurn said, taking his wife's free hand. "If your mother thought he was only a traveler, it makes sense that he wouldn't be forthright with the fact he was a landowner, especially to the working class of the Northeastern Mountains."

"Your grey eyes are proof," Weston added. "And I was there. I was there when Lord Dexarian confessed. He had already told Sabien as a boy thinking he was asleep. You were named after Lord Dexarian's mother, T'maya."

"I thought my grey eyes were given to me from a distant relative in my family's past. It's been known to happen."

"May I see the parchment, Mother?" F'lorna asked.

T'maya handed her daughter the letter. The group watched F'lorna read with speed, finishing both sides in less than a minute. She faced Weston. "You have known about this for many phases of the moon—since before I came back home. Why did you not tell us? My mother could have visited her father!"

Merriton intervened. "She wouldn't have been received by the family. Lord Dexarian was very old. He stayed in his room unless he was helped outdoors to sit in the sun in the mornings. In this situation, she would have to be called upon by the family."

F'lorna listened to Merriton, but her gaze stayed on Weston.

Weston fidgeted under her stare. "I didn't want to tell you right when you arrived. Your foot was broken. You had been lost for so long. I didn't want to burden you with more information about your family's lineage, particularly after finding out you are half Lake-keeper. And…" he paused, struggling with what he should say. "Lemmeck came and talked with me before traveling north to Left River Hook. He explained to me what you were going through and for me to look out for you. I noticed you had lost weight, and you appeared to be struggling internally with something when you arrived at our village. The last thing I wanted to do was add to your burden. And now"—he looked down at the ground—"it is too late. I am so sorry."

F'lorna glanced back at the letter and then back at Weston. She was about to speak but then stopped.

Her mother walked up to Weston and placed her hand on his shoulder. "I wouldn't have gone, Weston, so please do not carry any guilt. I made my peace with not having a physical father long ago. Ra'ash is my Father. I know the traditions of the Sand-shapers. They would not have accepted me."

"Unless they want to use you to coerce their son into marrying who they want," F'lorna said, holding up the parchment. Then she sighed and rolled it back up and handed it to her mother. "You should have this, Mother." Then she looked at Weston whose head was still hung low. "You were right not to tell me, Weston. This information would have complicated my thoughts with more confusion. Ra'ash saw fit to send this letter when the time was right." She squeezed his shoulder and his face lifted. She noted the tears building up in the corners of his eyes. "I offer you my apology of healing. Ra'ash knew best. You and Lemmeck are good friends." Then she turned to her parents and placed both her hands on her father's hand which was still holding her mother's hand. "My family," she began. "It seems that our lineage has taken another twist."

Jaquarn took his other hand and placed it on his daughter's. "Like the River. Our family lineage moves the way Ra'ash sees fit."

Everyone stood silently and waited while the tender moment unfolded. A family being faced with trials but still holding onto one another caught everyone in a pause of self-reflection. Then F'lorna began to laugh. Her jovial countenance became infectious, and the others began to laugh as well. "Ra'ash does have a sense of humor," she said. "If Raecli marries Lord Sabien, we will be related."

"Of sorts," Merriton said.

"Yes, illegitimate children are not well received," T'maya explained.

"Except you are the daughter of the father," Merriton noted. "It is sad to say, but in the Sand-shaper culture, an illegitimate child of the father has more rights than an illegitimate child of the mother. If anything happens to Lord Tarmian or Lord Sabien and if Lord Sabien never has an heir, T'maya would be next in line and then F'lorna, which is why Lord Tarmian threatened Lord Sabien with leaving the estate to F'lorna. He could theoretically do it, but Lady Rosarian would have to agree, and that would never happen. She probably only allowed him to mention it, so she could get the daughter-in-law with violet eyes that she has always wanted. Violet and grey mixed, she would say. What a wonderful pairing."

T'maya felt the warmth of her husband's and daughter's hands on hers. There was nothing she needed more than what she had right here. "I am glad to know my family history. It makes knowing who I truly am that much more poignant. I am the wife of Jaquarn. I am the mother to F'lorna. I am friends of the Marsh-landers. And I am the daughter of Ra'ash. That is more than I could ever ask for or desire."

Chapter 17

Overheard Letter

L e'ana rubbed the sweat from her freckled face with her dirty
tunic sleeve. Several strands of her curly scarlet hair stuck to
her cheeks and forehead. She stood straight and stretched her
back. It ached from the constant hunching over each of the plants.
She felt the woven basket in her hand. It was almost time to drop
off this load of leaf beans into the netted crate for washing. This
crop was one of several of the early summer crops that needed
harvesting. Her father and mother were harvesting the herb
potatoes and the baby bulb onions with the help of Lemmeck and
his twin brothers. She glanced at Sage just beside her doing her
best at twisting the top of a pod away from the stem of the stalk.
Sage hated working in the dirt, but she volunteered to help when
she saw Lemmeck and his brothers walking in the direction of
Right River Hook.

Le'ana noticed that Sage's basket wasn't even a fourth full. "Here, Sage. Let me have what you have gathered so far, and I'll add it to my basket and take it to the washing crate. That way we can start with fresh baskets."

Sage eyed Le'ana's basket. Her eyes were a lighter shade of green than Le'ana's dark green eyes that matched the River Pine needles. "I can't believe you've gathered so much already!" Then she looked down at her own basket. "I'm sorry I'm not much help. I never did like playing in the dirt. I think it is because my mother did not like it when my clothes became soiled."

"You are a great help!" Le'ana insisted. "When Elder Trenton made a new rule that the families of Right River Hook no longer needed to help in the harvesting, my parents were so surprised. The villagers have always helped in the task of harvesting. It is very grueling work for one family, and we provide food for every evening meal and for trade."

"I heard Elder Trenton has been making many new rules since Elder Jaquarn has left," Sage said not hiding her irritation.

Le'ana bit her lip. She missed F'lorna so much. The entire village has changed since her family decided not to return. "The first thing Elder Trenton did was to take all F'lorna's family's lands. He said they were needed for his fishing. Since Lemmeck's family went to Left River Hook when your family left, all we eat is fish. We rarely get meat harvested from the forest. And we don't have F'lorna's mother's cooking. She always made any meat taste good. We eat fish the same way every evening. I would rather not eat the evening meal than to taste one more bite of Elder Trenton's bland fish."

Sage walked up to her friend. "I'm sorry we left too."

"Don't be," Le'ana said, raising her chin so as not to let the tears flow. "If my family could go, we would. But we are planters. Where else can we find all the land we need to sow and harvest our crops? And now that Elder Trenton has banned the communal Shoam-sha, the families of Right River Hook rarely see each other. I feel sorry for Zelara. She is a singer like you, but there is no place for her to sing without the Shoam-sha. The dancers, musicians and singers all have Adorations that now can only be used in their own Achion Clusters. How is that benefiting the village? F'lorna was right all along. We need to have a communal Shoam-sha. It unites the villagers together."

Sage placed her basket on the ground. Despite working in the dirt, she managed to keep her cream tunic clean. Her burgundy hair was braided over her horns and then pulled together at the nape of her neck. Her umber skin glistened with perspiration. "He may have canceled the Shoam-sha at Right River Hook, but we still have ours at Left River Hook. I am singing, and my sister, Blaklin, will be telling a grand story she learned as a child. You and your family should join us. It is not far to walk, and it is a pleasant stroll under the shade of the trees."

"We better attend soon before Elder Trenton bans everyone from going to other villages as well. I wish Elder Jaquarn would come back for a rise of the Heat Source just to see what Elder Trenton has done to our village. He would not like any of it."

Suddenly, Le'ana heard her name being spoken by the winds. She looked west from where the wind blew and saw a figure in the distance running toward them. "I think it's Zelara."

Sage shielded her eyes from the sun. "Yes, and she is carrying something. It looks like a tube plant that grows on soggy land."

"Let us go to her, so she doesn't have to cross through the rows of plants. Her father will want to know why her clothes are so dirty, and he'll accuse her of helping me with the harvest."

Le'ana and Sage left their baskets and carefully made their way through the crops to meet Zelara. When she finally got to them, she hunched over and grabbed her knees, breathing heavily. Le'ana noticed the tube plant in her hand. It had been dried and the ends were stuffed with rolled pieces of material.

Zelara breathed deeply. "Give me a moment. I ran as fast as I could when I got it. My father hounds over me the entire rise of the Heat Source. He never gives me a moment of peace!" She stood up and took several more breaths. "I need to hurry because I know he will ask where I went if he finds me missing, and I hate lying to him."

"Why are you carrying a tube plant?" Sage asked.

Zelara gave her mischievous grin. "I made it just in case. I've gotten more creative since my father stopped the communal Shoam-sha. I can't believe I ever agreed with him! I miss singing. I miss praising Ra'ash with the village. How stubborn and stupid I used to be!"

"Don't be hard on yourself. We all have made mistakes and are learning from them," Sage said. Then she pointed. "So what is it used for?"

"Since we have F'lorna's lands now, I constantly keep a lookout on her Achion tree. She still has the leather piece wrapped around the tree branch. Though I doubted we would hear from her or Weston anytime soon, I made it my duty to keep checking it. I made this out of the tube plants." She held up the wooden cylinder. "It's like those translucent cylinders from the Sand-shapers but much easier to make and care for."

"Did we get a parchment from F'lorna?" Le'ana asked with excitement. It felt too wonderful to be true. They had heard remarkable rumors of swords being made and F'lorna teaching a new Adoration. And, of course, the stories of Croga, F'lorna's Swarve, have become prolific. One traveler even insisted he had seen F'lorna flying over the Violet Moon upon her Swarve.

"Yes, I heard Banthem from a distance and waited for him to land. Then I gave him four of those dried critters that F'lorna left. He was very hungry. And the story gets even better," Zelara said unable to hide her elation. "The parchment is thick like there are several letters. I had to separate the pages and place them on either side of the tube plant. I'm glad I thought of making it longer than necessary."

Sage hugged Zelara. "Thank you! Ra'ash knew I needed to be here today. I want to hear every word."

"We can't stay here, though," Zelara said. "Le'ana's property is right next to ours. My father may see us."

148

"Let us go to the other crop where my parents and Lemmeck and his brothers are harvesting. It is closer to the forest on the other side of our property. We will tell my parents that we need Lemmeck's help with something. They'll leave us alone long enough for you to read it all to us," Le'ana said.

"What are we waiting for?" Sage said. "Let's run!" Sage ran through the rows of dirt, making sure not to harm the lines of leaf bean stalks on either side of her.

"Sage, don't you want to go around? Your tunic is getting dirty," Le'ana yelled after her.

Sage didn't answer, so Le'ana and Zelara followed Sage's lead and ran along her footprints in the dirt. When Sage made it out of the crop, Le'ana thought she would slow down, but she ran even faster. "I didn't know Sage could run like a White Diamond Stag!"

"I know! I can't feel my legs anymore," Zelara said, gasping for air.

Finally, Sage stopped running and began a brisk walk as she tried to get the mud droplets off her tunic. They only smeared more, so she gave up. Le'ana could see Lemmeck, Rashion and Dashion. "I don't see my parents."

"Lemmeck!" Sage yelled and waved him and his brothers over.

"What is it?" Lemmeck asked with obvious concern.

"We have a letter," Sage answered. "Zelara is going to read it to us."

"Where are my parents?" Le'ana asked looking around.

"They just left to bring what we have harvested to the netted crates," Dashion answered.

"Good. We have some time," Le'ana said.

"Is the parchment in that tube?" Rashion asked.

Zelara nodded. "I made it just in case."

"Good thinking," he answered.

"Follow me," Zelara said to the group. "We don't have much time. My father always wants to know where I've been and who I've been with."

The group followed Zelara into the forest that rimmed Le'ana's land opposite of Elder Trenton's land. She stopped when she found a big grouping of Achion trees shrouded in moss and bushes. The others circled around her as she carefully pulled out one of the rolled-up strips of cloth. She shook the tube gently until the scroll peaked out. Then she pulled it free. "Let me look," she said, reading. "No, this is the second half." Then she shook the tube a little more until the other half of the parchments popped out. Then she placed the second set of parchments over the first. "Okay, this should be in the right order."

"There are so many," Le'ana said in a whisper. "They must have a lot to say."

"I better get started," Zelara said and cleared her throat.

As she began reading, the others fell quiet. All that could be heard was the rustling of the leaves in the wind and an occasional chirp of a bird. Zelara read loud enough to be heard by the group but not so loud that Le'ana's parents would hear if they returned early.

Zelara became so enthralled in the story that she lapsed into reading silently.

"You are doing it again!" Le'ana said.

"I offer you my apology of healing. The words are so incredible that I forget I'm reading to others."

When she finally finished the last word on the last parchment, the circle of friends remained quiet for several seconds.

"They are going to need our help," Lemmeck said firmly. "They will need skilled bowmen to protect them while they extract the auraium from the land bridge. Those Sand-shapers will be back. They covet that golden metal."

"I can't believe Raecli is getting married to a landowner," Sage said.

"Yes, and that landowner is related to F'lorna's mother. It is all so confusing," Le'ana said, shaking her head. "F'lorna is not an ounce River-dweller. No wonder they're not coming back home. Our village would not accept them."

Zelara nodded. "My father has made a mental list of all the reasons Elder Jaquarn and his family will not be accepted back into Right River Hook if they should ever return. This will only add to his argument. I hear him repeating the list daily."

"We must tell our mother and father," Lemmeck said, turning to his brothers.

"We can't leave yet," Rashion said. "We are providing meat for Left River Hook, and the village is growing rapidly."

"I will ask Mother and Father if I can go. With Father's help, you two can harvest all the meat," Lemmeck said.

Dashion shook his head. "I know what Father will say. He will explain that your duty is first to the village. But…" He paused to think. "What if we take the next few rises of the Heat Source to harvest every animal we can? If we show Father that we have plenty of dried meat for the winter, he may be more receptive to let you go."

"It might be too late by then," Lemmeck countered.

"No," Zelara said, looking back at the pages of parchment. "They are still making the small swords and gathering villagers to help. I believe that will take time."

"I want to go too!" Sage yelled and quickly covered her mouth. "Sorry," she whispered. "I feel I need to be there. It was nice coming home, but I feel cramped. Blaklin is with child, and Jornan dotes on her constantly. My parents are there too, so I feel like I'm stuck in the middle and in the way."

"I wish I could go," Le'ana said disappointed. "But this is only our first harvest. We have many more crops that need harvesting all the way through fall."

Zelara squeezed Le'ana's shoulder. "I will be here for you."

Le'ana nodded and smiled. "And we have Banthem to bring us news."

"It is settled then," Lemmeck said. "Dashion, Rashion, let us finish the harvest here quickly for Elder Rengor. Starting tomorrow, we hunt. I will offer silent words that Ra'ash makes our work extremely profitable, so Father will let me leave south to help protect the land bridge. Sage, ask your parents if you can join me."

"They trust Elder Jaquarn and you. I am quite positive they will let me."

"Zelara, is Banthem still at F'lorna's tree?"

"Yes," she said. "He usually naps when he arrives. It is a long flight from the land bridge to here."

"Will you write Weston and let him know that Sage and I are hoping to join them soon?"

"Yes, but I better leave now. Banthem might leave and my father will return from fishing soon. The letter will have to be very short." Zelara rolled all the parchments and placed half into the tube plant and then placed the other half in, pushing the other one down the tube to fit them both. Then she took the rolled piece of cloth and plugged up the hole with it. "I will continue to keep watch for more letters from Banthem."

"What are we all waiting for?" Lemmeck asked. "We've got work to do." Then the circle disbanded. Lemmeck and his brothers went back to harvesting the herb potatoes, and Sage and Le'ana walked back to the crop of leaf beans. Zelara decided to stay hidden in the forest and make her way back to where Banthem was hopefully sleeping. The Heat Source was still above them. Her father would still be fishing the tributary.

Kytalia listened intently to every word the Novice Elders said until the group left in three different directions. Luckily, none came her way. They didn't know she was on the other side of the cluster of Achion trees shrouded by thick foliage. She was coming to Elder Rengor's land to offer her assistance in harvesting. She may be widowed and closer to being Twofold than she cared to admit, but she was still strong and resilient. She wanted to defy Elder Trenton's new rule that no one was to help in the harvest. He had transformed her beloved village into a depressing and stale place to live.

She was shocked to hear Zelara's voice reading the Sand-shaper symbols that her father hated so much. She felt much the same way as Elder Trenton did until F'lorna used the symbols to give her mother a piece of the *Divine Oracle* that was missing from her Eternal Memory. From what T'maya had told her, the symbols themselves were based on the *Forty-four Chants and Images of Jeyshen.* How could the symbols be an abomination if their roots were in the *Divine Oracle*? She watched T'maya read the *Chant of Acceptance* that her daughter wrote for her over and over again. Kytalia, of course, still repeated pieces of the *Divine Oracle* to T'maya, but she could tell that T'maya felt so much pleasure in being able to read a chant to herself whenever she wanted. T'maya no longer had to rely on others to speak the *Divine Oracle* to her from memory.

Still, Kytalia did miss reciting the chants to T'maya. She would listen enraptured by every word. Since Jaquarn decided that he and his family would leave Right River Hook, Kytalia felt useless, which was why she was going to ask to help with the harvest. The village had changed since Elder Trenton had taken over. He wasn't a Healer. He wasn't a Spiritual Elder. He was a Fishing Elder who had stolen leadership of Right River Hook even though he and his family were the newest members of the village. Kytalia sighed. He even took away the communal Shoam-sha—the one place Kytalia felt she belonged. Though Le'ana's family took care of her, she felt more like a burden. She wanted to move to Left River Hook, but she had no family there to take her into their Achion Cluster. Then the idea struck her. She could go with Lemmeck and Sage and travel south to where the Marsh-landers were building a village. Her Adoration was tanning. She didn't work on animal skins much anymore because it was labor intensive, but she could teach others.

"That's the answer then," she said to herself. "I will accompany Lemmeck and Sage to the south villages. Besides, they will need an elder to travel with them."

Kytalia knew what she had to do. She would talk with Lemmeck first. He had returned to the crop to help with the harvest. She would go assist in the harvest and get close enough to Lemmeck to explain her plan. "Besides," she said aloud, "I may be old, but I still have a lot of life left to live. I'd rather be where there are Swarves, auraium and steel swords than be stuck at Right River Hook with Elder Trenton controlling every detail of village life."

Chapter 18

Hunting Traps

Raecli breathed in as Cecil pulled the strings on her corset. She was in her old room at Lord Tarmian's estate. The furnishings were almost as gaudy as her room in the city. However, the items that Lady Rosarian adorned her estate with were all very old pieces handed down from her landowner family and pieces handed down from Lord Tarmian's family. Instead of glass and rock, they had many pieces carved out of wood and animal bone. She preferred the wood and bone. It was more like her home in the Achion Tree at Right River Hook. She had been back in the farmlands for only a few days, but she felt comfortable already, especially with her lady's maid, Cecil, with her.

"Well, don't make it so tight yet," Lainie said entering her room holding a tray with what looked like breakfast.

"I don't know why I have to wear this stomach squeezer," Raecli complained. "I didn't wear it last time."

"You're not a girl anymore. You are a lady intended for marriage. Comfortable clothing—except for bedtime—is no longer an option."

"I can hardly do anything active while wearing it."

"That is why you have us," Cecil said. "Right, Lainie? We don't wear the corsets because we do all the physical work for you. Your work as a lady is different. You will be expected to host guests, visit families and, of course, have babies."

"Oh, wouldn't a baby be so sublime? I can't wait! I hope you get pregnant right away after your wedding."

"Oh Ra'ash, help me," Raecli whispered under her breath. She couldn't stop her cheeks from turning bright pink. She needed a distraction and looked at the tray Lainie was holding. "Am I not dining downstairs with the family?"

Lainie shook her head. "No, it seems Lady Rosarian has left in her traveling case just this morning to visit with her sister. No doubt to plan your wedding next spring. Lord Sabien went hunting with his mongrels. And your father and Lord Tarmian have locked themselves in the gentlemen's room with Mr. Moirel and Mr. Barton."

Raecli's blush deepened. She couldn't believe she was getting married to Lord Sabien. They had shared some nice chats as they walked the perimeter of the rambling estate with its exquisite gardens and fruit and nut trees. He was benevolent toward her now that Kysha was gone. The poor girl was forced to marry Mr. Beal, the steward to Lord Steson who lived a few days' journey north of them. She honestly felt sympathy for Kysha, but at least she would be cared for. She had seen many homeless people on the streets in the city near her townhome. This situation could always be worse, which is what she told herself when her grandfather surprised her with the news of her intended marriage.

Raecli looked at the small, carved box on her vanity. It was a gift from Lord Sabien when she arrived with her grandfather. The broach was no doubt a gift chosen by his mother. It had an oval violet crystal that matched the color of her eyes, and it was fitted in an elaborate casing of auraium. An expensive gift, so Cecil had told her.

"Did you bring them their breakfast?" Cecil inquired.

"No, Miss Marva did," Lainie answered. "And I know what you're thinking, Cecil. You want to know if I overheard anything the men were discussing in there."

"The gentlemen's room is located between the kitchen and the staircase. You might have listened in a bit before coming up here."

Lainie smiled. "You know me too well. Right after Miss Marva left with her empty tray back to the kitchen, I put my ear against the door. Only for a few moments, mind you. I didn't want Lady Raecli's food getting cold, but I did hear them talk about the land bridge and the auraium. They want to dig it all out before the other merchants and landowners find out it is there, but the crops are still being harvested for some time now until late fall. But I think, if I heard right, they are going to send a dozen or so servants to the land bridge to stake their claim. Lord Recon is waiting for several of his servants to arrive from the city. It may take them a while because they are finishing up some jobs he has for them."

"Did they say when?" Raecli asked. She had been forming a plan to visit F'lorna, but that would be impossible if Moirel brought his men down there. She would surely be discovered.

"Now what are you thinking, Lady Raecli? I can tell your mind is scheming because you have that distant stance about you," Cecil said, tying the string on her corset securely.

Raecli faced Cecil and Lainie. "I need an excuse to travel for a day."

"Lady Rosarian and Lord Tarmian will never let you travel alone. You are too young and too valuable in their eyes," Lainie said. "The only traveling you'll be doing is walking around the estate."

"Are there no landowners whom I can say I will be visiting? I can visit them with a little detour south to where I saw the Marsh-landers," Raecli said.

Lainie shook her head. "Lord Tarmian owns all the lands south of here down to the forest that surrounds the marshlands. It would not be a quick detour. They would know that something else happened as you traveled."

Cecil snapped her fingers. "I've got it! Where does Lord Sabien hunt when he goes with his mongrels?"

Lainie shrugged her shoulders. "The only place he can really hunt is the south forest. That's where he sets up traps and checks them. It's not really hunting. He does have a bow and arrows that he brings, but he is much better at designing traps. We all call it hunting for his sake."

"Well, ladies, I have a grand idea," Cecil said. "And it is very customary for an intended couple to do so." She faced Raecli. "You must request to go on a hunt with Lord Sabien. I will come as your chaperone. Then you can try to find your friend. She shouldn't be difficult to find because news about her Swarve is spreading."

Raecli felt a glimmer of hope. "Lainie, do you think Lord Sabien would go? What if we run into the servants who left him, like Weston or his brothers?"

Lainie thought for a moment. "Lord Sabien is very different than his parents. He wants to institute the money ledger back to his servants. And regardless of what Lady Rosarian says, he and Weston were best friends since they weren't even able to walk, so says Miss Marva. It is a risk, though."

Raecli thought about her chats with Sabien over the past several days. "He does seem very interested in meeting his aunt, T'maya, and his cousin, F'lorna. He was very inquisitive about F'lorna's family. I believe we have talked most about that topic."

Lainie's eyes brightened. "And Lady Rosarian may love the fact that you want to spend time with Lord Sabien doing what he enjoys. She is set on you being her daughter-in-law, and spending time with her son is one of her top priorities."

"Then it is settled. Lainie, notify me immediately when Lord Sabien arrives home. I would like to have a nice walk with him around the estate," Raecli said enthusiastically. For the first time since she was taken from Right River Hook, she had hope that she would see her friend—even if for just one rise of the Heat Source. And Sabien will be able to meet his family that he has known about since his grandfather told him stories about his visits to the Northeastern Mountains when he thought the young lad was asleep.

"Though, it's not fair. I want to take a trip," Lainie complained.

Cecil countered. "No, Lainie. You are our eyes and ears here. We need you to listen to everything and tell us what you have learned when we get back to the estate. You play a valuable role in our little plan."

Lainie puffed out her chest. "I will be vigilant!"

"Just don't get caught eavesdropping," Raecli said giggling.

"What a ridiculous idea," Lady Rosarian said. "Why would Raecli want to go into a filthy forest and search for your animal traps with those mongrels of yours?" His mother wore one of her less formal dresses since no visitors would be arriving that day, but he knew even this dress made the servants' clothing look like rags.

"It's called hunting, Mother," Sabien said irritated. "Some hunters use spears, others bows and arrows, but I design traps to hunt."

"If you say so," she said. She was sitting in the drawing room enjoying a cup of herbal tea and boiled dough balls drizzled with honey. "You should have invited her to my sister's house with me."

"Mother, you went there to talk about Raecli and my wedding. Do you really want us there interfering with your plans?"

Lady Rosarian thought for a moment. "True. Her home is in shambles. I could barely relax in such a mess and with all the building going on. That's why I came home earlier than expected. I couldn't think with all the noise. But why do you want to take Raecli hunting? She's a lady now. Ladies don't hunt."

He sat down in the ornate chair next to his mother. He grabbed two of the dough balls and swallowed them down. "Look, you want Raecli and me to get to know each other, don't you?"

"Of course, I do, which is why I have you take your daily walks around the estate with her."

"Yes, we are talking, and we are getting to know each other, but I want to show her one of my passions. Even though you don't care for my hunting, I would like my future wife to enjoy it or at least appreciate it. I bring valuable food to the table. Are you not happy when I harvest an animal for Miss Marva to find a family recipe from our cylinders to give to the cooks?"

His mother sighed dramatically. "Okay, Son, you have made your point. But you cannot go with Raecli unsupervised."

Sabien pretended to be offended. "Mother, do you not trust your own son?"

"Yes, of course, I trust you, but moments of carelessness can happen, and I will not have my son's wedding ruined by being rushed because of an unplanned pregnancy!"

"I thought you wanted a baby," Sabien smirked. "With violet eyes."

"How dare you say that!"

"Mom, I'm only joking with you. I like to knock you off your constant decorum occasionally. Anyway, Cecil has agreed to go with us. And, of course, the servants carrying the traveling case will be there as well. We will be home before it gets too dark."

"That is one thing Lord Rencon has actually done well. Raecli's lady maid, Cecil, is a gem. I've seen Raecli blossom, and I know it is because of Cecil's invaluable insight. And she is an expert at styling Raecli's hair. I'm almost jealous. She knows the latest fashions from the city. I can tell that Cecil wants Lady Raecli to do very well in society. She is an asset to our estate. Yes, she can be your chaperon, and bring servants to carry the traveling case who are capable of warding off attacks."

"Mother, our lands go to the edge of the forest. We won't be seeing anyone."

"Those terrible River-dwellers often cross our lands."

"Yes, but they aren't warriors, Mother. And many of them think those lands around the forest are public lands."

"They are our lands!"

"Yes, but we don't farm down there. The land doesn't have the right soil."

"It's no matter. They are still our lands. If you see any of those River-dwellers, you tell them to stay off our property."

"Then it is settled. I will take Raecli and Cecil at first light in the morning."

"Dear, just don't take her too deep into the forest. You know it's all swamp in there. Check a few of your trap contraptions. Impress her with your design and the animals you harvest. Then bring her home. I hope she is more enthusiastic about your hobby than I am."

"You forget, Mother. She grew up a River-dweller. I think she'll feel right at home in the forest."

"Oh, don't remind me. That was her past life. She is a lady now and no one will speak a word of her living in trees. She is Lord Rencon's granddaughter and came from the city. That is all people need to know about her upbringing, and be sure to explain that to Raecli when you are traveling. It will sound better coming from the man she is intended to marry. Not a word of her growing up a feral River-dweller."

Sabien groaned and got up. "Yes, Mother. I will let her know. Thank you for allowing me to share with Raecli one of my passions. You have honored my request." With that said, he kissed his mother on the top of her head. "Enjoy your afternoon, Mother. I will see you and Father for dinner, and we can go over the details of tomorrow's excursion."

He turned away from his mother and grinned. He knew his mother was feeling pleased with herself. Little did she know, however, that hunting was not on his mind. He wanted to meet his cousin and his aunt. He also wanted to see his best friend, Weston, and apologize for what his father did and not being able to come to his aid.

Chapter 19

Meeting of Friends

Sage walked patiently next to Kytalia, the aged widow. They were halfway to the South Village, but they were going to take a detour and visit the Marsh-landers. Lemmeck had visited them on his way home and knew the way. They could see the forest surrounding the marshlands just ahead. Lemmeck ran to the line of dense trees to find food for the evening meal. He wouldn't come to the Marsh-landers empty-handed. Besides, Sage knew that he got restless walking Kytalia's slow pace. Sage didn't mind, though. It allowed her time to enjoy the changing view of their journey. Kytalia held many memories of Right River Hook from countless turns of the moon. She shared her stories enthusiastically to Sage's listening ear. Sage was accustomed to listening. Her sister, Blaklin, was a Storyteller, so she grew up learning to listen and finding enjoyment from the stories.

"I am very glad you requested to join Lemmeck and me. Our parents would not have allowed us to make the trek to South Village without a chaperone. What made you decide to join us?"

Sage looked over to Kytalia's pale, wrinkled face. She wore a mischievous grin.

"I overheard you and your friends reading the letter."

Sage's eyes opened in surprise. "You did? How did you find us?"

"I was making my way to Elder Rengor's land. I thought maybe I could help with the harvest. I may not be strong enough to tan my animal skins anymore, but I can still pick leaf peas. And the thought of Trenton telling the villagers that to help with the harvest was unfair to those who did not have a Planting Adoration just made me so angry. I have lived in Right River Hook all my life, and every villager always helped bring in the harvest. I wanted to speak my mind at the Village Achion Cluster but what can a lowly widow do? I hold no value."

"Yes, you do," Sage insisted. "Every child of Ra'ash holds value."

"I mean that I give nothing of value. When T'maya was living with us, I enjoyed reciting the *Divine Oracle* to her. It made me feel like I was adding value to our Spiritual Elder and his family; but now that she's gone, I feel useless. When I overheard you and your friends speaking, I found my chance to be useful again. I knew they wouldn't let you and Lemmeck travel unaccompanied, so I was determined to volunteer. And truth be told, Right River Hook has become so boring. The Shoam-sha is gone. Many families have left. The wonderful letter Zelara read— and, oh, if her father knew she discerns the Sand-shaper symbols, he would be as hot as a cooking stone!"

"You won't tell him, will you?" Sage asked, suddenly worried. She knew how Elder Trenton considered the symbols to be an abomination.

"Of course not! I will tell that Fishing Elder not a single word. I know that F'lorna wrote some of the *Divine Oracle* for T'maya, and I spoke nothing of it."

"How did you find that out?"

Kytalia pointed to her temple. "The undervalued go unseen, but I see everything. And T'maya told me. She trusts me, so Zelara's secret is safe with me. And about that amazing letter. When I heard Zelara read about F'lorna's Swarve, and Raecli getting married, and F'lorna's swordcraft and every exciting detail of what is going on in the south lands, I knew I wanted to be there. I may be old, but I still want to enjoy the last turns of the moon Ra'ash graciously decides to give me."

"I am glad you overheard us, and I am honored that you are traveling with us," Sage said. "When we walked back home with the villagers from South Village, they walked so fast. Le'ana and I barely had breath to chat, but now I get to chat, listen and enjoy the scenery."

"I think your friend gets irritated by my pace," Kytalia winked.

"If Lemmeck had his way, we would be running the entire journey. No thank you. Let him run off and survey and hunt while we take our time. My Adoration is Singing, which is not vigorous and suits me perfectly."

"Sage!" a voice cried out.

Sage turned around and saw an elaborate traveling case. "Oh no! It's the Sand-shapers. They are already going to the land bridge."

"But they know your name," Kytalia said, staring at the case. "Look! Someone is crawling out."

Sage squinted her eyes. "It's Raecli!" Sage began to run to her friend but stopped when she saw someone else crawl out of the traveling case. It wasn't her grandfather. He was young but a few turns older than they were. Raecli picked up her long, ornate dress and began to run to her—or at least jog. The gown she was wearing looked extremely cumbersome. Sage knew by Raecli's excited, carefree expression that it was safe, so she continued to run until they both fell into an embrace that knocked them to the ground. They laughed breathlessly.

"What are you doing here?" Sage finally asked, getting up on her elbow.

"I'm supposed to be hunting with my intended, but we are actually on a secret mission to find F'lorna and Weston."

"I'm guessing you know this River-dweller," the young man said, smiling at Sage as he walked up to them.

He was tall with skin that matched Raecli's olive coloring, though a shade darker from being out in the Heat Source more. He also had grey eyes, and the shape of them was extremely familiar. "You must be F'lorna's long-lost cousin on her mother's side," she said getting up. "You look just like Elder T'maya. In fact, you look more like her than F'lorna does. She looks more like her father besides her grey eyes." Sage dusted herself off and squeezed his shoulder in greeting. "My name is Sage. Raecli and F'lorna are my birth friends. We were all born on the First Green Moon. We've known each other all our lives."

It was obvious the young man was enjoying himself. "My name is Sabien. I was born at the beginning of the Fourth Yellow Moon," he answered.

He awkwardly squeezed her shoulder in greeting, and she had to hold back a giggle.

"I guess I will help you up, Lady Raecli, since your intended and friend have forgotten you," Cecil said, coming up from behind.

Sage looked down at Raecli. "Why are you still on the ground?"

Raecli grimaced. "It's this stomach squeezer and this draping dress. You would think Lady Rosarian would allow me to wear travel clothes, but she insisted I dressed appropriately as a lady would."

Cecil and Sabien each took one of Raecli's hands and pulled her up.

Kytalia laughed. "You look like a stiff plank being straightened."

Raecli looked at the aged face. "Elder Kytalia! Is that you?"

"The very same," Kytalia said, holding out her arms. "Come here and give your old friend a hug."

Raecli's eyes began to water as she allowed Kytalia to embrace her. "I'm sorry. I do not mean to cry. But you bring back so many memories of my mother before she went to her Eternal Dwelling Place. Thank you for reciting to my mother the pieces of the *Divine Oracle* she didn't have in her Eternal Memory. My mother and Elder T'maya valued your willingness to recite to them even though the rest of the villagers frowned upon it."

"It was my honor," Kytalia said, looking at Raecli's hornless head. "I offer you my apology of healing. I heard you lost your horns."

Instinctively, Raecli reached up and touched the hairline above her temples. "I've forgotten the weight of them."

"What a monstrous thing to do—take out horns that have already been set."

Sage noticed that Raecli must have reflected on the night her horns were extracted and F'lorna fell over the land bridge because her expression turned somber. She knew that Raecli had to make the best of where Ra'ash had placed her. "Who is this then?" she asked, staring at Cecil. "You are very beautiful, and I know of twin brothers with your skin color and golden eyes. The color is very rare among River-dwellers."

Cecil gave the Sand-shaper curtsy. "Thank you. I am fond of my eye color. And I love the color of your hair," she said to Sage. "Reminds me of dark red vines I've seen in the forest near the Northeastern Mountains."

"Oh, I offer you my apology of healing," Raecli said, slipping into her River-dweller dialect. "This is my lady's maid, Cecil. She is a gift to me from Ra'ash."

"I don't know what a lady's maid is, but I am honored to meet you, Cecil. A friend of Raecli's is a friend of mine. Lemmeck is with us too. His brothers are the ones with golden eyes like yours. He is hunting in the forest. He doesn't want to visit the Marsh-landers without a gift of food. Oh no! I said too much!" she covered her mouth and stared at Sabien.

167

"Don't worry," Raecli said, grabbing Sabien's hand. "He knows about the Marsh-landers. He won't tell his father. He disagrees with his father's treatment of his servants, which is why so many of them have escaped."

Sabien's expression turned hard. "My father and I disagree on many issues. I can't undo the horrible precedencies he has made yet, but one day, when I inherit, I will make everything right again. For now, though, I must let him think that we agree. He has already threatened to disinherit me."

"How about them?" Kytalia gestured to the servants carrying the traveling case. "Will they tell your father where the Marsh-landers are?"

"They believe I am taking Raecli hunting. I directed them to stay by the traveling case to protect it from intruders and thieves. They have food. They'll appreciate the rest," Sabien said, turning to Sage. "Raecli has told me so much. And I must meet Croga, the Swarve. I still find it hard to believe that my cousin brought back a Swarve from the Lake-keepers. It seems too unbelievable to be true."

Sage nodded enthusiastically. "Yes, we saw Croga make his way up the land bridge by flapping his wings with F'lorna and her father on his back when the waters flooded the Desert Plains. But even before that, Le'ana and Elder T'maya were traveling with me through the caves under the Desert Plains, and we found a skeleton of a Swarve. We think it was F'lorna's grandmother's Swarve on her father's side. It appears that Swarves help with Mountain Terror, which F'lorna inherited from her father's mother."

"Fascinating. And you say that he flew up the land bridge?" Sabien asked, disbelieving.

"No, it wasn't like he was soaring. He was running up the land bridge while flapping. He sprouted wings when he found his original food source, Achion leaves. F'lorna said that the Lake-keepers don't have Achion trees, so the Swarves there are very sickly. But she fed Croga the leaves from the tunnels that connected the Lake-keepers to the south lands when she finally remembered who she was and escaped Chieftain Lothar. I shouldn't say anymore. It is way more interesting to listen to F'lorna tell stories of her time with the Lake-keepers."

"Stand away from my friends or I will shoot and not miss!" a shout came. Lemmeck held his bow ready with an arrow waiting to launch. He was about a tree's distance from them.

"Lemmeck!" Raecli called out.

He instantly dropped his bow to his side. "Raecli? Is that really you?"

"Yes, Sabien and I devised a plan to find F'lorna," Raecli said, looking very pleased with herself.

"Can he be trusted?" Lemmeck asked pointing to Sabien. "His father is the one who had Weston beaten."

Sabien walked up to Lemmeck. "I am truly sorry about my family's actions. I would have never let my father harm Weston. He is my best friend. My only true friend. I've known him my entire life. But I have no authority at my home. I may not be a servant, but I am a prisoner with no rights. I must ask my parents for everything. Not until I inherit the estate will I have real freedom. Raecli told me that you helped free Weston, and I am in your debt for risking your life for my friend. I would have done it myself, but my father had a servant at my door all that night and another one posted at my window. If you are willing, please take me to the Marsh-landers. I give you my solemn word that I will never reveal their location, not even if I am to be tortured."

Lemmeck seemed satisfied with Sabien's words. "Yes, you shall go with us. However, I wanted to harvest an animal for them, but I did not catch sight of anything worthy of my bow. I do not like going without a gift. Do you know these woods well?"

"In fact, I do, which surprised me when Raecli told me that Weston lives in the marshlands in the center of the forest. I always believed it to be uninhabitable. How do they get through the swamp?"

"They've built these paths made of planks that lead to the center of the marsh where the land is firm."

"Why haven't I seen them? I hunt in this forest, not as often as I would like, but I should have seen at least one path by now."

Lemmeck shook his head. "They only have the paths coming from the south and the southeast and southwest. They stay clear of the north forest where your land ends."

"Oh, I see. I do stay in the north of the forest. They really chose an ingenious place to establish their village. My father would never suspect they would be so close to his lands."

"Why has your father allowed you and Raecli to leave the estate?" Lemmeck asked.

"He thinks we are hunting," Raecli said, smiling.

"Where is your bow and arrows? Or do you use a spear? Maybe you can help me harvest an animal or two. It is getting late, and we must hurry."

"My hunting is a little different," Sabien said. Then he gave a piercing whistle. Three mongrels who were waiting obediently by the traveling case ran to their owner. "These are my mongrels. I build and set up traps. They have been trained to find the ones with captured animals. I am sure we will harvest an animal or two or maybe even three to bring to the Marsh-landers."

"I've never heard of such a thing. You must show me this new way of hunting," Lemmeck said.

Sabien turned to the traveling case where the four servants waited for instructions. He gave the signal to stay put. Then he turned back to the group. "Let us be on our way then. I'm anxious to meet my aunt and cousin. And I would like to make plans with Weston and Merriton about keeping their village safe. We must part ways here and meet in the forest. My servants believe I am hunting, and they will tell my father we ran into River-dwellers. I'm supposed to be telling you to stay clear of our lands, but it cannot be helped that we met friends of Raecli. My parents will be annoyed but will understand."

"Agreed," Lemmeck said. "We will walk the perimeter of the forest until the traveling case is out of sight. Then we will enter and walk back north under the cover of the trees. I want to see these traps you build. Hopefully, Ra'ash will allow us to bring the evening meal to the Marsh-landers. Then I will lead us to their village."

Sabien looked at the sky. "The sun is getting high already. We must hurry. My parents will want us home before dark."

"Until we meet again," Lemmeck said, squeezing Sabien's shoulder. Then he turned to Sage and Kytalia. "We will have to pick up the pace a bit."

"Fine by me," Kytalia said. "I feel a renewed energy in my bones."

Sage watched Raecli, Sabien and Cecil walk back to the traveling case with the mongrels following by Sabien's side. She gave silent words to Ra'ash that Sabien's parents wouldn't be suspicious when they found out that Raecli ran into friends while traveling. But from what she has seen of Sabien so far, he was capable and accustomed to dealing with his parents' strict ways. He would ease their concerns.

Chapter 20

The Way of Peace

Sabien followed behind Raecli making sure to keep his feet in the middle of the plank path that led through the marsh. The planks were only about a foot wide, and he had to balance his body with every step. He had two wood rabbits tied around his shoulder, and Lemmeck carried a meadow deer on his back that got too close to the forest and stepped into one of Sabien's rope traps. It was still alive when his mongrels sniffed him out. Lemmeck took out a Tarnezian Crystal Blade that his parents had given him for something called a Doublemoon Ceremony. Sabien admired the way Lemmeck sliced the animal's throat so fast that it appeared to have suffered no pain. Then Lemmeck offered a prayer to his God, Ra'ash, for the deer's offering of sustenance. Sabien thought he might institute a gesture of appreciation when he harvested his animals in the future. Lemmeck's moment of gratitude made the harvest seem worthier.

"This place is ingenious," Sabien said, trying to look around but almost losing his balance.

Lemmeck was in the lead since he knew the way through the marsh. Then Sage and Raecli were in the middle, and Sabien followed the rear in case one of the girls fell into the swampy waters. Raecli's long dress had to be tied up on both sides, so she wouldn't trip on the material. His mother would be suspicious if the rim of her skirt was overly muddy when they returned to the estate. The wood planks that made up the narrow path through the marsh were stripped of bark and scraped to almost perfect rectangular shapes with what he assumed to be sharp rock splinters. The rocks were probably taken from his lands just north of the forest rim. They were very heavy and sturdy rocks, but if slammed just right would splinter off very sharp pieces that then could be attached to handles and used as tools. The rocks were what made the land unfarmable. They changed the topography of the soil, and there were too many of them to haul off. Regardless, his family had more than enough land further north.

"The Marsh-landers are very inventive, aren't they?" Lemmeck asked, looking behind him briefly to ensure Sage and Raecli were still closely following him on the plank path.

"They have to be," Sabien added. "My father gives them very little, so they have learned to use basic resources of the land to make their clothes, tend their small gardens and even make toys and games. They are a resourceful people. I have no doubt they will do well here—as long as my father doesn't find out where they are located."

"What I have to show you will definitely surprise you. I believe that the Marsh-landers have found a way to defend themselves. In fact, the River-dwellers of the south lands have been learning this new form of protection, as well. We have suspicions that now F'lorna has come back, the Lake-keepers will know there are more cultures on the other side of the new south waters. From what F'lorna has said, many of the Lake-keepers are peaceful, but there are also chieftains who crave power."

Sabien doubted Lemmeck's words. How could the River-dwellers and now the Marsh-landers protect themselves from the landowners and merchants of the Sand-shapers? His father had influence with all the landowners. It would be simple to gather all the landowners' servants, which would accumulate to thousands, and use them as an army to take over a small village. Now that Lord Rencon was in alliance with his father, they had access to the city merchants' strength and servants also. What he learned about the Lake-keepers from overhearing Lord Rencon and his father speaking is that they may have a material that makes weapons stronger than obsidian blades and stronger than Lemmeck's Tarnezian blade. What chance did any of them have against an unbreakable weapon?

Finally, Sabien noticed Lemmeck jump from the plank path onto dry land. He helped Sage onto the land and then Raecli. He scanned the area. He couldn't believe it. The center of the marsh held vast dry land, like a hidden island of sorts. Once he jumped onto land, he bent over and picked up some soil. "The soil here is excellent for farming."

Lemmeck nodded. "Yes, we think because the marsh keeps the land hydrated when it rains, the marsh soaks up the excess water. This land never floods—except for during the earth shakes—but that changed all of Rodesh."

"I want to find F'lorna," Sage said impatiently. "Lemmeck, do you remember where the village meeting plot is? I know your hunting skills see more than just trees and shrubs. I would get lost on my own and walk in circles."

"Me too," Raecli agreed, looking around.

"Follow me," Lemmeck said. "The trees become less dense once we make it to where the villagers' plots are located."

Sabien had a trained eye, but he knew it would take him several guided trips to make his way alone through this new land. "I hear voices," he said.

"Yes, we are almost there," Lemmeck answered. "I think we should visit Merriton and Weston first. Merriton is the chosen leader of the village. I don't want to alarm the villagers when they see you, Sabien. You are the son of the landowner who oppresses them."

Lemmeck took the long way to Merriton's plot. He wanted to avoid as many Marsh-landers as possible. When his plot came into view, he saw Merriton's wife, Saleat, mashing a root in a bowl. He walked briskly to get her attention before she saw the others traveling with him.

"Hello, Saleat," Lemmeck said.

She dropped her masher. "Oh, Lemmeck! You've come back so soon to visit us!" Then she noticed Sage, Raecli and Sabien. "You brought Sabien to our village? Do you know what his family will do to us if his father finds out?"

Sabien quickly stood before Saleat and bent one knee on the ground. "I promise you, Saleat. I mean your people no harm. I was content with not knowing where you all were, and I hoped you were doing well. My father does not treat his servants fairly, and you had every right to escape, especially after what they did to Merriton's face. And then what they did to Weston. Believe me. I wanted to free him, but my father locked me into my own room like a prisoner."

Saleat looked skeptical. "So why come now? What changed your mind?"

"I want to meet my Aunt T'maya and my Cousin F'lorna. To have family beyond what I have at the estate has revived me and given me renewed purpose. Also, I would like to see Weston and apologize on my father's behalf. We have been best friends since before we could walk. I was devastated when my mother refused to let me see him anymore. We can't stay long. My mother thinks I am taking Raecli hunting."

Saleat examined the two wood rabbits he carried around his shoulders. "It seems you are hunting."

"Yes, Sabien caught these in his hunting traps. Here is a deer also for your villagers' evening meal. We wanted to honor your village with meat."

"We don't get many animals around here. The swamp keeps them away. The meat will be appreciated. We will make a soup with the rabbits and roast the deer. Thank you. You can set them on my cooking table."

Sabien took the rabbits from his shoulder and gently placed them next to the deer that Lemmeck had set down.

"Sage, I've been so distracted by these young men that I haven't given you a proper welcome," Saleat said, squeezing Sage's shoulder. "I still remember the customary greeting of the River-dwellers."

"Thank you for the welcome," Sage said.

Saleat turned to Raecli. "And this must be the infamous Raecli. I am sorry about what Moirel did to you. Your grandfather should have never extracted your horns at such an age."

Raecli did the customary curtsy of the Sand-shapers.

"Oh, no formalities here," Saleat said. "Let me take you to the guest plot. That is where Merriton and Weston are. They are visiting with T'maya and Jaquarn. F'lorna may be there. I bet you are anxious to see your friend again and in better circumstances," she said, winking at Raecli.

"Yes, very much," Raecli said.

Saleat covered the two rabbits and the deer with a large piece of fabric and set rocks on the perimeter of the table to keep the fabric from blowing away. "These should be safe for a while. Follow me."

Sabien walked next to Saleat. "Thank you again for trusting me."

She smiled. "You always thought differently than your parents, but I know you couldn't show it. Maybe someday you can make right the damage that has been done, and we can finally live in peace."

Sabien felt the weight of her words, but he knew it would be years before he would inherit the estate.

"You know, you look just like her," she said, staring at his face for a brief second.

"Like my aunt. That is what Sage said."

"I didn't notice it at first, but now that you are before my eyes, and I have seen T'maya every day, I can now see the resemblance. You will like her very much. And F'lorna—well, she is quite unique."

"I've heard stories from Raecli and Sage, and Lemmeck has hinted to some sort of protection your village is learning. It is all very fascinating."

"Yes, quite true," she answered.

A light suddenly shined into Sabien's eyes. "What is that?" he asked squinting.

"Those are the swords we have fashioned. We have made so many that I've lost count. We are sharing them with the southland villages. Jaquarn, Weston and Merriton are going over the details on how to distribute them."

"So the Lake-keepers really do have weapons that are unbreakable?" he said in awe. "Did F'lorna teach you how to make them?"

"Yes. They are made of a rock with ore in it. Once we extract the ore, we make steel and fashion the swords and daggers. We can protect our village from enemies to the north and enemies across the waters."

Clinking was heard and Sabien saw Weston making his way to him after he set the sword he was holding down onto the pile. He didn't look happy.

"Why have you come here?" he demanded.

Sabien held out his hands in surrender. "I wanted to apologize for my family's treatment of you and Merriton and the other servants. What my father is doing is wrong, and you had every right to leave. You know I disapprove of his actions, but there was nothing I could do. But if there is any way I can help now, I will do everything necessary."

"You can start by not telling your father where our village is located," Merriton said, roughly. He had caught up with his brother and stood by his side with his arms crossed. Seeing the scar across his cheek still pained Sabien with cruel memories.

"I would never do that. I came here only to meet my Aunt T'maya and my Cousin F'lorna. Otherwise, I would have never ventured to find you. And Raecli," he said, motioning to her, "she desperately wants to see F'lorna. We cannot stay long. My family thinks that Raecli and I are hunting. We just happened to meet Lemmeck, Sage and Kytalia on the way."

"Kytalia is here?" T'maya asked looking around. "I don't see her."

Sabien stared at his aunt. They did look alike, chiefly their eyes. "Raecli's lady's maid, Cecil, stayed behind with her where the southeast path begins. Kytalia doubted she could make it by walking the narrow plank path. We were hoping you had a rowboat or another way to get her to the dry land through the swamp. My mongrels are protecting them."

"Promise me on your life that you will not reveal our home and that you intend us no harm," Weston said.

Sabien looked sincerely into Weston's eyes. "You were my brother. I hurt for months when Mother made you stay away from me. Now we can be family again, and I promise to protect your village just as I would protect my estate."

Weston thought for a moment and then his face turned into a wide grin. "I knew you were missing me. I would catch you staring at me as I walked to the fields. That is until you fell for Mr. Barton's daughter."

Sabien cleared his throat and looked at Raecli from the side of his eyes. "Kysha is married now. Raecli is my intended. We marry next year."

"So I've heard. Raecli sent us a letter when she returned to your estate."

"Where is this Banthem of yours?" Sabien asked. "I can't believe you trained your little bird of prey to carry letters. I remember when you found him fallen from his nest."

"He's asleep at my plot and not so little anymore. His journey to Right River Hook took its toll on him, but apparently, my very long letter was well received and now I have Sage and Lemmeck back with the Marsh-landers."

Sabien turned his attention back to his aunt. "Your father is my grandfather. He told me stories about your mother when he thought I was asleep. I've known for a long time that I had an aunt, but I did not want to disrespect my grandfather by sharing his stories he believed were confidential. And now I find that I have a cousin, as well. I don't expect to be treated like family, but I would greatly enjoy getting to know your family."

T'maya reached up and touched Sabien's face. "You don't look much like my mother but neither did I. I guess I take after my father and you take after your grandfather, and that makes us family."

Sabien couldn't help himself. He grabbed his aunt in an embrace and swung her around.

When he finally put her down, she shook the dizziness off. "I haven't been swung like that in ages."

Jaquarn laughed and squeezed Sabien's shoulder. "I am united with T'maya and F'lorna is our daughter, so I guess that makes me your uncle of sorts. I welcome you to our family. May Ra'ash shine brightly on your future."

"F'lorna very much looks like you," Sabien said to Jaquarn. "I saw Weston's drawing of her. I would very much like to meet her. We don't have much time left."

"Weston, you bring them to F'lorna," Merriton ordered. "She's watching Ruvarren for me. I believe they are with Croga. I'll go see about getting the village boat. We will use it to take Raecli and Sabien back to where Kytalia and Raecli's friend are waiting. Then we will bring Kytalia back here. We have just enough time to get Sabien and Raecli home before dark."

"T'maya, would you mind coming with me?" Saleat asked. "Sabien brought us several animals to prepare for our village evening meal."

T'maya nodded at Saleat. Then she turned to Sabien. "I'm glad you came to meet us. You are welcome anytime."

"Thank you, Aunt T'maya. Raecli and I will find ways to visit." He turned to go but faced his aunt once more. "By the way, do you know who you were named after?"

She nodded her head. "I think the letter said I was named after your great-grandmother. My father's mother."

"Yes, and it means *the way of the unknown leads to peace*."

T'maya was silent for a moment. "I have definitely been down many unknown paths."

"Did they lead to peace?" he asked. He needed to know if doing something new with unknown results led to peace or if it was easier to do what was expected of you.

"I've had to overcome many obstacles and hardships along the way, but, yes, I have much peace because I chose a different life than what I was accustomed to."

"Thank you, Aunt T'maya. We will see you again. I know Raecli is anxious to see F'lorna."

"Yes, you both best go. The Heat Source will start creeping west soon. F'lorna will be so pleased to see you both."

Chapter 21

Awaited Reunion

F'lorna watched as Ruvarren slept against Croga's fur. The fur didn't attach its strands to the young toddler like it did to her skin because the boy's innocence created no need for reassurance. Nonetheless, his fur made for a soft pillow and the boy finally fell asleep after asking a forest of questions. He asked her about her sword, about Croga and about the Lake-keepers. She tried to keep her answers as simple as possible because she knew that he would be absorbing all the information into his Eternal Memory. Even though Croga's fur didn't wrap around the boy's skin, Croga had a way about him that made people relax. Though his size was massive, his heart was even bigger. Croga by nature was not a fierce animal. She could see why the Lake-keepers had to keep constant watch over them. She glanced back at Merriton's young son. He wore his horn binding. The very same one

Lemmeck gave to Merriton. Then she looked at the sky. She had some time to herself before the evening meal.

"I shall practice my swordcraft," she said to herself. She went to where her sword rested against one of the baskets used to bring Croga's beloved Achion leaves in from the forest. It took a lot of work to keep Croga fed, and she appreciated the villagers' help. But she sensed she couldn't stay much longer. Croga was becoming restless with being confined to such a small space. He needed space to run freely—or maybe one day even fly. She doubted it, though. He had no one to teach him. The Swarves stopped flying long before *The Great Engulfing*. Even then, there were only a handful of flying Swarves spoken about in the *Divine Oracle*.

During F'lorna's down time, she worked on creating her own swordcraft. She taught a less aggressive version of the bar Haven craft to the villagers of South Village and to the Marsh-landers. She knew the full extent of the craft would be too difficult and dangerous for most of the villagers to learn. Her Dancing Adoration truly was a blessing. It helped her body with the supple yet swift moves of the sword. "Don't squeeze the grip so tightly," Aunt Dalia would tell her. "You will tire your hand while the rest of your body still wants to fight."

She imagined the aged woman in her mind. She kept her beauty even as her youth evaded her. She wondered if she would ever see her again. Now that she was coming to grips with having two Eternal Memories, she had a better understanding of how valuable her time was with the Lake-keepers. She missed Voddie's chatter and holding her younglings. Morgo too. He had an easy, genuine way about him. She admired the relationship he and Voddie had. Then she thought of Chieftain Lothar. She had wanted nothing more than to make him proud of her when she lived as his daughter. Jaquarn, her true father, feared that Lothar would come looking for her to make her his heiress. She doubted it, though. Now that she remembered what true acceptance of a father was, she realized Lothar had never really accepted her. And then there was Boru. Would she even know what to say to him now that her F'lorna identity had asserted herself?

She tucked the memories of her Lake-keeper friends back into her mind. It was time to practice her swordcraft. She had learned several swordcrafts during her time with the sages. They didn't perform the moves, but they did describe them in detail. She wanted to combine what she learned from Dalia and create a new swordcraft with what she learned from the sages. She also wanted to learn the new swordcraft with her dominant right hand and her non-dominant left hand. If she could fight with both hands, it wouldn't matter if one tired. She would simply switch the sword to the fresh hand. That would give her an edge over her opponent.

She grabbed the hilt of the sword with her left hand and began the moves she had been practicing with her right. Her left arm wasn't as strong as her right yet, but she would force it to catch up. She was already using it more to eat, pick leaves, greet others and write symbols. She began her practice by thrusting forward with the blade and her left foot. Then she swung the sword delicately during the transition to her next attack. Jab like a lightning storm. Move like a spring breeze. Reserve energy. Fear only made the body rigid. Faith allowed the body to be fluid. Trust the sword. Never hold onto to panic. It left no room for certainty.

F'lorna felt perspiration creeping down her cheeks, arms and back, but she continued to dance the warrior's craft. She would finish stronger than she began. That was how victory was won. The opponent would eventually make a crucial mistake because of exhaustion. She could hear the words of her aunt speaking to her, guiding her moves and thoughts. Finally, she gave the final slice of her sword as she bowed her head and lowered her stance. The opponent was down, and with respect, she would honor the injured or dead.

Suddenly, she heard hollers and what sounded like a loud cackle from the earth. She looked to where the sound was coming from and saw a young group of villagers pounding rocks together in applause. Then her breath heaved from her lungs. "Raecli!" She dropped the sword and ran to her friend. Her horns were gone, but her smile beamed like it did under the very first Violet Moon they witnessed together. She hugged her friend tightly. She looked exactly the same but smaller. Or maybe it was she who had grown taller.

"How are you here? Where is your grandfather?" F'lorna asked, looking around. "Did he discover the Marsh-landers' location?"

"No, not at all," Raecli assured. "Sabien and I devised a plan to come here and find you. I didn't know quite where your village was located, but by the power of Ra'ash, Lemmeck and Sage happened to meet us on our way here. F'lorna, you move so beautifully, yet I have a fear of that shiny weapon you were wielding. I have forgotten the name. It is very deadly, I think."

"Yes, very deadly. But I offer voiceless words that I will only use what I learned to defend, not to attack. It is a severe sort of dance, which is why I don't practice so fiercely in front of others. My weapon is called a sword, and I'm developing my very own swordcraft." F'lorna looked at each face. "I didn't realize you all were watching." F'lorna felt her cheeks blush, so she looked back to where she dropped her sword. She saw Ruvarren reaching for it. "Ruvarren, do not touch it!" she yelled. He stopped suddenly, and F'lorna quickly went to retrieve the sword and swiftly placed it back into its scabbard at her hip.

When she was sure the sword was safe, she turned to find Raecli, but the entire group had followed her. They all had strange looks on their faces. She reached for Lemmeck's shoulder. "It is good to see you, my friend. Zelara must have received our letter and read it to you." Then she turned to Sage and squeezed her shoulder. "We must find time to sing together. I think the Marsh-landers will enjoy the way our voices complement each other."

Weston nodded his head with anticipation. "I can confidently speak for each member of our village that we would greatly enjoy hearing you both sing."

F'lorna giggled. Weston had no qualms about showing his appreciation for her and Sage's singing.

Finally, she turned to the young man next to Raecli. He was a few inches taller than she but not as tall as her father. He had tan skin and no horns. She stared into his eyes and the image of her mother came into her mind. "You must be Sabien, my mother's nephew," she said feeling an unexpected joy warm her chest. "I've always wondered about my mother's family, and now I have the honor of meeting one."

"Don't forget that we too are family. I am your cousin," he added proudly. He bowed slightly. "I am very pleased to meet you, F'lorna. What you did just then with the sword—that was extremely impressive. I don't know what to ask you about more: your Swarve over there or about the way you danced with your weapon."

F'lorna felt Croga's fur grope around her hand, so she began to stroke the golden strands. He had come up beside her. Unexpectedly, she felt his excitement about seeing Raecli, and he began to whine. He had experienced her grief in losing her best birth friend once he began to assimilate F'lorna's memories along with Amorfia's. F'lorna smiled and looked at Raecli. "He wants to meet you."

"Me?" Raecli asked, pointing to herself and looking a bit frightened.

"Don't worry. He knows all about you from my memories. He feels my joy in seeing you, so he too is experiencing joy—and a little anticipation. Swarves are extremely docile animals unless there is a need. Then they can bind up a broken foot and run up a mountain." F'lorna thought of when her father found her when her foot was crushed under the rock. Croga's fur had secured her broken foot. It did not hurt even as he ran from the crashing waves of the new south seas up the land bridge.

"Oh, okay," Raecli said. She tentatively walked toward Croga with her hand slowly reaching out. Croga bridged the distance between them and pushed his furry head gently against her hand. He closed his eyes and began to grunt and purr, willing Raecli to pet more.

Raecli then brought her other hand to his head and began to rub both sides. "Oh, F'lorna! He is more than I ever imagined! It is wondrous how our lives have become so complicated yet spectacular since I was taken from your Achion hole."

F'lorna smiled as she motioned for the others to pet Croga. Sabien instantly reached out and began to pet Croga's cheeks.

"You are much softer than my mongrels," he complimented. "I wish they were here to meet Croga. I know they would love to play chase with him."

Lemmeck and Sage—who were already accustomed to Croga—went to either side to rub on the flanks of his giant belly.

"How big you have gotten," Sage said.

"I noticed many of the Achion trees on our journey through the forest were void of their leaves. Good thing the forest around the marsh is full of Achion leaves," Lemmeck added. "Croga has a big appetite."

"I've started feeding him other plants. I once tried to give him meat, but he is strictly a plant eater. He'll eat tree nuts, any kind of berry, some roots. However, he won't eat grasses. That's all the Swarves eat with the Lake-keepers, and they don't live very long—only around five years."

"Croga is going to live a long, long life!" Ruvarren exclaimed. The boy was now under Croga's chin, scratching his neck with both hands. Croga soaked up the attention like the marsh soaked up water.

As F'lorna watched her friends and family rub on her Swarve, she repeated Raecli's words in her mind. Raecli was right. She and Raecli have both lived through difficulty since Raecli was taken from her, but look at how spectacular their lives were at this very moment! The atmosphere around them swelled with feelings of joy and excitement—even awe. If she could have seen this moment and trusted Ra'ash like she trusted her sword, the process she went through to get here wouldn't have been so painful. F'lorna didn't know what future obstacles awaited her. She knew that life many times seemed unfair, and circumstances could cut so deep that help was needed to heal. However, she also realized that wounds could mend, and circumstances could honor the conviction of the persistent with joy and excitement. She was glad she and Raecli didn't give up. She would reflect on this moment every day as a reminder of what Ra'ash could accomplish through those who trusted His ways.

Chapter 22

Golden Piles

Jaquarn stood at the edge of the land bridge analyzing the work of removing the auraium from the rock face. Both Marsh-landers and several southern River-dweller communities, including South Village, chipped diligently around the golden material weaving through the rock. They dangled under the water's flow over the edge of the land bridge, sitting upon planks of wood secured by tightly woven ropes attached to the trees near the River. He looked over to Limmian, the Spiritual Elder of South Village. Her umber skin glistened with sweat, and her usual silver, tight bun had fallen loose from the water's current.

"How is it under the waterfall?" he asked her.

"Wet," Limmian said simply. "Every time I pulled a golden rock out of the face of the land bridge, there would be another one behind it. I hate to admit it, but I think the auraium may fill the inside of this land for several tree lengths." She examined their area. "We started work five rises ago, and we are surrounded by piles of auraium. What are we going to do with it all? It's a good material but keeping it would lead to major problems for our villages. I will not risk the lives of my villagers over these golden stones."

"None of us want that, and I wasn't expecting so much either. We can't keep extracting it or we will cover all the southland with auraium, and all the merchants and landowners will start coming south. In fact, Raecli has warned us that several of her grandfather's servants will be here soon."

"Why can't they find their gold in the Northeastern Mountains? Why has Ra'ash put something so desired by the Sand-shapers in River-dweller territory?"

Jaquarn glanced at the many piles of golden rock around them. Then he felt his mother's dagger at his side. Kytalia had analyzed F'lorna's sword holster that she wore at her hip. Then she recreated a smaller one for him. She didn't do the labor part of tanning and sewing the hide, but she oversaw it and taught several Marsh-landers with their Eternal Memory still open how to tan raw hide from the animals they harvested.

"Not only that," he said taking the dagger into his hand. "We also brought steel to our shores. I don't know if I made the right choice by bringing all of us together and bringing these foreign materials to our people. Our way of life may be lost."

"It was lost when the Sand-shapers found the auraium. I didn't want to believe it, but I think Ra'ash sent your daughter before us to get us ready."

"Have you seen F'lorna?" Jaquarn asked. "I haven't seen her since morning meal."

"Yes, after we ate, F'lorna took Dezzy, my granddaughter, to give her private swordcraft lessons. Her Eternal Memory is on the verge of shutting, and she wants to learn everything F'lorna can teach her. I see her practicing almost every day. She feels the burden of keeping our village safe, but she is much too young."

"They are all much too young in my eyes, but Ra'ash has chosen them," Jaquarn said. "F'lorna should be done with her lesson by now. The Heat Source is directly above us. Maybe she is with Croga."

"Good, I am glad you are both here."

Jaquarn turned to see Merriton coming his way. "What did you find?"

"I talked to the Spiritual Elder of the Riverend Village, the one just west of the land bridge. They are the makers of the boats," Merriton said.

"Yes, they are the ones who gave the steward of Raecli's grandfather a boat to cross the new waters. Apparently, he was going to the Lake-keepers. Did he ever return?"

Merriton shook his head. "No, he and his servant oared away and never came back, which gave me an idea for this auraium," he said sweeping his hands wide. "Let's put all of this on boats and push them into the waters to be lost."

"What if they go to the Lake-keepers? Will they think we are sending them gifts or enticing them to come here for more?"

"I asked Lear, he's the Spiritual Elder of Riverend Village, and he said the water's current has changed since Corven and his servant left. Now would be the best time to put the boats into the waters because, hopefully, they will go in a different direction than the Lake-keepers. And we can offer the voiceless words of the River-dwellers for a storm to hit these new waters and sink every boat, bringing the auraium to the watery depths below. We must start hauling the auraium and the rocks now. I fear the servants of Lord Recon and Lord Tarmian will be here at any moment. They must not see this."

"What about the auraium still in the rock face? They are bound to discover there is much more than what lies on the surface," Jaquarn said.

"I was thinking on that, as well. There are thick, dense rocks at the north of the forest surrounding the marshlands. Lord Tarmian owns that land, but he won't miss the rocks. Those rocks are what we used to make the planks for our walkways once they've been splintered, but they would also be useful at filling holes. They are heavy and if fitted just right, you can hide anything beneath them."

"What do you think, Elder Limmian?" Jaquarn asked. Her village was the closest to the land bridge, and therefore her village was in the most danger.

"I agree with Merriton. Let us remove what we have found as quickly as possible. Merriton, can you prepare the Marsh-landers to get the rocks from the land north of the forest? I know Elder Lear. I will ask him what he would want as trade for the boats."

Merriton held up his hands. "He already said we have given him enough. They have found more rock ore on their shores. They are making more swords for themselves and practicing the swordcraft F'lorna taught a few of them. He said getting rid of the lure of auraium for Sand-shapers is more than enough payment for his boats."

"Yes, every village is indebted to the Marsh-landers and F'lorna for offering steel swords and teaching us how to defend ourselves. Let us begin the work of cleaning up, shall we? I'll start my villagers hauling the auraium to Riverend Village," Limmian said.

"I'll get the Marsh-landers to excavate the rocks in the north forest," Merriton added.

"I have an idea," Jaquarn said. "Croga could help haul auraium. Let me speak with F'lorna."

Merriton clapped Jaquarn on the shoulder. "That Swarve could haul us all. I never thought of using him to help us carry loads."

"He carried F'lorna and me up the rock face. This will be simple in comparison. Let us begin. Maybe we can have the auraium loaded by the time the Violet Moon rises."

The elders parted ways. Jaquarn walked away from the land bridge and toward the south forest surrounding the marshlands. The Marsh-landers taught him how to string hammocks on trees for sleeping. He and his wife and F'lorna found a roomy, temporary space just inside the forest to keep Croga hidden—

though, he often came out of hiding to run along the forest rim much to the villagers' delight. The sight of a large, fluffy creature streaking golden along the green grass always ignited awe.

When Jaquarn got close to the temporary quarters, he slowed his steps. F'lorna tended to take naps with Croga on occasion from being over-exerted almost daily. She taught swordcraft, she taught how to make steel, she told stories of the Lake-keepers and she even repeated the *Divine Oracle* for the Marsha-lander younglings to learn. He crept quietly into their quarters and found F'lorna kneeling before something he had never seen before. Her lips were moving, and he sensed she was offering voiceless words to Ra'ash. He didn't want to disturb her, but he felt uncomfortable watching her. He finally cleared his throat and came into view.

"Almost done, Father," F'lorna said without lifting her head.

He waited. Croga who was lying on the ground next to her yawned and rolled onto his back, exposing his large belly. The wisps of his golden fur swayed in the wind. When she finally finished offering voiceless words, she sat on the ground and brought the large item onto her lap. He could see tears in her eyes, so he quickly sat beside her.

"What is that?" he said pointing. The item had wooden outer squares with what looked like the parchment that Weston made inside. Strings made from thinly woven fabric attached it all together.

"I am glad you are here, Father. I don't know if what I hold is of Ra'ash or of me. Is it something He wills or something I want?"

"It all depends," Jaquarn said. He was baffled, but he had learned that when it came to F'lorna, conviction had to be the sole motivator of all she did.

"Remember the first earth shudders we experienced at my Doublemoon Ceremony?"

He nodded. "Yes, that is when you became the Storm Dancer," he said, smiling.

"Sage's sister Blaklin loves to tell that story," F'lorna mused. "I remember it embarrassed me so much, but now it seems so small."

Jaquarn knew something was weighing on his daughter, so he wanted to redirect her thoughts. "That is the night you cracked your horn."

F'lorna felt for her left horn. She allowed her finger to gently touch the golden crest around it. "Yes, when I got to my Achion hole, I told Ra'ash I would give all my life to Him and follow Him where He led me. I didn't realize then how difficult my path would be, and how much I would have to endure and change. I am glad I went through what I did. It has made me stronger, and I have learned things that I can use to help others. But—" She stared at the item in her arms. "It is difficult to go against the traditions you have been taught your whole life even though you know what you are doing is right. I feel Ra'ash's pleasure in what I have done, but I know it will anger others. But it will also be a great benefit to many. And Ra'ash told me during the storm just before I fell asleep in my Achion tree what I would become."

Jaquarn looked down at the thick, square object F'lorna held to her chest. Then he looked at her fingers. They were stained black. "Have you been writing the symbols?"

She nodded as more tears fell down her already damp cheeks.

"What have you written?"

She stared into her father's cobalt blue eyes. "I have written the *Divine Oracle*."

Jaquarn exhaled and leaned back onto his palms. "How much of it?"

"I have written all the *Sacred Songs of the Prophets* and the Forty-four *Holy Images* and *Chants of Jeyshen*. The entire *Divine Oracle* rests in my arms, and now that it is finished, I am conflicted. I was raised that the symbols were an abomination. Mother almost never spoke of them. How can I write the divine with what is despised?"

"May I see it?"

She held the book to her chest tightly as if not wanting to ever let go. Then she bowed her head and handed the book to him. He took it and flipped through the pages.

"This must have taken you many phases of the moon. Why are some of the symbols bigger than the others?"

"The bigger symbols begin a new song, chant or image. I wanted a way the readers could know they were beginning a new section of the *Divine Oracle*."

"Fascinating," he said to himself. "I never thought the *Divine Oracle* would need so many symbols."

"The symbols were the easy part besides being tedious to write. The difficult part of writing the *Divine Oracle* was the timeline. I didn't learn the stories in order, so I had to write a list of them first and organize them. If you look at the first few pages, you will see the title of each song, chant and symbol in what I hope is sequential order. I fear I may have written incorrectly. Would that displease Ra'ash? What would others say if I did make a mistake?"

"Is that what is truly wrong? Do you fear you may have written the *Divine Oracle* incorrectly?"

F'lorna nodded her head. "When I wrote Mother the *Chant of Acceptance,* it felt more like writing a simple story. If I made a mistake, she wouldn't notice. But now I feel more of a weight. I don't want any mistakes, but I am not Jeyshen. I know what I have written will not be perfect, and should it not be thrown into a fire and burned if it is not perfectly written?"

Jaquarn thought for a moment. "F'lorna, your path is very different than mine. I can't give you clarity from a journey I am not walking on myself. But let me ask you this. You said you felt Ra'ash's pleasure when writing."

"Yes, it is what kept me going. I already had so much work to do, but I felt this deep need to get this written."

"Then from what I hear from you, Ra'ash is pleased with what you have accomplished, correct?"

"Yes, I believe He is."

"But you fear what others will say?"

She nodded slowly.

"Then you must decide who shall choose your steps: Ra'ash or others. We Rodeshians are a diverse group, and I am learning we are becoming more diverse every rise of the Heat Source. You will not please everyone, and you will offend many just like the Prophets did in the chronicles of the *Divine Oracle*, but you cannot let that stop you from doing the will of Ra'ash."

"I understand," she said.

Jaquarn handed the book back to his daughter. "When will you present this to your mother?"

"I wrote it in honor of Mother, but I would like to donate it to the Marsh-landers. Weston is the one who first taught me to read and write, and they know very little about Ra'ash and His teachings. I want them to read the *Divine Oracle and* experience their Creator."

"I think your mother would be honored," Jaquarn said. "And F'lorna, let me remind you of a truth you are missing."

She looked up at him. "What is that, Father?"

"Even the *Divine Oracle* found in the Eternal Memories of all the Right River Hook Villagers is a little different. The truths are the same, but as the *Divine Oracle* was passed down from family member to family member, wording evolved over the cycles of each colored moon. I remember an argument breaking out at the Village Achion Cluster when you were very young. I was leading the Shoam-sha, and my wording didn't match exactly with the wording of another family. They accused me of blaspheming the *Divine Oracle*. I had to have a village meeting to explain that the spirit of the *Divine Oracle* remains the same though our words may vary a bit. That is the same with what you have written here. I can sense the spirit of Ra'ash is in what you have accomplished because you desire to share His love with others. Don't be frightened by any mistakes you may have made. We all make them, but Ra'ash can still fulfill His perfect plan in our inadequacies."

F'lorna leaned in and wrapped her arms around her father's neck. The written *Divine Oracle* was wedged between them—

touching them chest to chest. "Thank you, Father. I will present the book to the Marsh-landers when we finish our work. How much longer do you think it will take?

Her father grinned. "That is what I came here to ask you. Can we put your lazy Croga to work like the rest of us? We will be done a lot sooner with his help."

Croga's head popped up when he heard his name.

"I was just thinking he needed some exercise," F'lorna said. "What did you have planned for him?"

Chapter 23

The Brandy Idea

Rashion listened for the whistle from his twin brother. Ra'ash had blessed their hunting even more since their younger brother, Lemmeck, left for South Village with Sage and Kytalia. The tanners of Left River Hook were busy creating clothing and other items from the animal hides and inners they had gathered so far. They were almost set for winter, and it was only mid-summer. Their family members weren't the only hunters in their village, but they were the best. He was happy when he shot a long, soft-haired male rabbit that was fully grown. He was having the skin made into a baby blanket for Blaklin's baby who would be arriving in early winter—one of the final members who would become the Third Violet Moon Children. He didn't want to admit it, but he had grown fond of Blaklin's sister, Sage. She'd sometimes sing at their communal Shoam-sha, and her voice was sweet like a breeze carrying the scent of honeyed yolk flowers.

"Brother, did you not hear me?" Dashion asked from behind him. "I whistled two times."

"I offer you my apology. I guess I was lost in thought."

"Thinking about a certain Novice Elder who sings?"

"What makes you say that?" Rashion asked trying to sound offended but appearing more embarrassed.

"I saw what you did with that rabbit fur. You asked for it to be made into a baby blanket for Blaklin. Now why would you want to impress her family unless you wanted to court Sage?"

"You ask too much, Dashion."

"You tell too little and force me to infer, Rashion. Besides, she's in the south lands with many willing Novice Elders gaping at her beauty and her sweet voice when she sings like you gape at her during our village Shoam-sha. But in all seriousness, she's had no advances from another at Left River Hook. Why don't you at least give her a hint?"

"I'm not as forward as you and Lemmeck. And look what happened to Lemmeck. He came home full of sadness because F'lorna refused to be courted by him."

"F'lorna has been through a lot this last turn of the Violet Moon. Lemmeck understands that he can't rush someone who is trying to sort through her feelings after being lost and forgetting who she was. I can't even imagine. Your situation with Sage is completely different."

"If you must know, I was planning on asking her if we could share a walk sometime, but then Zelara read that letter and she left the next day."

Dashion didn't answer. His stare was fixated on the forest leading to Right River Hook.

"We can't hunt there. Elder Trenton has declared the land property of Right River Hook. He is now claiming public land as his own just like the Sand-shapers," Rashion said. "Can you believe it?"

Dashion shook his head and put his finger to his lips. "Listen."

Rashion listened. "Voices," he whispered. "They are coming from Right River Hook. Let's hide and track them."

The twin brothers cut left and hid behind low-lying bushes next to the forest. They placed their bow and arrows in front of them, so they wouldn't stick out over the foliage.

Rashion peeked through a clearing in the bushes and squeezed his brother's arm. "It's Elder Trenton. He's with Layaton's father, Elder Bacheon, and Ralona's father, Elder Eotham. They are wearing traveling clothes and packs."

A piercing scream was heard from behind the three men. "Father! Don't go! Leave them alone!"

"It's Zelara," Dashion said. "Look what Elder Trenton is holding in his left hand."

Rashion caught a glimpse of a tube stick. "It's the case for the letters from the Marsh-landers. He has found out what they are up to."

Zelara grabbed at her father's right hand and tried to pull him still. He forcefully shook her off. "You are an abomination. I know that Sand-shaper woman taught you those symbols just to undermine me!"

"No, she didn't! I learned them when we lived near the Northeastern Mountains. One of the Sand-shaper children taught them to me. I was so young. I thought it was a game."

He held up the tube container. "And you mock me by reading them? And writing them? You should have forced those images back into your mind to be forgotten!"

"I tried, Father. I carried guilt for so long, but when F'lorna explained to me that the forty-four symbols come from the *Divine Oracle,* I felt my shame lessen."

Elder Trenton slapped Zelara across the face, and she fell to the ground. "You will never say that again! Those symbols are sacrilegious. I knew that F'lorna girl was an abomination when I saw her hornless mother. I told you not to become friends with her despite her father being the Spiritual and Healing Elder of the village. Now look at you. You have defied everything I have taught you. Go home. And when I return, you will repent of your choices or else you are no longer my daughter."

Elder Trenton turned away from his daughter. "Let us go. We need to stop whatever Jaquarn and those mixed-breed Marsh-landers are doing. Lies! Swarves! Lake-keepers! All lies to make us fear going south."

Rashion watched as the men walked past the bushes where he and his brother hid. Finally, he looked at his brother. "Go help Zelara. I will go to Sage's father and explain the situation. We must get to the south lands before Elder Trenton does. We need to warn them. If he finds out where the Marsh-landers live, there is no telling what he will do with that information. Meet me at our Achion cluster after you help her home. I believe Father will understand that we need to go south with haste. Thanks be to Ra'ash for providing us with so much meat so quickly."

Rashion watched his twin brother jump over the bushes while putting his bow and quiver of arrows back over his shoulder. Dashion ran to where Zelara lay crying on the ground. When she saw him, she wrapped her arms around him and began crying uncontrollably.

Rashion nodded. He knew she would be okay now that Dashion was with her. "Okay, time for me to make a visit to Sage's family," Rashion whispered to himself. "Ra'ash, give my brother and I swift feet. I must get to Sage and Lemmeck before Elder Trenton creates trouble."

Lord Tarmian sat in the parlor of his estate. He and Lord Rencon sipped on the glass of brandy poured by one of the servants. He watched his son sip on his evening tea. Something was different about him. He seemed contented somehow. Maybe he'd finally forgotten about Mr. Barton's daughter. Her pregnancy with Mr. Beal, the steward of Lord Steson, finally cut off all feelings for

Kysha in his son's mind. She was a lucky girl to find such an adequate station for lacking any qualities one would want in a wife. She was young and beautiful and now capable of pregnancy, which was all Mr. Beal was looking for when his barren wife died. But how could his son possibly grow feelings for Lord Recon's granddaughter so quickly, especially since his wife, Lady Rosarian, had pushed the poor girl on him so forcefully? Normally, a young man Sabien's age would not allow his mother to dictate his love life. Yet here he sat. Satisfied—almost like he had a valuable secret hidden somewhere. Sabien had nothing hidden, though. Lord Tarmian had his room checked regularly for any of those letters from the bird of prey. Raecli's room was checked by Lainie regularly, and she reported there were no more letters to be found. Even the one he had read had disappeared.

Lord Tarmian took a big swig of his brandy and set down the glass. Besides finding out that he had a half-sister and niece by his absent father, life was going very well for him. His merging via marriage with Lord Recon would be extremely advantageous, especially now that he was sharing information about the auraium found in the land bridge. First thing he would do with his share of the golden stones would be to build a townhouse that overlooked the Sapphire Bridge. Wouldn't Lady Rosarian be so pleased with him? Then he could take his grandchildren to visit the city whenever they wanted. He would be different than his own father who wandered off exploring the mountains by himself. The only traveling he did while growing up was visiting other landowners with his mother. She was the only reason his family name stayed relevant in social circles.

"Lord Rencon, any word from your servants?" he began. They had decided that morning after breakfast that they would expose Lord Sabien to more of their plans about the auraium. His son, though extremely quiet and private, was particularly smart and innovative. He would be an asset to their plans as long as he was in agreement with their ultimate goals: riches, power and expansion of their family name.

Lord Recon swallowed down the last of his brandy. "That earth shake really hit the city hard. I know you felt the shudders worse down south, but much of the city's construction is a blend of glass bricks and rocks from the mountains. Roads and buildings are being rebuilt. And it is taking time to move meat and produce from the farmlands to the cities. Manpower is weak. The servants are hungry and have no strength. I lose money if I feed them adequately, and I lose money if I don't."

"And you have tried a diverse number of animals?"

"Don't get me started on the animals. My father paid handsomely to get various animals over the years from the south lands to train them to move goods in bulk. They all failed. Either they are too weak, untrainable, or they get sickly and die. There is not a single animal on all of Rodesh powerful and adaptable enough to work in the cities. We are stuck with lowborn servants, and even they are slow and weak."

Lord Tarmian had a sudden realization that could be of great benefit for Lord Recon and himself. "Leave us," he commanded. The two servants serving them instantly bowed and left the room, shutting the door behind them.

"Should I leave, Father?" his son asked.

He watched his son's expression. He didn't seem too interested in staying or leaving, which was perfect.

"You can stay," he finally said. When he was sure he had both men's attention, he began. "Lord Recon, your steward, Mr. Corven, left with his servant on a boat in the new waters to what he believes is the land of the Lake-keepers."

"Don't remind me," Lord Recon said. "He's probably floating on the new south waters or down at the bottom of the ocean being consumed like fish food."

"Would you say this Corven is a smart man?"

"Sadly, yes. I do believe now that he has memorized the cylinders of countless merchants, including mine and his father's, which are the largest collections of cylinders by far. He was lame in the foot and had nothing better to do."

"So if he took the risk to journey to the Lake-keepers, he had to at least have valid evidence."

"Yes, I suppose he did."

"And now we hear a story of my niece, this F'lorna girl, who came back from the Lake-keepers with their crest on her horn—a horn that fell off during the earth shudders, but that has suddenly regrown."

"But can we really believe what we hear?"

"No, but we can believe what we read. You read that letter your granddaughter received."

"Yes, but still. These are kids' writing. They are prone to exaggeration."

"You forget one important mention in this letter?"

"Which is?"

"She brought a Swarve with her. A Swarve that could carry her and her father on his back up the steep land bridge."

Lord Recon's eyes widened. "Are you saying we can use Swarves as our workforce? Even if they do exist, I don't know the first thing about them. The River-dwellers carry more stories about them in their childhood memories than we do."

"However, you have a steward who if his research has led him correctly has made it to the Lake-keepers and must know a great deal by now," Lord Tarmian said.

"And you have a niece who has lived there for almost a year. She can tell us about the new metal she carries and about the Swarve she rides."

Lord Tarmian leaned back in his chair. "Maybe my father did leave me something better than a name. He left me a relative who can lead you and me into the next era of commerce. I think we need to make a visit to the south lands once her location is verified."

"Shall I send my servants?" Lord Rencon asked.

Lord Tarmian shook his head. "No, I don't trust lowborns with this task." Then he looked at Sabien. "Son, it is time for you to meet your cousin. Find her. Get as much information from her as you can. Tell her that I want to bring her and her mother into our family."

"Father, it may take me weeks to find her, and I know very little about the River-dwellers," Lord Sabien said.

"Didn't you say Raecli saw some of her horned friends by the forest near our lands?"

"Yes, they were just passing through."

"Then it is settled. You will take Raecli with her knowledge of the River-dwellers and get the information I need. You have one week. I want to know what village Corven left from. I want to know where my niece is living. I want to know about the metal she has brought back with her. I want to know about the Lake-keepers. And I want to know about that Swarve of hers."

Sabien sat stunned in his chair.

"Did you hear me, Son? I can only trust you."

"What if I run into some of the Marsh-landers during my search?"

"Ha! Forget about that small band of rebels. If we get Swarves, our use of servants will be minimal."

"Yes, Father. May I go tell Raecli and Cecil to pack for our trip?"

He gave a single nod. "You leave first thing in the morning."

Lord Tarmian watched as his son exited the room. He dutifully left the door open. "Servant!" Lord Tarmian yelled. "More brandy for Lord Rencon and me!"

A servant popped into the room only seconds later with a glass decanter of brandy. "Yes, Lord Tarmian."

Lord Tarmian watched as the servant poured ample, amber liquid into each of the glasses. "Now leave us. You may retire for the night."

The servant nodded and left the room closing the door behind him.

Lord Recon took another long drink. "Are you sure we can trust them?"

Lord Tarmian bided his time. He would allow his brandy to linger a bit. He didn't want the moment to be over. "If we can't trust my own son and your granddaughter, who can we trust? The legacy reaches through them. They will have to adjust and learn just as we did. However, I will be sending two of my servants to follow them."

Lord Recon smiled. "As will I."

Chapter 24

Basin Rumor

D urstin didn't want to tell Chieftain Rugar what he had discovered. He stood in the great hall of the Lowland Cliffs Castle. The ceilings weren't tall, but the length of the hall was impressive. Rugar's throne stood elevated on a smooth rock platform at the wall of the very left. The entrance to the hall was on the very right wall. More than two hundred steps had to be taken before reaching the foot of the throne. Rugar's prized Goliathan head was mounted over the throne. Durstin knelt and waited for Chieftain Rugar to motion for him to rise. When he got the signal, he straightened and spoke the words he dreaded to say.

"I've just come back from speaking with the Supreme Sage of the Atlatl Forest Temple," Durstin said.

"Did you discover where my daughter is? Is she hiding with the sages of Atlatl Forest? She always had a fascination with them."

"I believe the news is worse than we can imagine."

"Tell me where my Izzy has gone," Chieftain Rugar demanded.

Durstin breathed deeply adjusting the scabbard hanging from his waist. "Chieftess Izziatan asked the Second Supreme Sage if she could be the chaperone for the sages on Chieftain Lothar's vessels."

"What?" Chieftain Rugar stood. "How could this be? My daughter is surrounded by our mortal enemies. How could Corven do this to me after I adopted him into the bar Hathway family? She will be discovered and thrown off the vessels into the new waters."

Durstin shook his head. "Chieftess Izziatan is smarter than that. Corven explained that she has covered the golden crest of the Lowland Cliffs with her hair, and she wears the garb of a sage."

Rugar stepped down and faced Durstin. "That headstrong girl will be the ruin of me. Now there is no way to charge Dagor Le Armon with her safety. They have left our shores three days ago."

Durstin cleared his throat. "I believe she knew that Dagor is our informant."

"How could she possibly know that information? Only I, my wife and you know about his agreement with us."

Durstin looked at the ground. He needed to choose his words wisely. "It appears that Chieftess Panela told both Izzy and Karthia that we have an informant on Chieftain Lothar's vessels, but she never said who the informant was."

Rugar's face reddened and he came so close to Durstin that their noses almost touched. "And who told her the name of our informant?"

"I did, sir. Well, not exactly. She guessed it and demanded to know if she was right. I figured that since she knew there was an informant, there was no use keeping his name a secret."

"And now you've doomed my daughter to death!" Rugar raged.

Durstin knew he needed to take a stance or else he would be losing his position as Swordmaster. "No, I believe that is not true."

Rugar crossed his arms. "How so?"

"Chieftess Izziatan is extremely stubborn. I should know. I've trained her in the bar Hathway Swordcraft since before her youth memories shut. She is headstrong and gets what she wants except for one thing."

"Which is?"

"Her freedom. I could tell by her words that she was going to get on one of Lothar's vessels no matter what. I didn't want her to go. I even threatened her that I would go straight to you and tell you what she was planning. She said if I did, she would row right over to the Highland Cliffs and demand to speak to Chieftain Lothar himself. I finally relented and told her that Dagor le Armon was our informant. That was the only solution that would keep her safe."

Chieftain Rugar's expression softened only slightly. He turned and sat back on his throne. "So you figured if she knew who the informant was, he would keep her safe."

"Yes, Chieftain Rugar. She is your daughter. If I were in Dagor's position, I would do everything in my power to ensure her safety and secrecy. If he wants a position as my second, he better bring Chieftess Izzy home alive and healthy."

Chieftain Rugar thought for a moment. "And are you sure she could not be recognized?"

"Corven didn't recognize her at first because she wore a simple cape, and she unbraided her hair. The curls cover almost all of her horns. The golden crest cannot be seen. Plus, she brought her own sage with her from the Temple, so she can keep a record of all they see and do."

"Hmm," Rugar said. His body began to relax. "This may be a good thing. I know my Izzy. She will record everything from a point of view that will benefit my people. I can't trust Dagor fully until I see him dock those vessels at the Lowland Cliffs' piers. This plan of hers can be of great benefit to me, and you said yourself that she is a master at the sword."

Durstin's body was still stiff with apprehension, but a glimmer of hope took shape that he may not lose his position. "She is one of the best female swordsmen, and she can defeat many of my men. She is strong, but her bar Hathway sword is very heavy from the jewels set in it. I gave her another sword that is lighter but just as powerful. This will give her added strength, and I didn't want her boarding Lothar's vessels with a bar Hathway sword."

"Good thinking. Where is it now?"

"It's in the vaults of the chieftains' weapons. I wrapped it and placed it where no one would find it. I will return it to her when she returns home."

"No, save that moment for me. If she returns with victory, I will celebrate and return her sword in a grand show of honor. If she fails me, I will take her sword away, and she will not be allowed to practice swordcraft again. You better pray to the Befores that this little scheme of hers works out."

"Yes, Chieftain Rugar. I have two more important details I must tell you. I discovered while I was at the Atlatl Forest Temple that the Supreme Sage has already hired the builders from West Basin to build the additional quarters for the sages overseeing the cylinders and symbols. They will not be able to build our piers. We will have to ask Chieftain Darmin if we can use his builders from East and South Basin."

"I loathe working with that man," Rugar said. "He'll expect a gift and to dine with us for dinner. I'll have to flatter him." He exhaled in defeat. "Yes, send out one of your men to invite him and his family for dinner at the Lowland Cliffs Castle tomorrow evening. I forgot the name of the master builder from East Basin."

"His name is Jayston. His brother, Boru, is the one who designed Chieftain Lothar's galleys. They are on the vessels, as well. Probably to ensure there are no complications with the boats while they journey the waters to the new lands."

"Chieftain Lothar infuriates me! How does he always get the best? No matter. Dagor's father, Cresden, was able to sneak me the plans for the piers. I'm no builder, but they look simple enough. Just get me builders from East and South Basin who are adequate. They will need to begin the work soon. I don't know how long the galleys will be gone."

"I only see one problem with using his builders," Durstin said.

"Ah, yes. Chieftain Darmin will want to be a part of our plans to take Lothar's galleys. Now that I think about it, that isn't such a bad idea. He has an army of bowmen at his disposal. With my swordsmen and his bowmen, we will surely beat Lothar if he demands his galleys back."

"Yes, but Lothar's niece is meant to marry Chieftain Darmin's son, Rathtar."

Chieftain Rugar gave a mighty laugh. "Chieftain Lothar only gives false promises. He hates Chieftain Darmin and his unruly son more than I do. I can guarantee he will not give up his beloved F'lorna to Rathtar. She is heiress of the Highland Cliffs, and she can marry whom she chooses. Maybe even you Durstin le Guyel. Wouldn't that be something? After Lothar walks with the Befores, you can pursue his niece and the cliffs could be united once more."

"Maybe," was all Durstin could say.

"What was the other important detail you wanted to share with me?"

"Oh, it is nothing of too much interest. As I was making my way on the Swarve to Atlatl Forest, I took the shoreline. I wanted to see if there have been any changes since the last time I went."

"What did you find?"

"There is a new inn called the Fisherman's Inn in East Basin. It is quite nice."

"Is that the important detail? A new inn?"

"No, the interesting thing is that those symbols found in the cylinders that started floating into Domus Lake—they are being written by children in the sand. From what I can see, it is not simply a game. They are communicating."

"So," Chieftain Rugar said. "The Supreme Sage must deal with that. I had the impression that she wanted to keep the symbols for herself and the sages since she demanded them all from us. She even took the ones from Lothar."

"Understood, but if all the kids of the Basin know this new form of communication, shouldn't we know it too? I think we should send two of our sages to learn them. Otherwise, we may lack some knowledge that could be used as a disadvantage. Chieftain Lothar will have F'lorna, but we will have no one who understands them."

"You are right again, Durstin. You have proven yourself valuable today. Why don't you go to Chieftain Darmin's wooden fortress yourself and bring two of our sages. Invite his family to dinner and make sure our sages learn all of those symbols."

"It will be done as you have said," Durstin nodded.

"Dismissed. Now I have to face my wife with the information of her daughter's disappearance. She will not be happy, but I will show her that Izzy's rebelliousness can be used to our advantage."

Voddie entered her home and set Paxton on the ground in the living area. She brushed her wavy scarlet hair off her shoulders. Her son, Range, hadn't shown up for lunch at the Fisherman's Inn. She also didn't see him on the shoreline with the other children writing the symbols on the sand. "Range! Are you home?" She heard crying coming from the boys' room. "Is that you?"

She walked to the boys' room and opened the door. There was Range wearing his horn brace and crying on his bed. "What is wrong?" she asked sitting next to him on the bed.

"I did the one thing you and Father told me to never, ever do! But I didn't mean it!" He got up and curled up into his mother's arms and began to sob even louder.

"Did you steal something?"

He shook his head.

"Did you hurt someone?"

He slowly nodded. "But not physically. I hurt his heart. I didn't know who he was. I was just telling a story that I heard from the fishermen who eat at our inn."

"It can't be that bad," Voddie said, pulling her son away from her arms and setting him on the bed. "Just tell me what you said and who you said it to."

"You and Father already know the story, which is why you told me to never speak it aloud. It's dangerous to get involved, but I was with friends. I didn't think anyone except Basin kids was listening. I didn't know who the new boy was, but he was coming by to learn the symbols. And he's super fun to play with. I knew he was from West Basin, but I didn't know he was a chieftain!" Range began to cry again but louder.

Voddie felt a singe of fear in her stomach. "Are you speaking of Chieftain Valor, Chieftain Laninson's little brother?"

Fresh tears fell down his ruddy cheeks as he nodded.

"Oh no," she whispered. Then she felt a tug on her skirt. It was Paxton. She instantly picked him up and set him on her lap.

"What story did you tell? Not the one about Chieftain Dontonion bar Hudson's death?"

He nodded once more.

"Did you tell the entire story?"

"Yes," he said, drying his cheeks with the back of his tunic sleeve.

Voddie exhaled and leaned back against the wall next to the bed, setting Paxton on her chest. "Aye, it was bound to come out sooner or later, but I was hoping the story wouldn't lead back to our family. Boru and Jayston are gone on those galley boats. All the Basin children are making those symbols in the sand. And now Chieftain Valor knows that his father wasn't killed by the woodsmen nomads. They are a peaceful, quiet group. Who would have believed they would kill a chieftain for money anyway? They only trade for their goods."

212

She looked back at Range. "So you also told him how their Swordmaster, Barronne le Sharon, took the bribe from Chieftain Darmin to tell the bar Hudson family that it was the nomads who killed their father and not Darmin's son, Rathtar, and his rowdy friends?"

"Yes, and when I finished the story, the boy started screaming at me. He said I was lying, but I defended myself. I told him I heard it directly from a fisherman who heard one of Chieftain Rathtar's friends bragging about it at the inn. And that's when he told me who he was. He said he was going to tell his brother and mother and get me in trouble. He asked me my name, but I wouldn't give it. None of my friends gave him my name. Finally, he ran back into the Atlatl Forest back to West Basin. What if they send me to the Befores?"

She petted his head. "When your father comes home from fishing, we will explain everything to him. He will know what to do. And, Range, you did nothing wrong. Aye, you have my gift for gab. You simply need to train it a bit. You were merely telling a story you heard, and there is no crime in that. In fact, the crime has already been committed, and justice has not been executed. Nothing stays secret for long. Eventually, hidden deeds get out into the open."

Chapter 25

Sea-Breathers

It was day four and Chieftess Izzy's nausea had not subsided. Every time she ate something, she would only throw it back up. Thankfully, she could keep down water, or she would be in grave danger of not making it to the new lands. She laid on a small pallet in the room for the sages at the bow of the galley. They had to add a third and fourth pallet for her and her personal sage, which meant their room was extremely cramped. She could hear the oarsmen grunting and the splash of the oars hitting the water in unison as they swept the current behind them. Their journey so far already had many complications. The wind was directly against them, and the current of the waters went south toward the Lake-keepers. The oarsmen were tiring out quickly. Even Dagor took turns with the oars.

The only small respite she got was when the galleys stopped oaring at night and anchored up with their lines tied together. It wasn't quiet in her room until late into the evening after the men and the young sages finally went to sleep. Sometimes, she would lie on her pallet and wonder if she had made the right decision to come. Dagor kept her identity protected, but she never realized how difficult crossing the waters would be. She grew up with privilege as a Lowland Cliffs Chieftess. She was accustomed to servants helping her every whim. She never went hungry. She never went thirsty. She slept well every night in silence. She only tired when she practiced her swordcraft. She wouldn't pity herself, though. She wanted adventure, and she knew it would come at the price of not being comfortable. She would not give into discouragement or entitlement. Her passion to explore exceeded them both.

She heard a knock on the door and hurriedly ruffled her curly hair over her horns to cover up her golden crest. "Who is it?"

"It's Dagor. I wanted to check on you."

She could hear concern in his voice.

"You may enter."

He opened the door and the first thing she saw was his bright blonde hair. His normally pale skin had turned tan, but she could see peeling from a sunburn on his arms. He looked tired and his clothes were soaked in sweat and sea water.

"Have you been oaring?" she asked.

"Yes," he said. His chest still heaved rapidly from the exertion. "I have so much respect for fishermen now. Oaring is very hard work."

"This is a big boat," she said.

"It's a galley," he reminded her. Then he looked at her as if studying her. "Your face looks thinner. If I take you back home with your bones protruding under your skin, I do not think your father will be very happy with me. I need you to eat."

"I can't. Every time I try, I just throw it up."

"It's because you're down here. The fishermen say that when you look at the horizon, your nausea will go away. Come to the deck with me."

"But you're the one who told me to stay hidden down here," she said.

"I know. I didn't want the wind to blow through your hair and expose the crest of the Lowland Cliffs. That would not be good on this galley. Is there a way you can make sure your hair stays in place? Or can you wear your cape and hold the hood over your horns?"

"I'll take my cape. I have a metal clip to hold the hood in place." She reached for her bag that was at the bottom of her pallet and pulled out the cape. "I'll put it on before we walk up the stairs to the above level."

"Follow me," he said. "We have a few more hours of daylight to continue our journey. Let us see if any of the fishermen have caught us some fresh food."

She got up holding the cape against her. The galley hit a big wave and she fell into the back of Dagor. "I'm so sorry."

"Here," he said, offering to take her hand. "I'll help you."

She put her cape over her left arm, and he took her right hand into his. She could feel calluses and blisters across his palm. The calloses were from practicing swordcraft, and the blisters must be from oaring. Heat rose from her cheeks. She had never walked holding hands with a man as an adult. When she would swordfight, she'd shake hands with her opponent, but that was platonic. She was just like one of the men when she fought. The sensation was nice. Since she was the only grown female on board, she received several looks from the men oaring as they walked past the rows of benches with men holding their part of the long, wooden oar. However, no one said a word. Dagor made it very clear the first day of their voyage that no one was to approach her or talk to her.

When they got to the bottom of the stairs that led to the main deck, he let go of her hand and helped put her cape on. She clipped the cape at the neck right past her chin.

"Are you ready?" he asked. "The wind and sun will make you feel better. Then you can eat some bread and hopefully fresh fish."

"I'm ready."

216

He took her hand again and led her slowly up each step. When they finally made it to the top, she realized he was right. The wind and sun felt good. She threw the cape behind her leaving the hood in place and stared up at the sky. "It's nice to see you again, blue sky."

There were only a handful of men fishing on the large deck. The three sages were sitting on the wooden deck playing a clapping game she recognized from when she was a child. They were older sages, not having to bind their horns. But they still had just about a year before their youth memories were closed.

"Sage!" Dagor called out. One of the sage's instantly got up and walked up to him. He took off his shirt. "My shirt is wet. Tie it to one of the lines, so it can dry. Make sure to tie it securely."

The sage nodded and dutifully took the shirt and tied it to one of the lines on the port side of the galley.

Izzy wanted to look away. She felt even more heat rise from her cheeks. The swordsmen of the Lowland Cliffs never took off their shirts in front of her. She would see them from the castle windows shirtless, but having Dagor stand so close to her unclothed from the waist up made her feel oddly stirred. Dagor had a muscular, lean build. His chest and back were slightly paler than his arms. He was several inches taller than she, which she liked. The loose shirts he wore made him look almost scrawny, but as Swordmaster, he had to be both fit and intelligent. Thankfully, he left her side and walked up to one of the fishermen.

"Did you catch anything? The chaperone of the sages needs to eat."

The fisherman smiled. "We sure did. We have the heating stones ready. I just need to descale the fish and cut them in half. Give me a moment, and I'll get it ready for her. Would you like to try your hand at fishing?"

Dagor stared at the pole for a second. "I do have cousins from East Basin who taught me how to fish when I was younger. Let's just hope the information is still in there. Is this pole different than from ten years ago?"

"Aye, just a little. Let me show you," the fisherman said.

Izzy was glad for the distraction, so she could calm herself and suppress whatever feelings that were causing her to be unsettled. After the fisherman explained the rod, Dagor made his first cast.

"Perfect!" the fisherman exclaimed. "Now let me go get the fish ready for our sage."

The fisherman passed by her and gave her a quick glance and a nod. She gave him a slight smile back.

"Come over here!" Dagor yelled, smiling. "Look at the horizon. It makes you think that the waters are endless. My eyes have never beheld such a sight!"

She walked to the edge of the galley and looked straight ahead. "I've never seen endless waters like this. It's strange that our river feeding into Domus Lake from the north through the desert would become a colossal ocean. I wonder how much longer it will take us to get to our destination."

Dagor looked around to make sure no one could hear them. "I need you to have a name. People are beginning to ask, and I can't keep saying the grown-up sage."

She thought for a moment. "Call me Palashin. It was my doll's name growing up."

"Okay, Palashin it is. My father was told by your father that it took Corven and Reece almost two weeks to cross the waters. However, they had a small boat and only Reece was rowing."

"He's the one who threw the Tree Heart Fruits that Chieftain Laninson shot," she added.

"Yes, so he is most likely very strong. We do have much bigger vessels, but also we have seventy-two rowers on each of our galleys. Then again, these galleys weigh a lot. I didn't expect it to be so difficult to oar," Dagor said thinking over the details of the trip so far.

"You are thinking we will make it to the new lands in less than two weeks? It's only been four days," Izzy said, feeling disheartened.

"No, I talked to Boru and Jayston. They've calculated a week and maybe one or two days more. I believe we are halfway there from what the sages have told me."

A gust of wind rolled over them and her hood came off and her hair flowed back. Her golden crest shone in the sun. She hurriedly put the hood back over her horns and repined the clip under her chin. "Did anyone see?" she asked.

"Yes," he said, "but only your sage. Does she know who you are?"

She shook her head.

"You better explain everything to her later today. This will be in her youth memories, so she needs to have a clear understanding, or her story of the voyage may be complicated."

Izzy stared at her young sage, Remni, who was playing the game with her friends again. And she pushed her pointer finger to her lips as a sign to say nothing.

The sage looked confused again, but then she smiled and nodded.

Izzy looked back at Dagor. "She won't say anything. This isn't fair. You get to walk around half naked, and I have to wear a cape."

"You're lucky just to be on this trip. I just pray to the Befores that your father doesn't kill me."

"Which is why you are protecting me so much," she said. She wouldn't let him know that she liked the added attention.

"I need to return you back to your father alive and well," he said and took up the fishing rod again.

"I'm stronger than you know."

"I'm sure you are right," he said simply.

Izzy watched him fish for a moment then looked over the edge of the boat. "Boru had to design the galleys just perfectly, so the water wouldn't go through the holes for the oars."

"Sometimes when a big wave comes in, we get wet. Which is why I'm half naked as you said. But, otherwise, his design has been well executed. We've only had minor problems. I'm glad he brought his brother on board. I've heard from many fishermen that their galley is the fun one. It seems many of our men cross over to their deck each night."

"And I'm glad I'm not on it," Izzy said. "I'm barely getting enough sleep as it is on your galley."

"What can I say? The men need a little time to relax after working all day. I can't stop them from playing music and having a few drinks."

"I know. I'm not complaining," she said. Then she glimpsed movement in the waters. "What was that?"

"What?" he asked looking where she pointed.

"I saw sharp horns. They look like ours, but shorter and pointed."

"It's probably just a sea shark or a fish with odd fins," he said continuing to look at the waters.

"There!" she shouted.

Suddenly, a figure came up out of the water and stared at them for several seconds. He had a silver hook through his mouth that clamped his lips shut. His horns went straight up but were short and sharp. He had short, white hair that landed just above his eyes. He wore no shirt, and his skin was white and oddly shiny. He cocked his head to the side like he was analyzing them.

"Hello," Izzy called out.

Her voice must have startled him because he dove back into the water.

"Keep your eyes open. He'll have to come back up to breathe," Dagor said.

By now the other fishermen and the sages were next to them at the edge of the galley.

"What was that?" one of the fishermen asked. "He looked like a Rodeshian of the water."

"You four, go to every corner of the galley. He may swim under the galley to escape us!" Dagor commanded.

Instantly the fishermen and the three young sages took position all around the galley. Izzy stayed next to Dagor.

"He can't go far. He will have to take a breath soon," he said.

Izzy turned to him. "I don't think so."

"What do you mean?"

"I stared at the hook going through his mouth, and I could see what looked like the brown weeds that float along the waters wedged in between his lips. Then I looked at his nose. I could see the same brown weeds poking out from of his nostrils."

"What does that mean? What are you trying to say?" he asked, looking confused.

"I think he breathes underwater," she answered. "We haven't seen any boats for days. How did he get here? Do you think he's from the new lands? Are we closer than we thought?"

Dagor shook his head. "No, I don't remember your father saying anything about those who breathe the sea. I would remember that."

"Yes, I met with Corven and asked him many questions. He talked about several kinds of Rodeshians, but never ones who breathe water. I am sure he would have mentioned that."

They continued to stare at the waters, waiting for the figure to come back up again.

"Anything?" Dagor called out.

"Nothing," the others said in unison.

"He swam away from us but not toward the Lake-keepers. If he is not from the new lands and he is not a Lake-keeper, who is he?"

"I know who he is," a shy voice said.

Izzy looked down to see her sage. "Remni, do you have information about his people in your youth memories?"

The girl nodded. "Yes, he is what's known as a Sea-breather. They are thought to be extinct, but I will add a note to my memories that they are not—at least not one of them."

"Fascinating," Izzy said. "What was in his mouth, and why was his skin so white and the texture almost looked like those of the tree mushrooms?"

"They inhale a special seaweed into their throat and nose that goes deep into their chest."

"Is it the seaweed we see floating on the waters?" Izzy asked.

The young sage shook her head. "No, it's a special seaweed that they only know how to grow and cultivate. They use the seaweed to breath underwater for long periods of time. Breathing underwater with their seaweed is a difficult process to learn, and they must be trained very young. They clasp their lips together with the circle piercing to remind themselves to breath only through their nose. They exhale excess water through their slightly parted lips."

"And what about his skin? If he swims in the waters with the sun over him, why is his skin so white?"

"They make a thick paste that they put all over their skin every day since the time they are born. The ointment protects them from the sun and allows them to swim faster. But it turns their skin white and transforms the texture. How they make this paste or where it comes from is unknown to me."

"We haven't seen any other boats on our journey. Maybe his land is be nearby?" Dagor asked.

The girl shrugged. "His land is either nearby or the Wind-wielders are not extinct, as well."

"What? Who are the Wind-wielders?" he asked sounding very baffled now.

"They are the masters of the Sea-breathers. They have boats like yours but bigger. And instead of oars, they have learned to control the wind."

"How can they possibly control the wind?" he asked skeptically.

"I don't know. That answer is not in my youth memories either. We just know they had large boats that could control the wind."

"Is there anything else you know that we should know?" Izzy asked.

The girl gestured for Izzy to come closer, so Izzy knelt. Then she whispered in her ear. "I know you are Chieftess Izziatan bar Hathway, but the Second Supreme Sage told me I was to tell no one. I am a gift to your people for bringing the sages of Atlatl Forest home safely and with their youth memories filled with fresh information from these new lands. I am honored to serve your family."

Chapter 26

Kairo Tunas

Jayston and Boru stood on the side of their galley looking over the unceasing waters. Boru began to pace the wooden planks of the deck while Jayston scanned the waters for any sign of movement.

"Boru, the men are starving. Not even I can keep a hungry belly cheerful. They can't oar the galleys anymore. Their clothes fall from their bodies," Jayston said, casting his line yet again. "We've been at sea for eight days, and there is no land in sight."

"Today's the ninth day," Boru corrected.

"Yes, but this day doesn't count because we are not oaring toward land. We are stuck here in the middle of these great waters that we know nothing about except for what an unknown, hornless foreigner told the young sages."

"We can't continue oaring if the fishermen have no food," Boru said. "That is why Dagor has us stopped."

All six galleys were anchored and tied together. Fisherman were at the edge of the galley. Some were casting their rods, but since there were more fishermen than rods, others were on the lookout for any signs of fish below. There were only a handful of cast nets to catch the smaller fish as bait; however, there were very few small fish in such deep waters. They were quickly running out of bait to lure the bigger fish. Dagor insisted that they would save every fish they caught in the empty wooden barrels that once stored food that had all been eaten. Then, that evening, the fish would be divided between the six galleys. Almost five hundred mouths to feed. The task seemed impossible. It would take days to catch enough fish to feed everyone but by then the hunger cycle would begin again.

Boru wouldn't admit it, but his boat design was too heavy for oars. Even with seventy-two men oaring, the heavy wood and waterproofing tar made the galleys slow to move. The weight of around eighty people on board each galley didn't help either. If he would have had enough time, he would have built only one vessel, not six. And he would have tested it first. Then he could make changes to the next design, but Chieftain Lothar wanted the galleys right away, and he too was so anxious to see Amorfia—or F'lorna—again that he didn't think the entire process through.

"The sages are talking about the Wind-wielders. They have boats that control the wind. That would help us, but I can't imagine how they could possibly harness something unseen," Jayston said. He gave a heavy exhale. "We can use all the lines and create a bigger cast net that can catch the bigger fish."

"You know that would take days to weave a cast net so big. We'd starve to death by then. I wish we could just catch bigger fish. When I was younger, I heard stories of the woodsmen who lived on the shores beyond Atlatl Forest who would bring giant fish home to feed the village."

"How is that possible, Boru? They don't have boats or metal for fishing hooks," Jayston said.

"No, I remember those stories too," a fisherman said coming up beside them. "They didn't catch them in boats and with hooks."

"Then how did they possibly bring them in?" Jayston asked. "With prayers to the Befores?"

"They would go out into the waters. A big group of them with spears. They'd swim out and only one of them would have the long rope held by the others on the shore. They wouldn't have to go far. The waters there are not like Domus Lake. It gets deep quickly, and the deeper waters have the bigger fish. Once a large fish was spotted, they would take their spears and jab it until it died. Then the woodsmen with the rope would wrap it around the great fish, and the others on shore would pull it in while the ones with the spears swam next to it, making sure no other bigger fish tried to take their kill."

"I've spotted several giant fish," Boru said. "But our fishing poles can't handle them. They come right up to the boat, especially when we throw out the bones and skins of the fish we eat. I even think I saw a Kairo Tuna. That would feed everyone on a single galley for days."

"We've all seen them," the fisherman said. "I've been to every galley to visit with the fishermen and trade stories. They've all seen Kairo Tuna. There must be a pod of them swimming around us, eating our leftovers."

"Wait. I have an idea," Jayston said and looked at the fisherman. "What is your name?"

"Briar," he said.

"Briar, take the small boat and get Dagor."

"And make sure he brings his sword," Boru added.

"Yes, sir," Briar said. He instantly left to the stern of the galley where the small boat was tied.

"What are you thinking, Jayston?" Boru asked his brother. "We don't have spears."

"Yes, but we have a boat full of fisherman, and most of them are also bowmen."

Boru thought. "Yes, every man was supposed to bring their weapon of choice in case we ran into trouble in the new lands." He was now catching up with the plan his older brother was formulating. "If we can catch a Kairo Tuna for our galley, we can show the other fishermen how to catch one for theirs."

"How much fish do we have in the barrel? Is it enough to entice the Kairo Tuna to us?" Jayston asked.

"I just checked before coming here. We have about three dozen. Let's try cutting up one dozen first and see if that will be enough, but we need to wait for Dagor. He must approve of our plan."

"What plan?" Dagor asked.

"How did you get here so quickly?" Boru asked. He noticed that Palashin, the older sage, was standing next to him, wearing the cape over her head. He wondered if she was truly cold or if she was hiding something. He figured it was the latter. It was too hot outside to feel cold. Her young sage, Remni, was with her.

"We were on our way here. We met up with Briar just as he was launching off. He says you needed to see me," Dagor said. "I hope it is because you found a plan to either feed us or get us to the land faster. I already feel the tension from the fishermen. If we don't solve this problem now, I fear we will have a bigger problem on our hands than food shortage."

"We do have a plan," Jayston said. "But we are still working out the details."

"I'm listening," Dagor said.

"We want to lure the pod of Kairo Tuna that has been staying nearby to our galleys. It would have to be a collaborated effort of all six galleys if we are all to be fed. We will use the fish we have caught and cut them up to chum the water," Boru began.

"Chum the water? Please remember. I am not from the basin. I know very little of fishing."

"We would be dumping the pieces of fish as bait across the water. It will have to be a large amount to attract the entire pod of Kairo," Jayston offered.

"We will have the swordsmen on the smaller boats with their swords and the bowmen at the edge of the boat with bows ready. Once the Kairo Tunas emerge to feast, we strike. Oh, and we will need one fisherman with a line to wrap around the fish to bring it on the deck."

"He will probably need two or three lines. We are not dragging it on shore like the woodsmen. We are dragging it up a galley," Jayston countered.

"You're right. One man on the boat will have several lines. And…" Boru paused.

"And what?" Dagor asked. "This plan of yours is getting more interesting every moment. I would hate for you to stop now."

Boru noted the sarcasm in his voice. "It would also be good if we could have some men in the water with spears."

"We have no spears," Dagor said.

"We will use your sword to make some," Boru answered.

"Out of what? A piece of the boat?"

"I would want at least two men with spears in the water for each galley's Kairo Tuna, so we will need twelve spears. One of my oars can probably make two spears, so we will need six oars. One from every galley."

"I will not let you destroy this boat. You most of all shouldn't want to harm your own creation," Dagor said. "And you want me to use the only fish we have left as *chum* for a bigger fish we may never see again, let alone catch?"

"A creation that is too heavy and too slow. If I made galleys again, I would make changes. And you know as well as I do that the fish we are catching will not feed all of us. There are too many of us on each galley. Which would be another thing I'd change."

"Now you tell me," Dagor said, rubbing his chin with his palm.

"You know Chieftain Lothar pushed us hard to get these done. No tests were done. The galleys are good. They float and we can oar, but right now, we need food. I am willing to sacrifice one oar per galley to feed your people," Boru said. He hated being honest about his design flaws, but he had to get over his pride in order to save their journey to the new lands.

Dagor said nothing for several moments. "Let's do your plan. I'll gather my swordsmen, and we will get the spears and the small boats ready. Jayston, get the bowmen ready and find the men who are good with the spear. Boru, get the chum and the lines ready. We are losing daylight. We will go when I raise my sword to the sky but do not begin the strike until I bring my sword down. Understood?"

"Yes, sir!"

Izzy held her sword in her right hand and grabbed hold of the edge of the small boat with her left. Against Dagor's wishes, she demanded that she be a part of catching the Kairo Tunas. She looked up to her galley's deck and saw her sage, Remni. She would be recording this day in her youth memories. Izzy would not fail. She would prove to herself and to her family that she was up for adventure. She couldn't wear her cape, so she twisted several braids tightly around her horns and secured the braids with numerous knots of string. No one even gave her hair a second glance. Everyone was preoccupied with implementing Boru's and Jayston's plan to catch their food for the duration of the trip. Dagor was at the front of their small boat. He waited for the signals from each galley to see if they were ready.

Bowmen lined the wooden edge of the galleys with bows and arrows at the ready. Even the holes for the oars had outstretched hands with bows ready to fly. Each of the smaller boats floated in front of the galleys with the swordsmen with their weapons at the ready. There was one fisherman in each boat holding several lines to bring up the Kairo Tuna once it died. Plus, another man held the smaller oars to maneuver the boat. The fishermen with spear ability were already in the water holding onto the edge with spear ready. She looked over at the last boat where Boru and Jayston held their spears on either side of the small boat. This would be a bloody and gruesome way to catch the large fish, but hunger pains forced actions that were not pretty.

She could feel the tension rise as the fishermen holding the barrels of chum moved the lip of the barrels up to the edge of the galleys ready to pour all the food they had left into the waters in hopes of more food. Now all they needed was for Dagor to give the signal. She looked over to him. His face was stern. His blonde hair was wet and swept back, and his blue eyes emulated the blue of the waters. He glanced side to side ensuring that all six galleys were ready. If they were going to have victory, they would need at least six Kairo Tunas to feed everyone on each galley for several days. Dagor closed his eyes for a moment. She wondered if he was praying to the Befores or rethinking the plan. Either way, a second later he thrusts his sword into the air.

Six barrels of diced up fish spilled into the water and began to spread a slick of oil across the waves. There was some movement, but it was only smaller fish taking advantage of an easy bite. Everyone remained still and waited. All that could be heard was the splashing of waves against the anchored galleys and the wind blowing through the few lines left tied on. Then the waters began to shiver as more fish came to eat the free meal. Izzy bit her lip to keep from sighing. The small fish were eating all the bait. It would be gone before the Kairo Tunas smelled it. She looked at Dagor. His arm was still in the air holding his sword. Suddenly, their small boat jolted left as something big underneath swam underneath them. She noticed the boat next to theirs also lurched. Then came another hit even harder than before. Finally, she could see them. Great blue beasts circling around them just beneath the surface. They were surrounded.

"Strike!" Dagor yelled, bringing down his sword.

Immediately, she took her sword and began to thrust it into the back of thick, tough skin of the great fish. She realized quickly that she would need to strike her sword with two hands to penetrate it. The fish began to swim down, but one of the men with the

230

spears must have struck it from underneath because he came back up to her. She held her sword with both hands and thrust with all her might. Red blood flowed across the waters. She pulled it out and plunged the sword even deeper into the wound. The whistle of arrows was all around them. The bowmen were accurate, but in this chaos, one arrow was bound to go array. That's when she felt the sting across her right cheek. She ignored the pain and continued thrusting her sword deeper into the fish's back.

"It's dead, Palashin!"

She kept cutting deeper not hearing the name of her childhood doll.

"Palashin!" Dagor shouted again and grabbed her shoulders, bringing her back fully into the small boat and his arms. "Now wrap the lines around the fish before they begin to sink!" he yelled to the men. "You, up there! Help them!"

She heard splashes as bowmen from the deck jumped into the waters to help tie up their kills.

"You've been cut," Dagor said, looking at her with concern. He held her in his arms as her sword rested on her torso. "An arrow has sliced your cheek. I don't think it's deep, but you may have a thin scar. I don't believe you will need bindings."

Izzy tried to catch her breath as she looked up at the face of Dagor. "Did we get six Kairo Tunas?" she asked.

"They are tying them up now. I am sure Boru and Jayston are taking count. You did good. I think you single handedly killed that one yourself."

"I had help from someone underneath," she said.

He smiled at her. "You ready to get up now or would you like to stay in my lap?"

"I can get up," she answered embarrassed.

"Wait," he said, suddenly. "Let me fix your hair. You can see your golden crest."

She stared at him as he secured the braided hair wrapped around her horns with the ties. With his face so close to hers, she could gaze upon him without being noticed. He was handsome for being from the Highland Cliffs.

"There," he said. "No one will see now."

"Thank you." Izzy got up and surveyed the scene hoping Dagor didn't notice her gaping at him. Men were everywhere tying up the great fish. Boru was on his galley counting. She couldn't see Remni. Fear crept in. "Remni!" she yelled. She saw two tiny hands reach up on the ledge of the galley and Remni's head pop up over the edge. She had a frightened look on her face. "It's all finished now! Why don't you go to our quarters with the others?"

The girl nodded fervently and left the ledge.

"Why did you send her away?" Dagor asked.

"She doesn't need to record this bloodbath. We need the food, but the way we got it was not respectful to Rodesh or its creatures."

Dagor looked around. "I see your point. I wouldn't want my future children to know all the details of this catch. Best just to say we were able to get food."

"Nine!" Boru yelled out.

Dagor looked up. "What?"

"We caught nine Kairo Tunas!"

Whistling and cheering rang out through the vast waters as the men continued to tie up the great fish and hoist them into the galleys.

"I guess we aren't going to starve to death after all," Izzy said. She wiped her cheek and blood was all over her sleeve.

"Here," Dagor said, taking off his shirt. "Put this against the wound to stop the bleeding." He balled up the material and handed it to her.

She placed the shirt against her cheek. "Seems to me that you like taking your shirt off in front of me."

He laughed. "Then stop giving me a reason to." He surprised her by standing up. He held his sword to the sky and waited for everyone to look at him. It didn't take long for him to command the attention of all the men working to get the great fish out of the waters. "I am proud of each of you—the fishermen, bowmen, swordsmen and spearmen. Men of Domus Lake! I am grateful to Boru and Jayston for scheming up this ridiculous but successful plan. Tonight, we celebrate, and tomorrow morning we set off again to explore new lands!"

Again, cheers rang out over the waters, and something deep within Izzy felt satisfied. She had successfully achieved her first victory on her own adventure, and she had a scar to prove it.

Chapter 27

Hooting Danger

Cecil was enjoying herself immensely. She got to replace her maid's uniform with traveling clothes. Lady Rosarian was in an uproar about it, but Raecli demanded that they be able to wear comfortable clothing if they were to travel, especially since they would not be taking the traveling case. It was too noticeable where they were going. Here she was a lady's maid, walking to the southern part of River-dweller territory through vibrant green grasses and shady trees. Her mother would never believe it. Cecil watched as Lady Raecli walked with Lord Sabien two steps in front of her. They were deep in conversation. She hoped that their marriage would take place. She liked living in the farmlands. The air and water were clearer and fresher in the south. Raecli's townhome in the city was impressive, but there was more freedom in the country. Etiquette was not so stringent—even though Lady Rosarian tried very much to hold tightly onto highborn customs.

She didn't much care for Lord Tarmian, though Lord Sabien was different. He was genuine and nice and treated the servants with dignity.

When Lady Raecli did marry Lord Sabien, she would make sure that Lady Raecli rose to be the highest esteemed lady in all the farmlands. And when they visited their townhomes in the city, she would ensure that Lady Raecli had the latest fashion of hair and clothing. She had overheard Lady Rosarian telling Miss Marva that she, Cecil, was a good influence for Lady Raecli. Her mother had taught her everything she knew, and everything her grandmother knew and everything her great-grandmother knew about being a lady's maid.

"It's called an Adoration?" she overheard Lord Sabien ask.

"Yes, our chosen Adoration is our chosen purpose that would fulfill a need in our village. When we became two turns or fourteen years old as you say, we celebrated our Doublemoon Celebration by doing a demonstration of our Adoration," Lady Raecli said.

Cecil listened fascinated. She knew Lady Raecli grew up most of her life as a River-dweller, but she never dared ask about it. It was deemed a disgrace to be a River-dweller.

Lord Sabien stopped. "What was your Adoration?"

"Both F'lorna and I chose singing as our Adoration. We would be able to use it to praise and worship at our communal Shoam-sha. But when my mother died, F'lorna changed hers to dance. I never knew why. She was the best singer of all our birth friends," Lady Raecli said. Then she looked at her hands. "Maybe she changed it for me since I was so sad that my mother died from Smoke Sickness. She didn't want to overshadow me." She looked back and smiled at Sabien. "F'lorna and I would sing the *Divine Oracle* to our mothers."

"You two were best friends?" he asked.

"We were inseparable because both our mothers were Sand-shapers, but my mother moved to the River-dweller territory earlier than F'lorna's mother. She knew some of the *Divine Oracle*."

"Aunt T'maya?" he asked.

"Oh, yes. I forget that you are related to F'lorna. It still feels odd to me."

"This *Divine Oracle*. I must read it," he said.

"You can't," she said. "It is passed down verbally through our Eternal Memories."

"Will you sing some of it to me?" he asked.

Cecil could see that Sabien was enraptured by the River-dweller customs of having an Adoration. "I didn't know you could sing, Lady Raecli. If I had, I would have told the housemaids of the townhomes we visited. The ladies of the house always love having those who can entertain at their dinner parties."

"No, I couldn't. Sand-shapers think so lowly of River-dwellers. If I sang one of our songs, I would embarrass my grandfather."

"That isn't true," Lord Sabien said. "Sand-shapers don't know your *Divine Oracle*. Maybe a few of our old scrolls have some of it written down, but no one reads them. Please sing for us?" he asked again.

Lady Raecli looked at Cecil with pleading eyes for help. "I must side with Lord Sabien. I would love to hear you sing." Cecil had heard many daughters of merchants sing. If Lady Raecli was remotely good, this would be a huge asset for them both.

"It seems I am outnumbered," Lady Raecli said. "Please note that I haven't sung in quite some time. Only when Grandfather was away, and the servants were far from my room would I sing."

Lord Sabien and Cecil nodded simultaneously.

"Okay, let me pick out a song that wouldn't be too offensive to Sand-shapers," she whispered closing her eyes to think. "I have it."

Lady Raecli hesitated.

"Go on," Lord Sabien said. "I am going to have to hear you sing eventually if we are to marry."

Cecil could see Lady Raecli's blush instantly. She wore traveling pants and a tunic with leather ankle boots. Lady Rosarian said she looked like a boy when she walked into the drawing room, but Lord Sabien's mouth had gaped opened. He quickly replaced his stunned look with an easy-going smile, but Cecil had seen it. Good indicator of attraction. Now Cecil wanted his mouth to gape again when Lady Raecli sang. If so, their marriage would absolutely take place.

Lady Raecli started to sing but stopped. "Sorry, give me one moment." She turned around and made several wide smiles with her lips. Then she used her voice like steps going from the bottom to the top level of pitch and then back down again. Cecil had never seen or heard someone do that before singing, so it must be a River-dweller custom.

"Now, I am ready. I needed to prepare my voice."

Cecil watched as Raecli closed her eyes. The first sound of her voice was sweet and gentle but had strength to it. One would think the wind could steal her voice away, but her voice continued to push forth brightly into the resistance. She sang of something called a prophet. The prophet was angry because the creation had abandoned the Creator. That was why the creation was dying of thirst. It no longer had its roots in the fertile soil where the rain could water it. Suddenly, Raecli's voice rocketed into the highest pitch Cecil had ever heard a voice make, and she kept the pitch for many seconds until it lightly faded into the wind. Then in a resounding undertone, she sang for the creation to remember its first love. Finally, she bowed her head. Cecil noticed a tear forming at the crease of one of her eyes. She looked at Lord Sabien. He was gaping. She needed to act fast, or they would be stuck in an embarrassing moment.

"Beautifully sung!" Cecil exclaimed and began to clap.

Lord Sabien closed his mouth, but he continued to stare at Raecli. When Raecli opened her eyes, his gaze did not cease.

Lady Raecli paused waiting for him to say something. "Did you like it?"

"You have the most marvelous voice I have ever heard. And your song. It reminds me of my grandfather's funeral. My father read something about what you sang about."

Raecli brought her hands to her eyes. "The wind must have dried my eyes. They have watered a bit."

"Here, Lady Raecli. Take my handkerchief. I always have one ready," Cecil said and brought out the white fabric from a pocket in her traveling bag.

When Lady Raecli finished dabbing her eyes, she faced Lord Sabien who was still staring. "If you like my singing, you will love your cousin's. She has a voice that makes people stop what they are doing."

He shook his head. "No voice could be sweeter than yours."

Raecli giggled, but she must have noticed the seriousness of his expression. "Thank you, Sabien. I'm glad you appreciate my Adoration to Ra'ash."

Cecil tried very hard not to grin. She caught a moment that few lady's maids got to see—the dawning of love.

The spell of Raecli's voice finally broke and Sabien looked to the sky. "The sun is high. We must continue walking if we are going to make it to the Marsh-landers before the evening meal. I want to check my traps before we get there. I am sure my traps have harvested at least one animal to offer them."

They took only a few steps before Lady Raecli grabbed Lord Sabien's arm. "Stop!"

"What? What is it?"

"The hoot. Did you hear it?"

"It's just an owl," he said.

Cecil listened. "There it is again, but it's coming from somewhere else."

"Those aren't owls' hoots," Raecli said. "Those are the hoots of Lemmeck's twin brothers, Dashion and Rashion. I know their hoots from anywhere."

"Are you sure?" Lord Sabien asked. "I don't recognize the sound, but it could just be a bird I've never heard."

The hoots echoed across the field again. Now with more vigor.

"No," Raecli demanded. "Dashion and Rashion are here. That means something is wrong."

"What does the hoot mean?" Sabien asked.

"If you hear it, you are supposed to stop right away and not move."

"What does that mean? Why would they not want us to move?"

Cecil thought. "Maybe they don't want us to go any further. They must have heard you singing, Lady Raecli. They know you are here."

"Maybe they don't want us going into the Marsha-lander's village," Lord Sabien said. Then he looked to Cecil. "Did you see any of my father's or Raecli's grandfather's servants packing up this morning, like for traveling?"

Cecil thought. "No, but Lord Recon and Lord Tarmian were talking to four servants behind the back patio this morning. I remember because I was packing food for our journey in the kitchen."

"Did you hear what they were talking about?" he asked.

"No, they were too far away, but I did find something odd."

"What?"

"There were two of Lord Recon's servants and two of yours," she said looking at Lord Sabien.

Lord Sabien breathed deeply and bowed his head. "We are being followed."

"Are you sure?" Raecli asked.

He looked at her. "Yes, I knew it was all too simple. My father is always looking over my shoulder. He never lets me take charge. I should have known he would send servants to follow us."

"And my grandfather," Raecli added.

Cecil heaved a sigh. And they were having so much fun too. "Well, nothing left to do then."

"What do you mean?" Lord Sabien asked.

"We can't go showing them where the Marsh-landers are living, now can we?" She turned to face the pair. "Let's go ahead and take a few steps, and Lady Raecli you need to cry out and fall.

You're about to have a twisted ankle." She looked to Lord Sabien. "You'll be carrying Lady Raecli back to the estate. Make sure you look concerned when you bring her into the house. Lady Rosarian will love the drama. And Raecli, you need to be genuinely hurt if Lord Rencon and Lord Tarmian are going to believe you two willingly cut your journey and stretch of freedom short."

"Get up there, Cecil! You aren't trying hard enough!" Raecli yelled. Lainie had tried to climb the tree, but she could barely pull her weight up the first branch. Cecil had only made it to the second branch.

"No use about it, Lady Raecli. We ladies aren't meant to be climbing up trees," Lainie said, reaching up to help Cecil down.

"But you both told me that as a lady, I am to wear this stomach squeezer because you two were able to do the harder labor. Now you are telling me you can't even climb up a simple tree?"

"It's a mighty big one, if you ask me," Lainie said still looking up to where Cecil was trying to make her way down. Cecil finally fell from the branch closest to the ground into Lainie's outstretched arms.

"Thank you, Lainie," she said standing up. Then she swept the leaves and bark from her apron. "Lady Raecli, climbing that tree is impossible."

Raecli held out the leather swatch. "I must get this leather wrapped around the highest branch or else Banthem won't see it. I need to send Weston the letter I wrote. Lainie, you know my room is checked often. I can't bring it back there."

"Lord Tarmian tells me to check your room and Sabien's, but you know I wouldn't go looking through your private things," Lainie said indignantly.

"Yes, but he may send another servant. My grandfather and Lord Tarmian know about the tree by my window, but they'll never venture to this tree in the middle of the estate's farmlands. You must help me!"

"Lady Raecli, we are going to have to find another way. There is no way up that tree."

"I can't leave the estate. My ankle is twisted, remember? They'd have me followed anyway," Raecli said. "There is no other way!"

"Why don't you tell Lord Sabien to climb the tree?" Cecil asked.

"If I ask for his help, he will want to read the letter, and he'll discover that his father is planning on stealing F'lorna's Swarve and her sword. He never intended to welcome her or T'maya into their family. Then what do you think Lord Sabien will do once he discovers the truth?"

"He would confront Lord Tarmian," Lainie said.

"Yes, he would," Raecli said. "He considers F'lorna family, and he can't stop talking about her Swarve. He's in love with Croga. And he is so impressed with F'lorna's swordcraft. Whenever we are together, he makes plans on how we can visit them, but we can't visit them if Lord Sabien confronts Lord Tarmian with the truth. Lord Tarmian may disown Sabien for his defiance. Do you two want that? For us to be disowned?" she asked, looking at them both.

"No, my lady," they answered in unison.

Raecli took a breath. "Look, I trust Lord Sabien to do the right thing, but right now he's very emotionally involved with all that is happening in the south. If he learns of his father's and my grandfather's plans, he will not think objectively. His father almost disowned him once to get his way, and I know he will do it again. It is better for me to send this letter, so that Weston and F'lorna can prepare everyone for what may come. F'lorna is strong, and she has a large group of villagers working with her. There is nothing Sabien or I can do from here. We must trust Ra'ash with this one."

Cecil and Lainie both nodded.

Raecli quickly took off her blouse. Then she began to undo her skirt. "Come here, Cecil. You put me into this thing. Take me out. And get this stomach squeezer off me. Lainie, hand me the bag of dead rodents."

"You can't seriously be thinking about climbing up that tree?" Cecil asked as she untied the skirt and moved it down. "Lady Raecli, you must not be seen in just your undergarments."

"No one is going to see me. This is the servants' day off. Now hurry and untie this confounded stomach squeezer."

"Here is the bag of food for Banthem," Laine said, placing the item into Raecli's free hand.

"Finally," Raecli said. "I can breathe." Then she went to the first branch and easily hoisted herself up.

"Don't do it, Lady Raecli. Or you will truly twist an ankle!" Cecil said, anxiously.

"Don't forget. I grew up as a River-dweller. I used to live in trees." Raecli placed the leather swatch and the lip of the bag with dead rodents between her teeth and grabbed the next branch.

The servants watched as Raecli effortlessly made her way up the tree. She straddled a thick branch and grabbed the highest branch above her with one hand. She could hear gasps from below. With the other hand, she brought up the swatch of leather and wrapped it around the branch. Then she tied the leather string attached to it over the leather to secure it. Finally, she opened the lip of the bag wide, and tied the leather cords around the branch next to the leather. "Banthem should be able to stick his beak into the bag for his treats," she whispered.

When she was finished, she cautiously made her way down limb by limb. She grabbed the final branch with both hands and swung her feet to the ground. "Easy as taking a stroll," she said.

"Wow, Lady Raecli. I've never seen a lady do something so amazing," Lainie said in awe.

Cecil came right up to Raecli and began putting her clothing back on. "I hope we never have to see you do that again. I'm telling you; I won't be able to sleep for a week with images of you falling and breaking something."

"I have to go back up," Raecli said sheepishly, as Cecil tightened the stomach squeezer. "When Banthem arrives, who do you think is going to put the letter into the cylinder around his claw?"

Cecil and Lainie both moaned.

"Make sure to keep an eye out for Banthem. I've described him to you, and he'll be circling this area. Right when you see him, tell me. We need to get to him straightaway. He'll eat and rest for a while, but he won't wait forever. He'll want to get back home to Weston. There is a lot at stake. I'm trusting you both to stay vigilant."

"Yes, my lady," they said.

"You're all dressed," Cecil said after tucking in the final piece of fabric. "Your undergarments are soiled and ripped. I'll have to sew and clean them before Miss Marva notices, but other than your mischievous grin, you look presentable."

Raecli stared at Cecil and Lainie. They both looked like they had seen something horribly fearful. "Aww, come here," Raecli said, bringing the pair into a hug. "Ra'ash loves to bring me the best servants and friends I could imagine."

After the hug, both Cecil and Lainie looked pleased but extremely embarrassed. As Raecli turned to walk back to the estate before anyone noticed her absence, she realized something. "You know what? This stomach squeezer doesn't feel so bad anymore. Now let's get your injured lady home before anyone realizes she can climb trees."

Chapter 28

Sailing Gold

Nine wooden boats filled with golden stones lined the shore of Riverend Village—the village located on the west part of the land bridge where Corven and his servant, Reece, had bartered for a boat and oared to the Lake-keepers. The local villagers mixed with villagers from South Village, located on the east side of the land bridge, and the Marsh-landers gathered around the rocky shore to watch the great exhibition of sailing auraium. F'lorna sat upon Croga's back bringing in the final load of stones. Croga wore a harness designed by Kytalia and created by her growing number of apprentices. Though aged, Kytalia could show her students how to work the hide, cut it and thread it together through the holes they made with sharpened stone. Though many of the villagers now had steel swords and daggers to slice animal hide and make holes, she preferred to teach them the way of stone in case the new material of steel was not available.

F'lorna engaged in the process of creating the harness so Croga could haul the stones in large quantities. She knew what Croga would like and not like around his head and over his shoulders. They finally came up with a simple, yet large harness design where he could pull several hides sewn together and folded upon themselves like a basket attached to Croga's harness with ropes. The villagers filled the hide basket with stones, and Croga's muscular frame easily pulled the auraium over the land bridge and to the opposite shore. Then the villagers emptied the hide basket and began the process of putting the auraium in the boats. The task of getting rid of the auraium was almost complete.

F'lorna slid down Croga's back and began to untie the harness from around his shoulders. "Good job, Croga. You made quick work of moving those rocks."

Croga gave his usual grunting response to her when she talked to him. She rubbed his large face. "I think you need another bath. Too bad you can't swim or else I would have you jump into the new waters."

"How is your Swarve holding up from all his hard work?" a voice asked from behind her. It was Elder Lear, the Spiritual Elder of Riverend Village. He had tan skin and light brown eyes. He was just about F'lorna's height but much stockier. His eyes were angular like her mothers.

"I think he enjoys the work," F'lorna said. "It's better than lounging by a large, shady tree all day."

"Never did I think our village would be pushing off boats into the new South Great Expanse carrying auraium hauled in by a Swarve," Elder Lear said. "In fact, I never thought we would be making boats at all. It is a new Adoration in our village. The first younglings are being trained by Marlow," he said motioning to the hornless villager standing next to him. "We are pleased to have it now that we are surrounded by water instead of the Desert Plains."

"A lot is changing in Rodesh," F'lorna agreed. She looked to Marlow. "I like the design of your boats. I was told you used them for transport of goods in the cities along the coast of the northern ocean." She used the word *ocean* knowing that was the word Sand-shapers used for Great Expanse. "What brought you into River-dweller territory?" she asked. Every Sand-shaper who came south from the Northwestern Coast or the Northeastern Mountains had a unique story.

"I brought a treat for your Swarve," he said, heartily. "I hear Achion leaves are his favorite. Do you mind if I feed them to him while I tell you my story? Some of my ancestor's old cylinders mention Swarves, but I was always told they were more of a myth."

"He would actually love a snack," F'lorna said pleased she didn't have to go pick them herself. Though riding Croga looked easy, it took a lot of balance to lead him, especially when he was hauling the rocks.

Marlow slung the leather bag he was carrying off his shoulder and opened it up. Then he grabbed a handful of leaves and brought them to Croga's mouth. Croga was used to being fed by others and instantly used his soft lips to suck up the leaves.

Marlow laughed. "His lips tickle. The fur on him is softer than feathers. The myth has become a reality," he mused.

"What are the pieces of white fabric tied to the long wooden poles on the boats?" F'lorna couldn't help but ask.

"My family comes from a long line of transporters," Marlow began. "We use boats to transport produce and goods from one city to the next across the shoreline of the ocean. Normally, the boats have oars and are manned, but I knew these would not have oars because they would not be manned. As a kid, I read many our family's cylinders—generations of boat transporters—and I read a parchment about using the wind to move boats. The process wasn't explained. It was only mentioned that in ancient times, a group of Rodeshians could harness the wind. It wasn't until I saw the curtain of a traveling case flapping in the wind that I got the idea to use fabric to hold the wind in place, forcing it to move the boat. I've never tested my theory, so I don't know if it will work."

"We will find out soon," Elder Lear said.

"I guess we will," Marlow said, feeding Croga another handful of leaves. "If not, the current will hopefully be strong enough to pull them out."

"And why did you come south?" F'lorna asked, still curious about his story.

"I have no family. No wife. No siblings. After the earth shudders happened, I lost everything. All my cylinders were gone. The shakes demolished my business in seconds. I could either rebuild or do something new. That's when I heard that an ocean had opened up in the south. I thought to myself that the River-dwellers may want boats to fish their new ocean or to travel. So I made my way through River-dweller territory. Some of the River-dwellers were accepting of me, but many were not. But, thankfully, once I got to the south ocean, the Rive-dwellers were very inviting."

"That's when he met our Fishing Elder, Sekuna," Elder Lear said with a grin.

"Yes, that's when Sekuna stole my heart. I saw her fishing from the shore, and I asked her if she would like to fish from within the waters on a boat. Then she began asking me questions and hasn't stopped asking me questions from that day. We are now joined and expecting our first son or daughter."

"Your story sounds a lot like how my mother and father met," F'lorna said. "Your child will be as I. Born of two worlds." She didn't mention the truth that she was now of three worlds. "I offer voiceless words to Ra'ash that the purpose for your child will be great."

Marlow appeared surprised by her comment. "If he or she is anything like you, I will be most pleased."

Weston came up to where they were talking and gave Croga a hardy scratch on his belly. "You better be staying out of the water, Croga. F'lorna and I don't want to go rescue you again!" Croga grumbled a low rumbling greeting to Weston. After several more scratches and pets of the Swarve's fur, Weston turned to the group. "I think we are ready to launch the boats. All the auraium is on board."

F'lorna couldn't help her concern. "Elder Lear, are you sure the wind and current are going a different way than when Corven and his servant left on one of your boats? The Lake-keepers value gold as the Sand-shapers. I would not like them to receive our boats of gold. It may cause fighting between the Highland Cliffs and Lowland Cliffs because they will be the first to see them."

"I can't be certain about anything, and now that we have the wind catching fabric attached to the boats, I have even less knowledge. However, I do know for certain the wind is going westward, not eastward as it was when Corven's servant, Reece, oared away. And the current has changed."

Satisfied, F'lorna nodded her head. "Then let's get these golden stones as far away from South Village and Riverend Village as we can."

"Agreed," Elder Lear said. "Let me offer a few words to the villagers. Will you join me, Marlow?"

"It would be an honor," Marlow said giving Croga the last of the leaves and a brisk pat on his head.

As the two men left, Weston turned to her. "Elder Limmian heard you wanted to speak with her about the celebration tonight. The Marsh-landers and the villagers from Riverend Village will be joining us at South Village."

F'lorna felt a little nervous about what she needed to ask the Spiritual Elder of South Village, but she wanted permission to move forward with her plan. "Thank you, Weston. I will speak with her after the boats launch. How did the work at the land bridge go? Were you and Merriton able to fill most of the holes from our excavating the auraium with the rocks from Sabien's lands?"

"It was a lot of work, but we believe our work will conceal our digging—at least for a while. If Sand-shapers start burrowing around with their obsidian blades, they will find it very difficult to get any auraium. I am still amazed we got nine boat loads," he said looking toward the shoreline where the boats were being prepared to launch and the crowd was gathering.

She looked at the leather swatch on his arm. "Banthem hasn't come back yet?"

"No, I don't know if he is going to Right River Hook or attempting to find Raecli's leather piece. She took her leather down because Lord Tarmian and her grandfather discovered it. Banthem will circle several times looking for a piece of leather to land on, but if none is found, he will rest, find food and come back to me. May take a few more days."

"I wish the leather would not have been found on Raecli's tree. It would be nice to communicate with her whenever we wanted. I am so glad she risked coming to see us at the Marsh-land Village."

When Weston didn't respond, she looked at his face. He was staring at something in the distance.

"What is it?" she asked. When she turned to look, she saw Lemmeck walking with his brothers, Rashion and Dashion. "That can't be good if the twins have traveled all the way south from Left River Hook to meet us."

"Let us find out," Weston said, taking her hand.

He had taken her hand another time when they were going to get treatment for their wounds when they saved Croga from drowning, but they had been alone then. Now Lemmeck was in front of them and getting closer, but she realized he was so engaged in his conversation with his brothers that he didn't notice. Luckily, Croga came up next to her and bumped up against her, breaking Weston's grip.

"I think Croga is mad that we left him," she said, but Weston was already talking with the brothers.

"What's happening?" Weston asked Lemmeck.

"Elder Trenton, Zelara's father, found the parchments we sent her. I don't think he knows what's written on them, but he raged against Zelara."

"He slapped her!" Dashion exclaimed.

"What's going on?" Sage asked out of breath holding a basket. "I saw you coming while Elder Lear was giving his speech. They are about to launch the boats."

"Boats?" Dashion asked.

"Boats?" Rashion repeated.

"Yes, with the auraium," Lemmeck said. His brothers looked confused. "It's a long story," Lemmeck said. "Look, we need to get over there with the others, but before we do, Rashion," he said looking at his brother, "tell them."

Rashion waited a moment until all eyes were on him. "Elder Trenton, Elder Bacheon and Elder Eotham are all coming to South Village. We waited for them in the forest around the marsh to see if they would try to enter the Marsh-lander Village, but they didn't. I don't think they know where your village is located. That's when my brother and I decided to get here first to warn you, but when we got to South Village, only a few villagers were there. They told us where to find you."

"But what can this Elder Trenton do? He doesn't belong down here," Weston said.

"He's very good at using his divisive words to stir up trouble. I don't think he will have much influence this far south, but it is better to warn Elder Limmian and Elder Lear once the boats are launched," F'lorna said.

"I agree," Lemmeck said. "Now my brothers, I am glad to Ra'ash you are here. You are about to witness something spectacular."

"We'd enjoy it even more if you could offer us a meal," Rashion said.

"Yes, we have been traveling so fast that we haven't been able to stop to refill our stomachs," Dashion agreed.

"I have just what you need," Sage said, holding up the basket she was carrying. "This is supposed to be for the ceremony tonight, but we can spare a few." She pulled up the fabric that was covering the basket to expose sweet sap rolls.

"Oh, my favorite," Dashion said, grabbing two and taking a large bite of one.

"Mine too," Rashion said, grabbing two as well.

"These are delicious. Who made them?" Rashion asked with a full mouth.

"Elder T'maya, of course," Sage said. "She's been supervising the preparation of the celebratory food all day."

"Eat as you walk," Lemmeck said, and the group made their way to the shore.

"Weston," Rashion said coming alongside the Marshlander. "I forgot to tell you. When we were waiting to see if Elder Trenton would travel into your lands, we saw Raecli, Sabien and another girl. They were being followed by servants of Lord Tarmian, and we believe our friends were heading into Marshland territory to see you all. We stopped them, though."

"With your hoots?" Lemmeck asked.

Dashion nodded. "I don't think it is safe for Raecli and Sabien to visit the marshlands for a while. We waited to make sure they made their way back to the farmlands."

Rashion smiled. "It seems Raecli faked a twisted ankle because Sabien carried her back to the estate. I'm sure Raecli told them the hoot meant it was unsafe to travel. They more than likely realized they were being followed and faked her injury as an excuse to return home."

"And as we made our way south," Dashion added. "We saw Banthem headed north. It appears he is flying to Lord Tarmian's estate. He was too far west to be going to Right River Hook."

F'lorna listened intently to Rashion and Weston's conversation. "Let us give voiceless words that Raecli finds another place to put the leather where Banthem can see it."

The group of friends made it to the shoreline just as the boats were being launched. F'lorna leaned against Croga. The rocky land on the shore caused her to feel anxious, but Croga's fur gently wrapped around her exposed arm. She immediately felt a sense of well-being. Sage came up next to her.

Sage gave a sap roll to Lemmeck and Weston. "We didn't see you at afternoon meal. I know you must be hungry." They took it gladly. "And here," she said to F'lorna. "I know you haven't eaten."

"Thank you, my friend," F'lorna said. "My mother's sweet sap rolls have been in my Eternal Memory since before I could walk."

Sage stood next to her with Weston, Lemmeck and the twins on the other side of her. They all stood eating their sweet sap rolls and watched as the boats swayed unsteadily at first upon the shallow, rocky shores. F'lorna observed Marlow. She could tell his shoulders were tense. He didn't know if the boats would catch the wind or not. His wife, Sekuna, stood beside him assuring him by rubbing his back with her hand. Elder Limmian and Elder Lear stood at the center of the crowd, watching the boats gain momentum. She would find Elder Limmian once the crowd dispersed to get ready for that evening's ceremony to celebrate the sailing of the auraium.

F'lorna took a bite of her roll and stopped chewing. "The fabric has puffed out on one of the boats! It's moving faster than the rest!"

"Look!" Sage exclaimed. "Another one has billowed!"

Then, suddenly, as if all the boats agreed it was safe to allow the wind to move them, all the fabric sails blew out, catching the ocean breeze and using it to push them farther out to sea. The sight was one that F'lorna never wanted to forget.

"Weston, will you draw this for us, so we will never forget?" F'lorna asked.

He nodded. "The younglings will always remember this moment. I will draw something, but I doubt it will look as stunning."

F'lorna kept her eyes fixed on the image of the boats growing smaller in the distance as they made their way to the horizon. The rays of the Heat Source bounced off the edges of the auraium creating a dance of lights. She understood a little more of why the Sand-shapers and the Lake-keepers valued the stone so much. She felt the golden crest on her left horn. The crest held great value not only in wealth but in prestige. Very few Lake-keepers wore the crest of a chieftain. Her journey over the last turn of the Violet Moon had been difficult, and she came close to allowing confusion to cause her defeat. However, now she was stronger and more compassionate because of the struggle. She would never doubt Ra'ash's ways again even when she didn't understand them at first.

Chapter 29

The First Book

The villagers from South Village and Riverend Village intermingled with the Marsh-landers. Those with horns and those without stood side by side as comrades in the Village Achion Cluster of South Village. F'lorna stood in the front of the crowd next to her mother and father. Merriton and Weston also sat near them with Sage, Lemmeck and his brothers. They all stood in a place of honor. F'lorna looked down at the box near her feet. She had talked with Elder Limmian after the boat launch and told her what she wanted to do. Elder Limmian was hesitant about it at first, but she soon realized that what F'lorna achieved was inevitable. Yes, there would be those who would resist and those who would vehemently disagree. But there would also be those who would benefit greatly from her work, including F'lorna's mother and the Marsh-landers.

Sword Heiress by Alisa Hope Wagner

Elder Limmian stepped up on the small speaking platform and faced the audience. Her silver hair was neatly braided into a bun at the nape of her neck in her traditional style. The creases around her eyes and on the brow of her umber skin did not make her look aged but rather wise beyond countable seasons. She winked at Dezzy, her eldest granddaughter, who also stood in the front with the rest of their family.

"Before I commence with my congratulatory words, I want to thank Elder T'maya for organizing and leading the Cooking Elders and Novices in creating the amazing feast we enjoyed for our evening meal," she said, nodding her chin toward T'maya.

The villagers stomped their feet and many knocked rocks together in applause. F'lorna looked to her mother. She nodded and smiled, but F'lorna knew that her mother disliked so much attention. She handled it well, though. In that sense, F'lorna and her mother were a lot alike. They did not enjoy a field of eyes staring at them all at once.

"Tonight, we are celebrating the teamwork of three villages: South Village, Riverend Village and our newest friends, the Marsh-landers of the Marsh-land Village." Again, she waited for the applause to die down. "Many aspects of Rodesh are changing. The Great Expanse now greets us on the north and south. The Desert Plains are no more. The River has opened up her mouth and exposed the waters that were buried deep within Rodesh. We've seen boats that catch the wind today, carrying golden stones that are coveted by many. We have Sand-shaper and Marsh-lander friends who have become family. Now we have a new material that can crush the strength of the obsidian blades that have hurt and created fear. Finally, we know that the Lake-keepers thought to be destroyed in *The Great Engulfing* are alive and thriving. The Violet Moon has certainly brought with her a breath of the unknown beginning with the first ground shudders of the First Violet Moon. Ra'ash brings forth new waters with new currents, and we must move according to His flow. The markings we once used to chart our path are gone, and we must look to Ra'ash for fresh markings to navigate a new trail." She paused and

255

looked to her granddaughter. "Dezzy, would you mind coming here?" she asked. "Most of you know that Dezzy is the first of our village to offer two Adorations to Ra'ash. Novice Elder Lemmeck taught her Hunting, and Novice Elder F'lorna taught her Swordcraft. You ate of her first Adoration during our feast this evening, and now she will demonstrate the latter."

Dezzy stoically walked next to the speaking platform and faced the villagers as Elder Limmian stepped off behind the small wooden platform. Dezzy put her hand on the grip of her sheathed sword. She looked at F'lorna, and F'lorna gave her an encouraging nod. The young girl was nervous, but she was the best of all F'lorna's apprentices in the new Adoration of Swordcraft. Dezzy exhaled a long breath and closed her eyes. Then she swiftly brought out her sword and leapt as she forcedly thrust the point of her sword down inches from the forest floor. She turned and swiped the sword diagonally in front of her body and shot the blade back piercing the air behind her. She twisted and swung her arm left to right several times, keeping her wrist taut and the blade straight. Finally, she sent the final blow forward, into the belly of the night, and sheathed the sword in one move then bowed. The crowd applauded, and she couldn't help but beam from the praise. She returned to her place next to her family.

Elder Limmian returned to the platform. "My granddaughter has made our village proud. Not only with her new skills but her willingness to embrace the new current Ra'ash is sending us upon. As some of you may remember, steel was used in our territory many moon cycles ago to protect life. Elder Eline, the teacher of Healing Elders, who has gone to her Eternal Dwelling place, used a steel dagger to save Elder Jaquarn's life. He was a baby inside a breathless mother. Though Elder Eline didn't know what steel was, she did know to use it to give life to a baby without air. She too saw a fresh marking on her path and applied it to this new current with Ra'ash." Elder Limmian paused to look at the faces in the crowd. Her expression of compassion and concern could be felt in the hearts of the villagers. "With that said," she said, looking toward F'lorna, "we have another fresh marking for us to see and use to navigate our path." She was about to say more and stopped. "There is nothing more for me to add, so let me ask F'lorna to come up."

T'maya looked at her daughter. "I didn't know you would be presenting at the celebration."

F'lorna put her hand on her mother's shoulder and squeezed it gently. "This is for you, Mother." Then she smiled at her father who knowingly put his arm around T'maya's back. F'lorna knelt and grabbed the bottom of the box she brought with her. Then she walked up to the platform and set it down before stepping upon the wooden stage.

She cleared her throat and looked upon the faces. She wouldn't let fear of their reaction stop her from obeying the will of Ra'ash. "Before I present my new Adoration, I would like to sing a *Chant of Jeyshen* in honor of my mother, Elder T'maya. This is one my mother would have me sing repeatedly as a youngling—so much so I almost tired of it and took for granted the truths found within. It is a short chant but poignant. I will be singing the *Chant of Acceptance*," F'lorna said. She noticed her mother placing her hand on her tunic pouch where she kept the same chant that F'lorna wrote on parchment using the Sand-shaper symbols almost three moon turns ago.

Then F'lorna fixed her eyes on the Heat Source that was setting on the horizon. The song was not difficult. In fact, the simplicity of it caused it to be one of the first chants Novice Singers learned. She sang it, though, with a newness that she did not learn and that was not in her Eternal Memory. She allowed the significance of the moment to lead her voice. When the pitch went high, her voice went higher. When the pitch went low, her voice went lower. She did not add or subtract a single word, yet she changed the sound to match the new current of Ra'ash that Elder Limmian spoke about. When she finished, she welcomed the applause. Then she bent and opened the box, lifting the book from within. She held the book under her palms and forearms and presented it to the audience. Everything became quiet. "I created this according to the will of Ra'ash in honor of my mother and all who are void of the *Divine Oracle* in their Eternal Memory." She wavered but kept her eyes on the Heat Source drifting below the horizon. "It has taken me many phases of the moon to complete, and I have given many voiceless words to Ra'ash that, though I could not give Him perfection like Jeyshen, I could at least give Him my very best. It is with this intention of obedience and love that I present to you the *Divine Oracle* expressed in a written form using the Sand-shaper symbols to be read and received. It will be kept in the protection of the Marsh-landers until, hopefully, it can be duplicated."

Gasps and whispers permeated the otherwise silent atmosphere. F'lorna watched as the last crescent light of the Heat Source sunk below the rim of Rodesh. Then she turned her gaze to her mother. "Mother, will you be the first to read from this book?"

Her mother's hands were covering her mouth, and she looked toward father. He nodded and nudged her forward to where F'lorna waited. After several seconds of coaxing, T'maya finally went to the platform and stepped up next to F'lorna. She looked at the two words, *Divine Oracle*, written on the front of the book and tears began to pour down the sides of her face.

"Go ahead, Mother. Open and read. I will hold it for you."

T'maya nodded and did as her daughter directed. She flipped through several pages before stopping. Fresh tears streamed from her grey eyes, wetting her cheeks even more. Finally, she began to read softly, but the audience was so quiet that her voice sounded like thunder. *"But for Rodesh, there is only Ra'ash by whom all things were created and by whom we live. And there is one Savior, Jeyshen, through whom all things were saved, and through whom we receive new life."*

"Sacrilege!" a voice bellowed.

F'lorna instantly knew the voice of who shouted. She shut the book and placed it back in the box. "Go to Father," she said to her mother and led her off the platform. She placed her hand on the grip of her sword and watched as Elder Trenton followed by Elder Bacheon and Elder Eotham cut through the middle of the crowd.

The remnants of the Heat Source's light was almost gone, and the torch light illuminated the glow of the Violet Moon.

Drips of sweat trickled down Elder Trenton's furious expression. "How dare you use those symbols of abomination with our sacred *Divine Oracle*. May Ra'ash strike you down!"

"Do not curse my daughter," Jaquarn said, confronting Trenton.

Without a moment's notice, Trenton swung his fist hard into Jaquarn's jaw, and he fell to the ground. T'maya screamed and ran to her fallen husband. F'lorna instantly brought out her sword.

"Stand down!" she yelled.

Elder Trenton laughed. "What is this? A stick. You can't hurt me, youngling." He grabbed the edge of the sword with his palm and yelped. "It bit me!"

"This is a sword made of Lake-keeper steel. It can cut through anything. Now stand down!"

"You made me bleed!" he roared.

"You made yourself bleed with your ignorance," she said evenly.

"My ignorance! That abomination you've created must be burned. What did you call it? A book. Give it to me now, and I will leave. You have desecrated the *Divine Oracle*, and I will never allow it. Sand-shapers lost the *Divine Oracle* many moon cycles ago. They don't deserve to have it written in their sacrilegious symbols. No hornless Rodeshian deserves to have the words of Ra'ash if they are not already in their Eternal Memory. That is what they get for forsaking Ra'ash and the words of the Prophets! Your mother doesn't deserve to have it!"

F'lorna swiftly swung her sword four hand-lengths away from Elder Trenton's chest and guarded the box holding the book. Elder Bacheon and Elder Eotham came up next to Elder Trenton.

"You have no right to say who deserves to have the *Divine Oracle*. You are not Ra'ash. The words of Jeyshen and the Prophets were given to all Rodeshians. I will protect the will of Ra'ash! He asked me to write the *Divine Oracle* in the symbols, and I obeyed!" F'lorna said firmly. "Now stand down. Do not make me strike you!"

"You dare say you know the will of Ra'ash!" Elder Trenton lunged at F'lorna, but she evaded his attack, and he tumbled to the ground. He quickly got up and lunged for the box. She took the hilt of her sword and slammed his right hand. "Stand down! Don't make me use the blade."

"Circle her!" Elder Trenton yelled to the other two elders with him.

"No!" a young voice rang out. It was Dezzy. She ran to F'lorna, and the two stood back-to-back with their swords drawn.

Suddenly, sounds of swords and daggers being drawn echoed throughout the crowd. Weston and Merriton held swords. Lemmeck and his twin brothers had their bows at the ready. Then like a wave, villagers from the crowd with swords drawn walked up to where F'lorna and Dezzy stood. They made a wall of protection around F'lorna, Dezzy and the box holding the book of the *Divine Oracle*.

"Stand down!" Weston yelled at the elders.

"You hornless abomination!" Elder Trenton yelled and spat in Weston's face.

Merriton moved his blade inches from Elder Trenton's cheek. "You see this scar on my face," he said revealing the side of his cheek. "This was made by an obsidian blade. This blade of steel I hold will do far worse."

Elder Limmian made her way up to Merriton and Trenton. "My name is Elder Limmian," she said to Trenton. "You have no right to threaten and assault my guests, and you have no right to come into my village uninvited and interrupt our celebration."

Elder Trenton faced her. "You support this decimation of the *Divine Oracle*?"

"I support those who don't have the *Divine Oracle* and want the ability to receive it," she said with authority.

By this time Jaquarn had woken up from his knockout. He walked to face Elder Trenton. His swelling, red jaw was already bruising. "Go back to Right River Hook. Stay far away from the south and my daughter. If I hear a whisper that you are coming after her or her book, I will rip both your horns out with my bare hands. Say not another word. Turn around. And leave South Village!"

F'lorna gaped and almost loosened her grip on her sword. She had never seen her father make a such a heated threat.

Elder Trenton looked around at the dozens of swords at the ready, and his expression turned to one of fear. He backed away several paces. Then he looked to Elder Bacheon and Elder Eotham and nodded for them to leave. The villagers this time did not budge for them to pass. The three intruders had to weave through the crowd to get by. When they finally left, the villagers put up their weapons. Although tensions were still high, there was an unspoken conviction: they had fought for the book and won. Elder Limmian walked over to the box holding the *Divine Oracle*. She picked it up and brought it to Merriton. "As leader of the Marsh-land Village. Do you accept responsibility of the *Divine Oracle* written in Sand-shaper symbols?" she asked.

Merriton looked at his brother. Weston nodded. "Take it," he said.

Merriton squared his shoulders. "Yes, I take responsibility of it, and as F'lorna suggested, I will have it duplicated so others can benefit from reading it."

The crowd cheered. F'lorna couldn't stop the tears from falling. The villagers had taken her side. The *Divine Oracle* could now be received by those who didn't have it in their Eternal Memory. One by one, villagers came up to Merriton wanting to see the book. He took it out of the box and presented it to all who wanted to see. F'lorna felt her hand embraced by another. She looked to her left. It was Weston. He stared into her eyes and kept her hand in his.

"Looks like we Marsh-landers have a new Adoration to teach," he said, grinning.

"What?" she asked. She felt heat rising in her face. His hand held hers so tightly that she could feel the rhythm of his blood in his palm.

"Writing the *Divine Oracle*," he answered.

Chapter 30

Coins Uncovered

Barronne Le Sharon sat at the wooden, round table in the informal part of their home with windows facing the western and less sparse portion of Atlatl Forest. The front of his home looked over the waters of West Basin. His property was narrow yet wide, and his home built by his great-grandfather allowed onlookers to see both the forest and the basin from the main part of the living space when they glanced from the left to the right. His house, though full of memories, remained impossibly quiet like a well-kept secret—something rarer than gold. The burden of the quiet became his desperate plea for action. He exhaled and placed his elbows on the table. No need for formal etiquette at home. They were a small army but a well-trained one. He made sure of that.

Barronne looked over to his wife who sat across from him. She prepared a simple meal for them. Their demanding daughter, Karthia, married into the bar Hathway family of the Lowland Cliffs. A woman of the bow now in a swordsman's domain. She enjoyed her upgraded status, but her position as chieftess of the Lowland Cliffs did not change the le Sharon lineage in West Basin nor his resolve to live or die for his chieftain.

"You went to see Karthia today while I was training the bowmen. How is our grandson?"

"You would know if you had joined me," his wife, Celeste le Sharon, said giving him a teasing look. Her light brown skin was a few shades darker than his own. Her golden colored eyes always appealed to him—even when she teased him. His eyes were blue like many who dwelled in the Highland Cliffs. He went to the Temple of Atlatl Forest as a younger man, but there was no mention of any swordsmen in his family line. He came from a great family of bowmen, but that all changed when his grandson, Ruinne, was born. The baby was a bar Hathway and would be reared as a swordsman like his father and the fathers before him.

"Karthia came to visit us with Ruinne not yet three weeks ago. Has the boy changed in such a short amount of time?"

"You dislike the Lowland Cliffs and their steel, but they are family now. Your visits need not be so infrequent."

He exhaled and leaned back into his chair. Same conversation with the same answers. "I have young men to train. I have a chieftain to protect. When his father died, Laninson's life became my responsibility."

"Are you more responsible to him than to your own blood?" she queried.

"Am I not responsible to the blood of my family who have gone before me and who now walk with the Befores? To my great-grandfather who built this home? To my grandfather and father who were the Master Bowmen of West Basin? I have obligations that go both ways in time. My grandson may be of the Lowland Cliffs, but my lineage is here on the shores of West Basin backed by the trees of Atlatl Forest."

"It would be easier if Laninson would marry Izzy bar Hathway. Then West Basin and the Lowland Cliffs can finally be united," she said.

Barronne felt anger rise in his stomach, but he kept it at bay. His wife only spoke of what would be easy for her as a mother and now grandmother. She did not think beyond family to the legacy of West Basin. "You know very well that the basin and the cliffs do not merge neatly. The waves roar on the waters and the ground rises unsteadily from forest to cliffs. It is a dangerous union—bow and sword. And what would a Bow Master have to do with the cliffs?"

"Yes, I know what you will say. You don't belong on the cliffs," she said getting up. "It looks like dinner is done. I will wash up."

Suddenly, three loud bangs rang through the quiet. Celeste looked toward the main entrance. "Who would be visiting this late in the day and without warning?"

Another crash was heard, and the main entrance door swung open. Barronne instantly rose from his seat. "Chieftain Laninson," he said. "How may I assist you this evening?"

Laninson looked so much like his father in his younger years that it made Barronne wonder if he were not younger himself. He felt just as much life flowing through his body as he did twenty years ago when he became Master Bowman of West Basin for Chieftain Dontonion bar Hudson. Now his son, Laninson, wore the golden crest of his people on his horn.

"Why is there no fear in your eye?" Laninson asked. He stood in the doorway. The waves of West Basin rolled onto the shores in anticipation behind him.

"I have nothing to fear. Only those who cheat, lie, steal and kill have need for fear."

Laninson stepped into the Barronne's home. He had at least a dozen bowmen behind him at the ready. For the first time in six years, Barronne had hope that the quiet would finally be pierced by truth. "Have your ears found truth this day?"

Chieftain Laninson's eyes narrowed. "My young brother's ears have heard rumor from fishermen children. I come for the truth."

"Tell me this rumor, so I may tell you the truth," Barronne said. His heart raced in his chest, but he kept his breathing even. He did not want to break an oath if truth had not been exposed.

"If I did not trust you with my life in years past, I would not give you the dignity to defend yourself," Laninson said. His hand though looking rested by his side, and he could grab his bow and have an arrow through Barronne's throat in an instant. During the past six years, Barronne pushed the boy harder than the rest of the bowmen and gave him more of his time and words. Chieftain Laninson bar Hudson would be the best, and the Supreme Sage had quantified his attention to the boy with her declaration that Chieftain Laninson of West Basin, indeed, was the best bowmen of all the Lake-keepers.

Laninson's expression stayed fixed—though, Barronne knew the young chieftain's emotions were high. Yes, he had trained the boy well. It was time for the truth to lead the way for retribution.

"My brother hears rumor that the nomadic woodsmen of Atlatl Forest did not kill my father with a cowardly blow behind the head. My brother hears that Chieftain Rathtar and his friends in a drunken folly and lust for money are to blame for my father's death, and they paid you for your silence."

"You hear the truth then," Barronne said.

In less than a second, Chieftain Laninson had an arrow pointed at Barronne's throat. Celeste's screams were stifled by her own hands covering her mouth. Barronne didn't move. He kept his gaze steady on Laninson to see whether he would react with emotion or intention. "Would you like to hear the rest of the truth?"

"Yes," Laninson said without withdrawing the arrow. "Though the rumor may be true, the calculations do not add up."

"May I reveal what is unknown to you?" Barronne asked.

"Do not move," Laninson said. His eye was set down the line of his arrow's path. "Where is it?"

"It is under the very floorboards on which you stand."

Laninson briefly looked down. "I see two floorboards that have been reset."

"The truth lies inside," Barronne said.

Chieftain Laninson nodded to one of his men and moved three paces away from the floorboards without removing his gaze from Barronne.

The bowmen put his bow across his shoulder and knelt. "The floorboards are loose. I can lift them."

"Do it," Laninson commanded.

The bowmen lifted the floorboards and pulled out a large leather bag with the crest of East Basin burned into it.

"Open it and reveal what is hidden," Laninson said.

The bowmen opened the aged leather bag and poured out the contents onto the floor. Golden and steel coins fell upon the wood like a waterfall.

"Those are the coins of West Basin. They are the blood money given to you for your silence. Coins stolen from the dead bodies of my father and of his men," Laninson said.

"Not for my silence," Barronne said. "But for my patience."

"Go on," Laninson said. Though his arm was ready to strike, Barronne could tell the young Chieftain was listening, needing the last colors of unknowns to paint the fuller picture.

"My oath as Master Bowman of West Basin has been fulfilled to the scoundrel Rathtar of East Basin," Barronne began. "I have been holding this money for six years as a burden to train you and your men to be the best bowmen, so one day we could overpower our enemy. Simple nomads could not kill Chieftain Dontonion bar Hudson of West Basin. They are a peaceful lineage with no need for coins. No, Rathtar and his friends heard of a hunt of the West Basin bowmen. Rathtar owing money to an inn for his eating and drinking hid with his friends and waited to strike and raid the hunting party. Your father was not supposed to join us that day, but on a whim of anticipation he decided to go for the hunt. The sun had not even touched a finger to the horizon before we were stoned. When Rathtar saw the crest on your father's horn, he cried out like an infant. I awoke with blood weeping from a stone hit to the side of my forehead just under my right horn. Rathtar begged me not to tell anyone. He asked me to give him the oath of a Master Bowman that I would say nomads killed your father. He gave me the bag of money from my fallen comrades as payment for my silence."

"Why did you give the oath!" Laninson shouted. His stoic demeanor was now vibrating with anger.

"Because," Barronne said, "if I did not, they would have killed me. And if I died, I know Chieftain Darmin bar Holthen would use your father's death as an opportunity to overpower a thirteen-year-old chieftain and to take West Basin as his own. I played out the possibilities in my mind. The best course of action was to make the oath, take the money and wait for the truth to finally be told. The truth always comes out. And while I waited, I trained you as my own son. I trained your men to follow your every command. And now you are the best bowman of all the Lake-keepers. It is time to fulfill my second oath."

Barronne could see Laninson making the connections in his mind. He slowly brought down his bow and replaced the arrow in his quiver. "What was your second oath?"

Barronne walked three long strides to face Laninson. "When I buried your father in the Crested Tea Fields, I dug with my own hands until the soil became too hardened, and my fingers bled. Then once the soil covered my chieftain's body, the one who had been my friend since before our childhood memories shut, I made him an oath of a Master Bowman. I told him that I would destroy Chieftain Rugar and his insolent son, Rathtar, and make his son, Laninson bar Hudson, chieftain of all three basins of Domus Lake."

Laninson took in his words without blinking. "Do you ask me to seek the Lowland Cliffs for help? Our army is skilled, but we are few compared to both East and South Basin. The Lowland Cliffs Chieftain already takes resources from our lands and our forest. I have nothing more to offer him besides my lands, which is what Chieftain Rugar wants. He covets the fertile soil of West Basin."

Finally, Barronne could tell that Laninson almost had sight of the greater plan. "No, we go to Chieftain Lothar of the Highland Cliffs."

"Why would he help me take over the basin?"

"Many of the East and South Basin's bowmen are on the galleys that Chieftain Lothar has built. The basin is vulnerable, and we have an army trained and ready to fight. Now is the time to destroy the line of bar Holthen and take the entire basin under the name of bar Hudson."

"What does Chieftain Lothar get in return? The Highland Cliffs will be a heavier strain on our resources than the Lowland Cliffs."

"No," Barronne shook his head. "You give him what he wants. He has no need for our lands or our resources. He is in want of an heir to the Highland Cliffs. Marry his niece, the girl from the lands across the waters, and promise Lothar your firstborn in exchange for all Domus Lake Basin."

"I will never give up my first born!" Laninson exclaimed, repulsed. "What if I have only one heir?"

"Then your brother, Valor bar Hudson, will be Chieftain over the basin. Either way, your lineage and family name will remain and triple in size and power. And the insidious bar Holthen name will finally be vanquished."

"What if his niece does not return?" Laninson asked.

"That is no concern of ours. He provides you support for an attack against Darmin bar Holthen to secure the basin, and you offer your willingness to marry his niece and give him a true heir of the Lake-keepers."

Laninson reflected over Barronne's words for several seconds. Then his expression became resolute. "I will do as you say only because my hatred of the nomadic woodsmen has turned into rage against Rathtar bar Holthen." Then he looked at the coins on the floor. "What shall we do with my father's blood money?"

Barronne gazed at the scattered coins. The weight of them finally lifted. "Tithe ten percent to the Sages of Atlatl Forest Temple, and let the builders know to finish quickly. We need all our bowmen ready to fight. Then give the rest to the fisherman's son who finally exposed the truth and ended my years of silence."

"Come on, Croga! Faster!" F'lorna road upon Croga's back, coaxing him to run. His golden wings were spread. He could tuck his legs and drift across the ground for several seconds as the grasses rubbed against his barrel of a belly, but eventually the weight of his body would bring his legs back to a sprint. She had him running to the land bridge and back toward the rim of the forest and then back to the land bridge again. He needed exercise. The time of him lounging by trees eating Achion leaves was over. He couldn't be hidden anymore. The villagers would have to accept him, and he would become a normal part of life on Rodesh. F'lorna had a feeling that more Swarves would be making their way to their lands—though she didn't know how. The world of Rodesh they once knew was no more. Anything was possible now.

Croga jogged to a stop near the waters of the River and whined.

"Are you thirsty?" she asked, and he whined again. "Okay," she said, sliding off his back. "Let's take a quick break then it is back to running again. I need to get you back into shape. You won't make much of a warrior if you can't even outrun a villager."

Croga ambled to the waters and used his large tongue to lap up water. His drinking wasn't very graceful, and water splashed across his cheeks wetting his fur. When he was done, F'lorna couldn't help but laugh. "Does that water feel good?"

Croga sniffed and looked down the River toward the forest. She matched his gaze. It was Weston holding Banthem on his arm. He had a look of urgency on his face.

"Come on, Croga. Let's see what Weston has. Maybe it is a letter from Raecli." She put her arm against his wet cheeks and his fur caressed her skin. The land around the River was rocky and harsh, so she automatically sought comfort from Croga. "Is it from Raecli?" F'lorna asked when they finally got to speaking distance of Weston. He nodded his head.

270

"It is not good," he said when he reached F'lorna and Croga. "Sabien's father and Raecli's grandfather are planning on making a permanent presence at the land bridge."

F'lorna gently stroked Banthem's silky feathers. "We knew that was going to happen, which is why we got rid of the auraium," she said.

He shook his head. "Auraium is now only one of the things they want."

"What else?" she asked, thinking. "Steel. They want steel?"

"Yes, and there is one more thing, and you will not like it."

"What?" she asked leaning into Croga. "There is nothing more of value down here."

He pointed to Croga. "They want Swarves."

"How could they possibly use Swarves?"

He paused. "The same way we used Croga—for work. They want to use Swarves in the farmlands and cities to transport their goods instead of servants."

"But Swarves customarily only carry people. We only used Croga because we needed to get the job of moving the auraium done quickly."

"They only carry people with the Lake-keepers because they are sicklier and weaker. Remember telling me that? They don't have their needed food source over there, but if Lord Tarmian and Lord Recon are able to bring Swarves here, they can be used as a workforce for the Sand-shapers."

"But we don't have to worry about that. Swarves are too big. Even as babies they are the size and weight of boulders. They would have to build a boat as long as an Achion tree and as wide as ten Achion trees. It's impossible!"

Suddenly, Weston's eyes widened, and his jaw dropped. He stared at something behind her.

"What it is?" she asked turning around. "Oh, by Ra'ash! They are monstruous."

F'lorna turned to look beyond the River behind them. Six large boats with countless oars rowed over the horizon toward them on the new south waters. Their pace was slow, and she could barely see figures on the deck. As they crept forward, she discerned a symbol burned into each of the sides of the boats. She suddenly felt for the golden crest on her horn. "It is Chieftain Lothar. He has come for me."

"How do you know?"

"I see the Highland Cliffs Crest burned into the side of each boat."

"He wants an heir so badly that he would build those boats?"

"Yes," she nodded. "He is desperate for an heir. I just never thought he would want to find me. How could he possibly know where we are?"

Weston looked at her. "Corven and his servant, Reece. They must have made it to the Lake-keepers."

She looked at Weston. "I don't know what is going to happen, but we must expect the worst. Chieftain Lothar can't be trusted."

"Do you think he will take you by force?" Weston asked, grabbing her hand.

With her free hand, F'lorna felt for the glass pendant around her neck with the hair of the White Diamond Stag that Lemmeck gave her three moon turns ago. "You never know what Chieftain Lothar will do. When you think he will be angry, he shows compassion. When you think he'll overlook an offence, he presses in with violence. He is unpredictable," she said lost in memory. She shook her hand free from Weston's grip and let go of the pendant. Then she felt for the grip of her sword before turning toward Weston. "We don't have much time. You go warn the Marsh-landers and send a note to Raecli. I will warn South Village and Riverend Village. I'm glad Sage, Lemmeck and his brothers haven't left yet. I will tell them, and they can warn the villages on the way to Left River Hook. We must prepare to meet our new enemy or our new friend."

"And you say you have found seven boats filled with gold so far?"
Captain Larkson asked. He stood on the main deck of the massive
sailboat named after his daughter, Laurina. His uniform of blue and
white—the colors of the Olam Realm—maintained its pristine
condition though they had been sailing for over two months from
the Coastal Isles which was another two months from the Five
Realms. His light skin was completely covered by clothing save
his face, which was shadowed by his large captain's hat. His cut
and smoothly rounded horns poked out only two inches from his
hat. A clasp around each horn nub kept the hat fitted on his head,
so the ocean breeze wouldn't sweep it away. His hazel eyes held
years of experience, and to see them light up with anticipation was
a rarity.

"Yes, sir," Lieutenant Engles said. "Kelfy brought in two
more just this morning. There may be more. He will take another
swim tomorrow."

"The question stands: is this a gift blessing from the Good
Befores or a sinister scheme from the Evil Befores?" Captain
Larkson pondered.

"I wouldn't think the Evil Befores would give us such a
precious gift," Lieutenant Engles offered. "I'm sure they are an
offering from the Good Befores to help us enter new lands and
introduce ourselves to Rodeshians we have never met."

The captain looked at his lieutenant. "Kelfy said he saw the
oared galleys crossing the new sea heading north. They must be
leaving one land to go to another," he said thinking out loud. "Two
lands we know nothing about. Bring me Kelfy."

Lieutenant Engles whistled the call of the Sea-breathers.
Kelfy who was eating his afternoon portion for the day instantly
stopped and walked over the many lines running across the surface
of the ship to the main deck. His rubbery white skin still glistened
as if it were wet, but he had been out of the water for hours. The

ring attached to his mouth was out, leaving a large hole over and under his lips. His two sharpened horns were triple the length of the sailors.

"Yes, sir?" Kelfy asked, bowing.

"You saw six oared boats but no sails?" Captain Larkson began.

"Yes, sir. The galleys were large, but they had no sails to wield the wind."

"And they saw you and obviously did not harm you?"

"Yes, sir," Kelfy answered. "I saw no weapons, but they could have been stored inside. They appeared stunned to see me."

"I'm sure they were. You barely look Rodeshian."

"I am a Sea-breather from Coastal Isles. It is our custom," Kelfy said matter-of-factly.

"Yes, and a very useful custom too. Do you think they are the ones who sent the gold?"

Kelfy shook his head. "The design of their oared boats was strange to me, and they didn't have sails. The boats holding the gold had rudimentary sails. The sails may have worked at first, but by the time I found them, the sails were wrapped around the poles. Also, the oared boats had smaller boats aboard, and they were a different design than the ones with gold."

"What to do. What to do," the captain said. He looked back at Kelfy. "And you are sure this is the location you saw the galleys?"

He nodded. "Yes, I looked at the markings under the sea. They are the same ones I noted when I saw the oared galleys."

"What a puzzle. We have six oared galleys going north. We are in the location they were several days ago. Do we return to the Five Realms and give the news to the politicians of Olam Realm? If we do that, the other Realms are sure to set sail to find these new lands first or worse, Jorum Kingdom may hear the news of our find and send out their ships. Or do we continue sailing and meet our new friends?"

"I can speak on behalf of the sailors on board. We would like to continue and discover the new lands. Your daughter's name will go down in history of the Five Realms. Ship Laurina could be the first sailboat to touch uncharted territory," Lieutenant Engles said.

Captain Larkson put his hands to his chin and scratched. "I agree with you Lieutenant, but do we go south or north? Do we meet the makers of the oared galleys to the south first or do we meet those whom they travel to see in the north first?"

"The wind is going south," Kelfy said. "The sailing would be easier and faster."

"Yes, and the new lands north may not have room for the six oared galleys and our ship," Lieutenant Engles added.

"Quite right," Captain Larkson said. "Let us go south. I am sure they will have room for new visitors. They don't know how to use sails yet, so they will gladly listen to our advice as seasoned Wind-wielders."

"Yes, sir," Lieutenant Engles said. "I will prepare the sailors."

Captain Larkson turned to Kelfy. "Once you are done eating, why don't you take a quick swim south and see what you find? Report back to me when the sun is five finger lengths from the horizon. I need a safe place to anchor up."

Kelfy nodded.

Captain Larkson walked to the edge of the ship and stared over the waters. This was supposed to be his last assignment. His wife wanted him home to run for parliament, so they could have reason to keep more than one home in the Five Realms and travel. If retirement was indeed his future and this was to be his last assignment, he would make this voyage the best one yet. His name too would be made known in the history of the Five Realms.

Writer

Alisa Hope Wagner loves deep simplicity. She is home most days, but if you do see her out and about, you may actually be face-to-face with her extroverted identical twin sister. More than anything, Alisa adores being a wife to her high school sweetheart (Daniel), mother to her three awesome children (Isaac, Levi and Kiki) and daughter of the Most High King.

After hours of writing and editing at her computer, Alisa cannot wait to workout in her garage gym. When the day's work is finally done, she listens to smooth jazz and gets creative in the kitchen. But before she begins to write each morning, she sits with her Bible and journal and chats with God, letting the Holy Spirit encourage, correct and guide her.

Alisa is an award-winning writer of Christian fiction and non-fiction books. She has been writing for 20 years and has written and published over 30 books across all genres, including her speculative fiction books, the _Onoma Series_.

She lectures at churches and colleges about her four favorite topics: faith, family, fitness and fiction. Additionally, she writes about the topics on her blog, www.alisahopewagner.com.

Alisa competes in bodybuilding competitions and is a retired MMA fighter. She shares her health passion and knowledge in her 2 fitness books. She can be found on Instagram, Twitter, Facebook and Goodreads with her username: @alisahopewagner.

Alisa is the creator of *enLIVEn Devotional*: a writing ministry that brings the words of diverse writers together in order to support world missions. She and her co-coordinator, Holly Smith, produce devotional anthologies with proceeds going to the poor and needy of this world. You can find out how to get involved in this ministry at www.enlivendevotionals.com.

The most important thing Alisa would like to tell her readers is that God loves you so much that He sent His Son into this world to claim you as His brothers and sisters. No matter who you are or what you have done, Jesus loves you and died to have a supernatural relationship with you in this life and the next. Don't waste one single day. Ask Jesus into your heart, make Him your Lord and Savior and begin really living!

Artist

Albert Morales is an accomplished illustrator and painter with credits spread across the art board. He was a nominee for the 2018 CARTOON CROSSROADS Cartoonist of the year, where this year his strip joined the BILLY IRELAND CARTOON ART MUSEUM's collection of original art since the 1900's. His work is now curated and collected next to the likes of Charles Schultz (Peanuts), Bil Keane (Family Circus), and Bill Watterson (Calvin and Hobbes) to name a few.

Albert's creator owned comic strip SUPER IMPACTO VS. THE WORLD has also been recently published in a collection along with fellow cartoonists entitled TALES FROM LA VIDA by THE OHIO STATE UNIVERSITY.

Albert has had the opportunity to work with the HERO INITIATIVE on several of their 100 book projects including: Wolverine 100, New Avengers 100, Fantastic Four 100, Walking Dead 100, Hellboy 100, and TEENAGE MUTANT NINJA TURTLES 100.

Wrapping up his run with MARVEL / UPPERDECK as an official MARVEL - UPPERDECK artist (with SPIDER-MAN: Homecoming and FLEER ULTRA X-MEN), Albert is continuing doing creative projects in the way of publishing creator owned books. Slated for 2019 and already catching fire is his new book ANNIHILATION JONES and his just announced illustration duties for ALISA HOPE WAGNER'S new VIOLET MOON SERIES starting with *F'lorna of Rodesh*!

You can find Albert Morales at the following social media sites.
artwise310@hotmail.com
https://www.instagram.com/angryroosterstudios/
https://www.facebook.com/albert.morales.5477

If you love this book, please leave a review on Amazon and/or Goodreads. Your words will help other readers to discover F'lorna and her family and friends, so they too can experience the unveiling world of Rodesh.

www.ingramcontent.com/pod-product-compliance
Lightning Source LLC
Chambersburg PA
CBHW051525260626
47170CB00003B/789

* 9 7 8 1 9 6 3 1 9 0 0 1 4 *